TALE OF A BOON'S WIFE

# TALE OF A BOON'S WIFE

FARTUMO KUSOW

Second Story Press

Library and Archives Canada Cataloguing in Publication

Kusow, Fartumo, author
Tale of a boon's wife / by Fartumo Kusow.

ISBN 978-1-77260-047-6 (softcover)

I. Title.

PS8621.U86T35 2017      C813'.6      C2017-902647-X

Cover by Natalie Olsen
Cover images: GeorgePeters / istockphoto.com
hornsy / photocase.com

Editor: Kathryn Cole
Design: Melissa Kaita

Printed and bound in Canada

*Second Story Press gratefully acknowledges the support of the
Ontario Arts Council and the Canada Council for the Arts for our
publishing program. We acknowledge the financial support of the
Government of Canada through the Canada Book Fund.*

ONTARIO ARTS COUNCIL
CONSEIL DES ARTS DE L'ONTARIO
an Ontario government agency
un organisme du gouvernement de l'Ontario

Canada Council    Conseil des Arts
for the Arts      du Canada

Funded by the Government of Canada
Financé par le gouvernement du Canada | Canada

MIX
Paper from
responsible sources
FSC   FSC® C004071
www.fsc.org

Published by
SECOND STORY PRESS
20 Maud Street, Suite 401
Toronto, ON M5V 2M5
www.secondstorypress.ca

*To my dad, Mohamed Kusow, and my mom,*
*Timiro Mohamed, who always gave my sister and me*
*the opportunity to do what we chose, not what we must.*
*Thank you.*

# CHAPTER ONE

I GLIDED across the kitchen floor of our new house in awe. "This is so beautiful," I whispered and screwed up my eyes against the blinding brightness of the black-and-white tiles.

Mother put the bread in the built-in *tinaar*—clay oven—and closed the lid. She beckoned me to her and handed me a single sheet of paper. "Idil, read it for me."

I held it aloft. "It's a telegram!" I tilted my head and squinted at it as the afternoon sunlight splashed across my face. "Father has completed his training in the Soviet Union." The joy of telling her pushed the words out in one long string of syllables. "He is coming next Saturday!"

Mother took the paper out of my hand and pressed it against her chest. "What exciting news. Idil, I pray you marry a husband as grand as your father."

The thought of such a privilege awakened my senses and made me laugh.

"Take the bread out when it's done," Mother instructed Hawa, our kitchen girl, to finish the baking and led me into her bedroom. "Idil, come. We have work to do."

I sat on the bed and smoothed my hand over the covers, enjoying the luxurious feel of the Egyptian cotton sheets.

Mother dug into her wardrobe. "Idil, we must wear our best when Father comes." She pulled out a red and orange kaftan inlaid with yellow lilies and gilded with red thread around the flowers. A yellow silk underskirt and a black brassiere completed her outfit.

She opened a locked drawer in her dresser, unearthed a small wooden chest, and placed it next to me. Mother caressed the sides of the box. "The only jewelry that survived my stepmother is in this tiny thing." She took out pieces of gold jewelry and turned two bangles around her wrist, admiring them. "My father had to bury this box under his bed to protect it from her reptile hands." She'd told me the horror that was her childhood so often I could recite it verbatim. "It is better to lose a father and become an orphan, then live as a *rajo*." The stories of her upbringing as a motherless child followed us around the house like another being.

"Your father would likely never take another wife, but just in case, if I die before you are in your own home, run to the closest mountain and jump off. Death is more merciful than a stepmother's home."

The prospect scared me. "I don't want you to die. Promise you'll be with me forever and ever, and I with you," I wailed.

"I said *if.*" She walked over and kissed me on the forehead. "Idil, don't you worry. I won't allow bad things to happen to you."

Mother's commitment to my well-being awed me, and I wrapped my arms around her neck. "I love you, Mother."

"I love you more," she said as she put a small necklace around my neck. "I have to find a nice dress for you," she said and returned to the dresser.

I cringed. Even at thirteen, Mother's attempts to dress me up always led us to a week-long battle. I glared at the blue contraption she'd pulled out. "Do I have to wear that?"

Mother put it back in its place and sat next to me. "It's easy to dress your brothers. Give each a pair of pants and a shirt and Omar and Elmi are set. With you, it's a task." She smoothed my unraveling braids. "Even your hair refuses to be tamed."

❧

From the first light of that summer morning when Father was due home, Elmi and I roamed the yard. We pushed each other off the little hill between the soldiers' tents and the brick homes for the senior officers. Elmi landed on the red clay mud left behind by the heavy rain we'd had the day before. From the boulder above him, I extended my hand. He pretended to reach for help, but yanked me down. I lay beside him and laughed until my sides hurt. "That was cheating." The fresh scent of the damp earth made my nostrils tingle.

Mother forced Elmi and me to shower and change our clothes before lunch. "I should tie you to a chair to keep you clean. You should take notice of your older brother." She pointed at Omar standing stiff in his outfit with the dignity of a real man. "This is your last warning." Her stern tone told us we'd better not mess up.

Mother had organized a big celebration for Father. Her friends arrived well before dawn and occupied the *gembers*—four-legged stools—scuffing the scrubbed floor. The women drank tea, ate, and gossiped. They had spent hours making *odkac*, meat cut in the shape of black beans, cooked and soaked in melted butter.

Mother's friend, Safiya, led the meal preparation. "What a success. Hussein Nuur is an army general now." She smiled at Mother in a congratulatory way.

Mother glowed.

⁊⊱

Red-golden beams of sunlight shone on the prayer mats in the main part of the yard and danced upon the intricate designs.

At the sound of the approaching car, Safiya and several other ladies left the kitchen and stood by the driveway. They erupted into a loud and celebratory ululation at the sight of the car that brought Father from the airport in the Somali capital, Mogadishu.

My long braids, tied at the ends with two pink ribbons, bounced as I ran to him. "My father is here!" I announced as though others couldn't see him getting out of the car in his full glory.

The neighborhood children and their mothers darted from their homes and watched the marvel that was Father. I flew into his embrace and wrapped my arms around his neck as he exited the vehicle. "You are home!"

"And you are my girl." He lifted me to his level.

I buried my face in the curve of his shoulder and inhaled the strong smell of his cologne. "I missed you so."

Father stroked my hair and put me down. "I missed you, too."

I giggled with pride as I walked next to him toward the house.

Soldiers from the base lined up along the gravel driveway to greet him. Father smiled, but didn't join them for the evening prayer.

I followed his example, even after Mother reminded me to come and pray. "I want to do it with Father."

He led me away from the crowd and into the house. "Hold this and wait for me here." He handed me his belt, the gun and crest still attached to it. I traced my finger around the leopards on each side of the flag in the crest. My thumb rested on the crossed lances over the palm fronds.

Father returned, wearing a T-shirt and a *macawis*—sarong—wrapped around his waist. "Give me this." He collected his belt and extended his hand.

Hand in hand, Father and I left the house together. With every step we took toward the yard, now teaming with guests, I grew an inch taller.

Applause greeted us when we appeared. Father stopped to speak with two men who inquired about his experiences in the Soviet Union. After a while, their discussion bored me, and I drifted into the kitchen. Large pots sat atop the blazing *burjiko*—wood-burning clay oven. The aroma of the cumin, garlic, cardamom, cinnamon, and cilantro pouring from the soup and rice filled the air and drew me even closer. Mother served plates overflowing with meat, rice, and vegetables to the waiting guests.

Father hugged an elderly man. "Children, come meet my uncle. He's seventy and has never left his village, not before today. He raised me after my parents died." Father kissed him on each cheek.

A woman next to the man raised her open palms skyward. "May Allah keep you safe, my son." She recited prayers of thanksgiving at the sight of the food and hot tea. "May your enemies be struck blind."

❦

Tall and handsome in his seat, Father spent every night in the weeks that followed telling us stories of his travels to the Soviet Union. "You should've seen it, children." He showed us a postcard of an adult polar bear and two cubs looking at the camera, their dark eyes standing out against the snow-covered landscape.

Omar, Elmi, Mother, and I listened intently. "People live there?" I reached for his hand to urge him on.

His bright smile flashed. "You get used to the cold after a while." Father's handsome face was alight with pleasure. He recounted the last three years he'd spent in the Soviet Union military academy. "We did our training in the winter." He rested his hand on my shoulder as I moved my stool next to his armchair. "You're so beautiful, Idil, like your mother," he commented.

Even at a young age, I knew Father was wrong. Mother, a full head shorter than Father, with a slim build, long jet-black, wavy hair, and dark, subdued eyes, was like Elmi and Omar. With my broad shoulders and strong muscles—built more for roughhousing than feminine softness—I was Father's carbon copy. Mother worried from the time I was eight that I was growing too tall, too thick, and too rugged. She feared I wouldn't find a husband.

"Look at this." The muscles around Father's upper arms rippled as he lifted a Polaroid photo, and my eyes followed it in awe. In the picture, Father had a wool scarf wrapped around his face and neck. Two flaps attached to the hat dangled to protect his ears. Bundled in a heavy jacket and something dark and puffy over his pants, Father seemed large, like the balloons we bought when we visited Mogadishu. "You dress to survive," he said.

I noticed a small, white woman next to him in the photograph. "Who is that?" I pointed at the smiling figure.

Father directed his answer to Mother. "That is Nadia, one of my teachers."

Nadia was much closer to him than a teacher should have been. They huddled together against the mountains of snow that threatened to swallow them whole.

Mother smiled, shedding the unease such a picture brought.

Father continued with his stories. "This is the Kremlin. It is the center of the country and its government." He passed a postcard around and launched into a narrative about the building and its role within the Soviet society. The light reflection of the water adjacent to the building gave it an ethereal glow. "You could look at it for hours."

The attention, the status, and the stories made me happy. "I love it," I said.

My mother and brothers nodded in agreement.

❧

Mother invited her friends for tea in the afternoons to retell Father's stories. On one of those days I came upon them and hid behind the pillar that divided the sitting room from the bedrooms. Each guest listened, entranced.

"He met the president," Mother told her lady friends. "He can go back to the country anytime without a visa." Mother's glowing review of Father's work eventually led to talk of another woman's misfortunes. "Did you hear Muna's husband left her for Xabiba?"

"Did you see her children, so poorly dressed and unfed? No one can blame a man for leaving filth." The women shared a unanimous sigh in Muna's condemnation. "I walk the other way when I see her at the market."

After Mother's friends left, I came out from my hiding spot. "Would Father ever take another wife?"

"Any women who loses her husband has only herself to blame," Mother said. "What's a wife for, if not to comfort her husband, and care for the children?"

"Are you sure Father won't leave?" I shared my concern with Mother.

"A husband strays if the wife can't keep her home and children properly."

Mother, a model housekeeper, a great parent, and a proper wife made the risk of something similar happening to us seem non-existent. Relieved, I went to my room and started my homework.

❧

With Father home after his three-year absence, my excitement on the eve of *Eidul-Fitr*—the holiday marking the end of Ramadan—increased throughout the entire day. "Are you taking us to the light show?" I asked before I even changed from my school uniform.

Father pushed me aside. "I am meeting a friend this evening."

I stood in front of him and pouted, but my sad face did nothing to change his mind. "Your mother will take you tonight, and I will go with you to the prayer service tomorrow morning." He went into his room and a few minutes later, dressed in his best, he left.

Father didn't attend the Eid prayer service the next morning, blaming a severe headache. "I can't move," he said facing the back wall, away from us. "It's killing me." But when we returned, four hours later, Father was not home. He was still out when I went to bed.

The following evening Father dressed to leave again. I sat in the tiny hallway between his bedroom and the sitting room. As he stepped out, his strong cologne wafted in my direction. "Are you coming to tell us a story?" I attempted to guilt him into staying.

Father stopped for a moment, and a forced smile crept around his mouth. "Go play with you brothers."

I watched him with undisguised disappointment as he left.

From that night on, a great silence surrounded our dinner table. When Mother told us to give our thanks for the meal, I closed my eyes and prayed. "*Yaa Rabi*," I whispered, "stop Father from going out every night." It was to no avail.

We didn't gather in the sitting room anymore. We finished our schoolwork, and both Omar and Mother drifted into their rooms. I stayed behind for a while with Elmi, trying to fill the void. Later, I would follow Elmi to his room, but we'd say nothing to each other until fatigue from the day's activity dragged me off to bed.

# CHAPTER TWO

I OPENED the main door to the house. "Be quiet," I said cupping my hand around my mouth as a warning to Elmi. I didn't want to attract Mother's attention.

Elmi looked down at his clothing. "We are a total mess." A giggle escaped his lips.

Mother must have heard us for she called from her room. "Idil, Elmi? Is that you?"

I wanted to lunge at Elmi. *Look what you have done*, I mouthed in his direction.

Elmi knew we needed to avoid Mother. Thursday, the last day of the school week, Elmi and I played a game of Hide or Shove with our friends. The bell that ended the day marked the start of the hunt for opponents. In the game, if you were discovered, you were thrown into the dirt. It lasted for over an hour. We played it to celebrate the coming Friday, a day of rest for Muslims.

Mother made me wash and clean the whole of Friday if she caught me too dirty on Thursday. "A girl has no business walking around covered in filth," she always said.

Mother's comments reminded me of the gossip I'd heard—that Muna's husband had left her because of dirty children. The thought made me feel guilty. "Father might take another wife if we don't keep clean," I told Elmi.

He didn't believe me. "Men don't leave their wives because of dirty children. They do it because they want to; because they can."

I was shocked by Elmi's naiveté. "Muna lost her husband because of that. It's true. Mother told me."

Elmi laughed. "Women say that to convince themselves it won't happen to them." He scanned the area before he spoke again. "They take comfort that it's happening to some-one else."

As if she had forgotten we were there, Mother didn't call again. I moved closer to her door and, pressing my ear against it to listen, heard Safiya and Mother discussing something in a serious tone.

"I told you Ayan was a thief. I knew it from the first day I saw her in your sitting room," Safiya said. Safiya was an imposing, stout woman. What she'd lost in looks she made up for in size. She was a woman of few words and a sharp eye for thieves—those who preyed upon other women's hus-bands. "This has been done right under your own roof. He moved her into a house with servants."

"Why would he do that to me? I do everything right, exactly the way he wants it." Mother's words shook with emotion.

"Your husband didn't leave you. He was taken from you. There's a difference. Women like her are as sly as snakes. Thieves like Ayan slither in and take without warning."

Mother had not suspected Ayan, an eighteen-year-old wife who came to the military base with her husband four months before Father's return. Ayan's husband was a member of Father's battalion. She was tall and slim, and her skin glistened. She had perfectly aligned white teeth and a curved dimple on each side of her face when she smiled.

Mother invited her to our house when she learned that Ayan, a motherless young woman, had a baby. Since she'd lost her own mother when she was young, Mother always had a soft spot for people like Ayan. "I wanted to help her care for the child," she said.

"Two straight weeks and he hasn't left this one," Safiya continued. "If she wasn't married, your husband would've had a second wife by now." Safiya's deep sigh reached me outside the room.

"Hussein told me he'd never take another wife. He promised me I was the only one for him—he would never look at another woman," Mother sobbed.

"It's not his fault because he didn't choose this. Ayan tricked him. She did things to his mind to make him blind. We'll get back at her, we will." Safiya had dispensed with many of her husband's mistresses.

Mother's crying intensified. "I shouldn't have brought her into my house."

Safiya's voice was gentle. "Yes, true, but you should have gone to Moallim Hirsi when I first told you about Ayan and your husband. You should have believed me." Moallim Hirsi was a well-known witch doctor. My friends and I called him Hyena Man.

"I don't know what to do," Mother wailed.

"Moallim Hirsi will take care of it. He wants you to send two of your husband's undershirts—one red and one white. I told him the problem already."

"I am exhausted," Mother said, as if she were speaking to herself.

"Don't be afraid. He brought my husband back from a thief. Her family disowned her. She got what she deserved for stealing my husband with her witchcraft and making him fall in love with her." Safiya sounded almost jovial.

Mother continued to cry softly.

"Moallim Hirsi can do it," Safiya comforted. "I know he can. People from as far away as Mogadishu come for his services."

After a long minute of silence, punctuated by the ticking of the clock, Mother called me again. "Idil, I need you in here."

I entered her room, holding my books in front of my chest. Mother didn't notice the streaks of red dirt on the front of my blouse. Layers of mud coated my khaki pants from belt to ankle. She said nothing when I sat on the bed.

"I need you to take something for me." Mother searched inside Father's undergarment drawer with purpose. She put two undershirts in a cloth bag and pushed it into my lap as if the contents were on fire and she needed to be rid of it. "Here, take this to Moallim Hirsi."

I hid my hands behind my back, dropping the binder next to Mother's bed. "What does he want with Daddy's underwear?" I shivered. "Ask Omar to take it. Please." Omar was home. I saw him through the half-opened kitchen doorway. He was sitting at the table, eating.

"Omar?" Her eyes, tear-filled and thoughtful, rested upon my face. "No. This is ours to look after." She lifted my chin and held my gaze within hers. "You want to get Father back, do you not?"

"I want Father back, I do, but…"

Mother cut me off. "When you get there, wait until Moallim Hirsi is done and bring these back."

"What if Hyena Man kills Father?" I'd heard horror stories of what the man was capable of.

Mother took a deep breath. "He would do nothing of the sort."

I picked up the bag and my binder and left Mother's room.

⁂

Near a large and decaying tree trunk by the main gate, I scanned Hyena Man's yard. The L-shaped property appeared empty, except for the smoke that came from the kitchen. On either side of the narrow walkway, old scattered farm tools lay in the yard. I approached and came upon Hyena Man hunched over his workbench. He was hammering away at something I couldn't see. His lanky body was bent like a soft twig, and his fingers, long and thin, held the hammer tight. Every time he lifted his arm, my eyes followed, expecting him to drop the hammer, but it reached its target with practiced precision. I extended the bag I was holding. "My mother told me to bring this."

Hyena Man looked at me once and turned back to his work. He didn't speak until his daughter, Aisha, came out of the kitchen, carrying a teakettle. Aisha wore a tattered dress and had no shoes on her feet. She had been in my class until two years ago but quit after her mother's death to help her father run his healing business.

Aisha poured tea in a mug and handed it to him. "It's time for your rest," she said.

Hyena Man straightened up and took the mug.

Aisha moved closer to me "Are you here for my father?"

I extended my hand, Mother's bag still in my grasp. "Yes, to give him this."

"What is your father's name?" Hyena Man's brows arched, and the skin around his mouth creased deeply.

"Hussein Nuur."

He nodded and turned to his daughter. "Her mother is the woman Safiya was speaking of."

Aisha gave him a knowing smile. She took the bag from me. "Wait here." She opened it, took the shirts out, and placed them on the table next to her father's workbench.

They both clapped their hands twice.

Hyena Man spoke in a whisper, a hum, like the flow of a lazy river. The sound gained strength and definition by degrees until it reached a high pitch, an angry cry. "End of the adulterer with the adulteress!" His raspy voice echoed in my chest. "Death to the sin, save the sinner!" He swayed back and forth with its rhythm.

Hyena Man and his daughter walked over to the burjiko and held my father's undershirts over it. Smoke billowed and escaped as they moved the garments back and forth.

"We seek refuge from the evil of darkness, the evil of malignant witchcraft," he chanted along with his daughter. Their voices—loud, strong, and crisp rose beyond the walls of the house. "Seal Hussein Nuur's ears to her whisper, his eyes to her sight, and his limbs to her touch!" Hyena Man yelled. His head and mouth no longer belonged to him. Under the control of something far greater, he continued to shout.

As fast as it gained volume, the sound subsided and gave way to silence. His breathing was heavy and labored, the muscles around his neck tense. Large beads of sweat stood on his forehead as if he had been visited by a violent nightmare. Hyena Man walked back and sat on a tall stool near his workbench.

Aisha took a notebook and pen from a nearby wooden desk and motioned to her father that she was ready.

Hyena Man gave her instructions for Mother to follow. "Hussein should wear each shirt for two days without washing them." He wiped his brow with his hand. "He should wear the red shirt for the first two days."

Aisha wrote.

Hyena Man took a folded paper out of his shirt pocket. "This paper should be placed under his pillow for two weeks." He handed the paper to Aisha.

She put the red shirt in the bag, and placed the paper she'd been writing on along with the one her father gave her on top of it. She covered it with the white shirt and then handed me the bag. "Here. Take this to your mother."

I forced myself a look at the shirts. I expected the fabric to transform into a creature with fangs that would devour Father's flesh upon contact, but the articles seemed unchanged.

# CHAPTER THREE

"ALLAH, PLEASE bring Father back to us from Ayan," I prayed. "I'll be good and obey my parents. I promise I'll pray when Mother tells me to and I'll stop lying. I will never tell another lie ever again." I repeated different versions of this each day that week. Nothing! The two weeks Hyena Man prescribed ended, and Father's behavior only gained momentum. He stopped joining us for supper and soon was coming home only to sleep. The memory of his stories and happier times filled me with misery and made me wretched.

Mother's sadness also grew as time crept on. "He assigns Ayan's husband to patrol in nearby villages, so he can spend more time with her. I have lost him and I don't know why." She wiped her face with the end of her scarf. She wasn't like other women, and this wasn't supposed to happen to her. Father's actions made no sense. Nothing fit. She wasn't the filthy mother, the in-law hating witch, the unfitting barren wife, or the man-hungry whore. Husbands were supposed stay with women like her.

Mother decided to see Ayan, but she needed a cover to go to her house in case Father was there. "Idil, come with me. No need to change from your uniform." Mother took me the next day when I returned from school.

She didn't want Father to think she'd been spying on him. "If Daddy is there, pretend you have mistaken her door with that of a classmate." She held my hand so tight my fingers were tingling by the time we reached Ayan's house. She sent me to knock. "Wave once if your father is there and twice if he isn't."

Ayan opened the door. Her two long braids rested on her back, but she didn't have a shawl covering her shoulders like married women often did. She approached the door with a light step and retreated when she saw me, as if she were expecting someone else. "What do you want?" She asked in a harsh tone.

I ignored her question and peeked behind her to spot Father's boots or his uniform. I saw nothing, so I gave Mother the signal.

She came out of her hiding spot and joined us.

"What do you want?" Ayan threw the question at us.

Mother didn't bother with polite greetings. "I welcomed you into my house; treated you like my own."

Ayan stared at the ground beneath her feet.

"You are a married woman! You have a husband and yet you are after mine." Mother spoke as if Ayan's vows were far more binding than Father's.

"He is married, too," Ayan responded.

"He is a man. It is to be expected. With you it's different."

"It is not *my* fault if you can't keep your husband." She slammed the door.

We went to Ayan's house twice more that week. Both times, Mother hid behind the concrete pillar next to the gate and sent me to check.

The first time, a servant opened. He yelled at me and closed the door.

The second time Ayan came, the same servant right behind her. "If you don't stop, I will tell your father." Ayan waited by the door until I reached Mother, hiding behind the pillar.

Mother's anger shot out of her. "Does she think I am going to let her keep him? She didn't consider me when she opened her house, her bed, and her legs to him!" By the time she finished speaking, she was yelling, but she never went to Ayan again. "I'll tell her husband. Shire must know what his wife is doing. I am certain I won't be telling him anything new. All I am doing is asking him to control his wife. If he is ignorant to the matter, he has the right to know, to hear about the goings-on in his bed when he is away."

At home, Mother summoned our guard, Diriye. "Go tell Shire I need to see him Friday morning. Don't let anyone see you." Diriye set the meeting with Ayan's husband.

❦

Mother was ready for Shire's arrival. Early that morning, she stood in front of her mirror, talking as though the man was already before her. She'd raise a question and give her own answer, imagining what he might say.

Later, I opened the door for Shire and led him into the house.

Mother must have realized there was no reason to drag out the whole miserable tale. I could see that the man knew. It was written on his face, the way he stood, shifting his weight from one leg to the other, his eyes looking everywhere but at Mother's face.

She got right to the point. "Talk to your wife. She must understand she is in the wrong here."

He swallowed hard. "I've tried for weeks. I asked, I ordered, I begged." Shire, in his early twenties, was older than Ayan by four or five years. He looked weary.

Mother sat on Father's chair and pointed to the opposite one for Shire to take. "She is a wife, a mother. She should know better."

Shire didn't take the offer to sit. "General Hussein is there instead of me. He has my wife to himself." He inhaled a long, shuddering breath.

"She is *allowing* it. If she didn't continue, it would stop."

Shire's hands shook. He slipped them into his pockets. "She is not the only one in the wrong. He is my commander, my comrade."

"She must understand she is making a dreadful mistake."

"She won't, and neither will he."

"What are you going to do? Do you have a plan to remedy this?" Her tone was different, harsher than it was when she'd rehearsed in front of her mirror.

Shire looked at her. "I don't know. I have to go." He sighed and took his leave.

Mother followed him to the door. "Is there a plan to take care of this?" She asked him again two more times what he'd intended to do. He gave no answer.

❧

The news of the attack on Father and Ayan reached us four hours after Shire left our house.

"He went straight from here to his home," said Diriye, his ample body filling the chair across from Mother. "Ayan and General Hussein Nuur were in the bedroom."

Diriye saw me standing by the window, listening. He turned to Mother as if to see if she'd noticed me there. She hadn't.

"They hadn't expected Shire to arrive," Diriye continued. "He came upon them like a tiger. By the time her guard, and a nearby soldier responded to their cries for help, they'd each received a few blows."

Mother listened without interrupting.

Diriye closed his eyes tight. "Ayan was wearing a man's red undershirt and nothing else."

Mother sat up in her chair. "A man's red undershirt?" she repeated.

Diriye shrank back into his chair. "I am telling you the truth. I heard it from her servant—the man who was there. He told me right after he told the investigators." Diriye got up and walked toward the window. "It took the three of them to stop Shire: the soldier, the guard, and the general. Shire had death in his bones. That is what they told me."

"What happened to Shire?" Mother asked.

"You don't have to worry about him doing any more harm. The military will take care of him. They hauled him to the car in handcuffs and shackles." Diriye wiped his face with the back of his hand. "General Nuur is lucky to be alive."

*What had become of Father?* The thought flashed into my mind, but Mother didn't inquire after him.

"You can go back to work now," she said, dismissing Diriye.

❧

"I shouldn't have told the husband." Mother's regret was not for Ayan or Shire, but for Father.

Safiya kept a vigil by her side. "You did what you had to do. Maybe your husband will stop after such an attack. The military will make him."

Mother pulled her knees to her chest. "If he ever finds out I met with Shire, he will be furious."

"You just spoke about Ayan not him. We all know it's her fault." Safiya sat across from Mother for a long time.

The night seemed to go on forever with no end in sight. We waited. For what, I did not know.

"I have to go home, but I'll return after supper," Safiya finally said and gathered her shawl about her.

Mother remained seated. "Don't come back tonight. I'll send Idil if I need you." After Safiya left, she resumed her statue posture. "I'll be the subject of their gossip tonight. Safiya will not go home, but to their gathering places, retelling the story of my fall." She said it more to herself for she knew how a story grew, spinning into a new web of suppositions and additions. She often joined the circle as they spun the web of other women's troubles. The plate of dinner Hawa had placed on the corner table, next to Mother's chair, remained untouched.

When she spoke next her voice was weak, void of expression. "Time to go to bed," she told Elmi and me much earlier than usual.

Omar sat imperiously in Father's chair, his big shoulders squared. Heir to the throne in Father's absence, Mother avoided him.

"I didn't finish my work," I complained, because I didn't want to miss Father's homecoming that night.

Mother massaged her temples. "There will be plenty of time. *Later*. You get going now, to your bed."

She went to her room the same time Elmi and I did. Once inside, she cried with abandon. The house seemed to shiver with the depth of her sadness.

I wanted to go and sit with her as we often did in happier times with her telling me the stories of courting and marriage. "I married your father to escape my stepmother's grip," she always said. "Anything was better than serving that evil witch."

"You didn't love Father?" I once asked, my head resting on her lap.

"That came afterwards. After we were married and living together."

"I'll not marry a man I don't love," I'd said in earnest.

"You'll learn to love him. That's the best love there is." At the time, she laughed at my foolishness and kissed me on the head.

Tonight was different. I didn't go in to console her, knowing the remedy for her sorrow was beyond anything I could've done or said.

※

I awoke to a loud sound of heavy boots pounding the tiled floor, as the first sign of dawn penetrated the curtain panels. I listened to the tremors reverberating throughout the house and coming closer. "Who is there?" I shouted, but didn't get a response. I sat up on the bed and reached for my light and in the panic, knocked the lamp over. The crash on to the wooden floor added to my fear. I jumped out of bed and opened my bedroom door.

Elmi's silhouette filled the doorway. "What's going on?" he asked.

"I don't know. Is it Father?" Together, Elmi and I went to the sitting room. More than a dozen uniform-clad soldiers were taking furniture and other items out of the house.

Father, in full ceremonial military uniform, sat in his chair.

Mother stood next to him, whispering consoling phrases. "Don't you worry. It'll be fine." She massaged the back of his neck.

Omar was sitting on the floor cradling Father's hand. "It will get better," he comforted.

Father didn't respond to Mother's or Omar's kindness. The soldiers gave him quick salutes every time they passed, but he didn't acknowledge them either.

"What is happening?" I asked aloud.

"We are moving to Bledley," Mother said.

Bledley was described in my grade seven geography text-books as the region between the two rivers and the most fertile land in the country. Photos of banana plantations, mango groves, grain and cornfields covered the pages of the textbook. "What do you mean we're moving to Bledley?"

Mother's eyes met mine and I read their warning to be quiet. "Your father will be the commander of the largest base in the country."

"Yaaay!" Omar cheered. Even as a small boy he'd loved power, rank, and prestige.

Elmi tugged at Mother's elbow to get her attention. "What about my friends?" His question fell on deaf ears.

Bledley was beautiful to admire in a book, but I wasn't prepared to lose my friends and my home over it. "We have done nothing wrong. He should go alone. Why do we have to move?" In my mind, I thought Mother could exist away from him.

Without warning, Father slapped me with an open hand. "Don't you ever speak like that again."

I staggered backward, and Elmi caught me.

I ran to my room and closed the door. In the safety of my bed, I rubbed my burning face and buried my head in the pillow. I heard a knock and tried to ignore it, but gave in after a while. "Yes?"

Mother came into my room and pulled the curtains apart. Her wandering gaze went everywhere except to me. "Get your things ready."

The early morning sun poured in but did nothing to brighten my dampened spirit. "Why do we have to move in the middle of the school year—and so far away?" By the time I finished speaking I was sitting upright, charged with an anger I didn't know existed.

She left the dresser drawer she was emptying and sat next to me on the bed. "A man's dirt is his woman's wash, *always*."

"Why?"

She placed my head on her chest. "You will understand when you're older."

I hated when Mother said that, and she always did, every time I'd asked something she didn't want to discuss. "I'll never understand, not now, not later. Never," I said as defiantly as I could manage.

She stroked my hair and kissed me on the forehead. "The road to a man's heart is through the mounds of his mess. The sooner you accept that, the better."

I looked at her anew. My image of her as a fighter, a survivor who did what was right, not what was easy—shifted. She was no different from all the other women she'd gossiped about. Like the rest of them, she had given in and taken responsibility for what was not her mistake. I was incapable of such sad conviction. "I won't accept that," I said.

"You will. You might not want to, but you'll accept it all the same because there are no other options," Mother said, with a certainty that stunned me.

I opened my mouth to speak, but she dismissed me with a wave of her hand. She went back to the dresser. "You should pack if you don't want to leave your belongings."

I followed her lead, stuffing things into my large, black suitcase. "This is not fair," I said under my breath. "I'll not accept things like this when I'm older."

She shifted the bag upright and opened the door. "Let us go."

When I emerged, dragging my suitcase behind me, there was no furniture in the house except for the chair Father had sat in earlier.

Mother took Elmi and me outside to the truck.

The driver greeted us as we approached and loaded our luggage.

The trees in the yard swayed back and forth, fanning us in the light breeze. I wrapped my arms around myself, feeling a slight chill skitter across my skin.

Safiya appeared behind the truck carrying a thermos of tea and a sack of sweets. "My husband told me you are moving. Had I known, I would've prepared more food for the road. I am sorry to see you go. We were in Hodan's house just now discussing how to help." She turned to two other women standing at a distance.

"So, everyone's talking?" Mother posed the question to Safiya.

"Not in a negative way, not about a dear friend like you. We just wanted to help is all."

Mother scoffed at the lie, but said nothing more about it. She waved once to Safiya and the other women and fled toward the waiting vehicle.

The driver extended his hand and helped her in. His large frame filled the doorway, shielding her from the glaring eyes of the onlookers.

My friends stopped on their way to school, wearing bright smiles borrowed from happier times. "Bye Idil. We'll miss you."

My hugs lingered. "I'll miss you so much," I whispered in their ears.

"Come in," Mother called me from behind the driver.

I couldn't leave as easily as she'd done. For each step I should take forward, there were two I wished I could take back. I stood there, silent.

I heard Omar chattering to Father as they came toward Elmi and me. "Why are you standing there?" Omar's elbow landed on my ribs and I gasped for air. "Move," he snarled.

Elmi didn't have a chance to get out of the way before Omar pushed him down. Father didn't react to what Omar had done even after Elmi wailed in pain.

"You should learn to get out of the way," Omar said as he proceeded to sit in the front seat next to Mother. Father followed him in.

Elmi and I boarded last.

❧

The truck pulled out of the driveway, taking us away from everyone and everything familiar to a vast unknown.

My friends held their hands above their heads in a half-salute. I waved back and watched them grow smaller in the distance. An absolute longing filled me.

Mother touched my arm. "Here." She passed a thin blanket back to Elmi and me. I took it, although I knew no amount of cover could warm the icy feeling inside. Her attention lingered upon me. She poured Father a glass of his drink, then turned back to me. "Do you want something to eat?" An apologetic tone colored her words.

"I am not hungry."

She handed me a piece of cake from the sack Safiya had brought anyway. I took it, passed it to Elmi, and focused my attention outside the window. The landscape drifted away faster and faster as we drove in silence for what seemed like hours.

"It is your fault!" Father shouted at Mother shattering the quiet in the truck. "You set Shire against us." He held his head between his hands. "You met with him and chastised him." Anger oozed from him, filling the small cabin. "'Be a man.' Is that what you said to him?" Mother kept silent as he hurled accusations at her. "How did that help him? He's in jail now and single." He took her arm and tugged her toward him. "You had everything—house, children, money, servants—but you weren't satisfied. You wanted more."

For the first time, she faced him. "I didn't have what mattered. I wanted a husband."

Father turned to her, surprised. "I was coming home, spending nights. I fed you, clothed you, and shared your bed. That's what the vow said."

Mother didn't respond.

"Maybe I should marry three other wives or divorce you and take four." He growled. "That would teach you a lesson."

She said nothing.

He extended his glass.

She refilled it.

# CHAPTER FOUR

WE ARRIVED at Bledley late Sunday morning. The truck moved very slowly through a market, bustling with throngs of people, and my spirit lifted. The city was smaller than Gaalmaran, where we had come from, but stalls lined both sides of the road and our truck passed through a sea of color. A vibrant array of fruit and vegetables—bananas, mangoes, lemons, limes, four different kinds of peppers, and tomatoes—shone before us on high wooden tables. I rested my knees on the seat and hoisted myself into the half-open window. A warm breeze washed over me. The smell of fresh produce and damp earth filled the truck and I felt Bledley beckon me in a way that Gaalmaran never had.

Several children chased each other around the rectangular fruit tables, their bare feet covered with mud from a recent rain. The women shopkeepers tilted their heads and laughed. A boy and girl each swiped some fruit from a tray. They hid behind a stack of wood, their backs facing the truck, and bit into it. The woman in charge didn't seem to notice.

I nudged Elmi and pointed. "Did you see that?"

Elmi knelt beside me, but Mother saw us. "Sit," she ordered.

We did until she looked away to refill Father's glass. Then, taking care not to attract her attention, we snuck back up to watch the children playing through the window.

The city's busy market disappeared and was replaced by grain farms. The strong wind made little clouds of dust, which rolled up and fell back. Acres and acres of farmland spread before us. Big, old trees stood grandly atop their earthbound roots, their heavy, green leaves rustling in the soft breeze.

Father sat up and looked around. His mood had improved. "An airport is planned for here," he told Omar.

Omar pointed at a chain-link fence. "What is that?"

Father smiled. "That is the military base where we will be living."

Omar's eyes lit up with excitement. "How do you know this?"

Father squeezed Omar's shoulder. "I was here three times before I went away to the Soviet Union."

Desolation welcomed us at the gate. The base was as empty and quiet as the market was busy and loud. Rows and rows of cream-colored tent structures stood before us. Father waved his hands. "That is where the soldiers live."

Young children ran here and there in the field near the tents. Dust covered the black earth adding to the depressing landscape. I saw no adults.

Father pointed to a few dozen small buildings. "The junior officers live there."

Omar didn't ask questions as Father described different parts of the base. "My office is there, behind the embankment." A large metal gate came into view. "That is our new home."

Uniformed officers approached the truck before it came to a full stop. They greeted Father with a precise military salute and moved to the back to unload.

Once off the truck, my feet met an asphalt driveway leading to a big house, bigger than I could've imagined. It stood on guard in the middle of the base. Everything else—the administration quarters, the residence for the lower-ranking officers, and the tent structures for the soldiers—seemed insignificant against it.

Knee-high cement blocks served as perches for two marble lion statues resting on their hindquarters. Over the gate in front of the house were decorative wrought-iron okra leaves. A Somali flag—blue with a white star in the center—waved at us from a metal pole in the middle of the yard. We entered, led by two soldiers. The door to the main house opened, and the sadness I'd felt before evaporated and was replaced with excitement.

"This way sir!" One officer led Father into the house.

Yet another extended his hand to Mother. "Come with me, Madam."

She hesitated.

He pointed at the stairs. "Madam?"

She preceded him into the house. We followed.

Omar flew past us as though he were running from foreign invaders. "The biggest room is mine." He ascended the stairs by twos and disappeared.

I admired the spiral staircase, enjoying the luxurious feeling of the soft, cream-colored carpet beneath my feet. My hands caressed the smooth surface of the wooden railing. This house was a palace compared to where we had lived.

Elmi, only a few steps ahead, shrieked with excitement. "Look!" he yelled.

My eyes followed his finger. At the end of the stairwell hung a huge framed painting of the Indian Ocean. In the picture, it was dusk, and the beach was empty except for two children. Their hands outstretched, heads tilted back, smiling wide, they pointed at something out of sight. The contrast between the small figures and the roaring waves descending upon them was stunning.

Omar ran out of a room to get to Mother. "It's not fair!" he yelled.

"What is the matter?" she asked.

"The biggest room is a girl's room!"

A uniformed officer carrying a chair turned to Omar with understanding. "The other family had only girls."

Omar forgot his grievance. "All girls? How many?"

"Six."

He lowered his head to give condolences to a family he didn't know. "Six girls and no boys." It saddened him to hear a family stuck with such an abomination.

Mother looked at him with a reassuring gaze. "I'll take care of it." She assigned each one of us a room.

"Mine is the biggest, and I love it." I admired the décor of the soft yellow room, accented by lilac-filled bouquets drawn on three of the walls and on the back of the door panel.

Mother stared at me. "Be careful not to upset your

brother," she warned. She assigned Elmi the room next to mine, and he accepted with no complaint.

Omar opened the door to his bedroom. "I get the smallest?"

Mother took him in her arms. "You are on the men's side of the house, see? You are on your Father's side." She knew such a statement would appease him. "This is next to your father's study."

As the day grew old, the voices of the servants and the soldiers moving about the house faded to a soft murmur. Elmi and I wandered toward the study. "This is a library, not a study," I said. "Let us see." We entered and stood in front of magnificent hardwood bookcases that covered the walls from floor to ceiling. The middle section held volumes with wooden covers, while on the ends were thin paperbacks, memos, and copies of old newspapers. A handcrafted oak desk stood in the center of the room. On its polished top sat statues of camels and lions, and a wooden *dhiil*—milk pitcher—carved with decorative images of tribal symbols. Everything, from the penholder to the bookstand, boasted outstanding craftsmanship. On one wall was a photo of a young man dressed in white macawis. He held a wooden spear over his right shoulder, his left hand rested on his hip. White ink letters and symbols covered his dome-shaped hair.

Elmi ran his fingers over the books, from one end to the other. "I have never seen so many."

I didn't hear Omar come in until he was standing next to me. Marking his territory on the men's side of the house, he pushed me away. "Get out of here," he said, and sat on the big chair behind the desk. "Who said you could be in here?"

Elmi and I left the room silently.

❧

Mother called Elmi and me into the sitting room. It was three days after we moved to Bledley. She'd registered Omar at the high school first and then moved on to us. "It's time to go."

I'd expected the inevitable, but still I was disappointed. "Now? We are going now?"

She knitted her brows tight. "Did you hear what I said?"

There was no arguing with her, so Elmi and I resigned ourselves to the dreadful journey, got ready, and followed her to the car. Our arrival at the school coincided with the ringing of the morning recess bell. The yard was much larger than the one in my former school, but I saw no swing sets, basketball nets, or soccer pitches. Still, the playground welcomed the children leaving their classes with open arms, and they embraced it with glee. As their rubber-sandaled feet hit the ground, clouds of dust traveled up their legs. They paid no mind to it and moved into distinct groups, based on age or size. I couldn't tell which.

They pulled skipping ropes, empty cans for a kick-the-can game, balls made of yarn, and leftover fabric out of their pockets. The games began immediately. The yard, which had been empty a few seconds before, exploded with a chorus of happy laughter. Every child wore a pair of khaki pants and a white shirt or blouse. I scanned the area to find a group I might fit into as a pang of loneliness stabbed at me. My mind rushed back to the comfort of the long-established friendships I'd left behind, and I cursed Father under my breath.

The principal stepped out of his office and greeted Mother. "I am ready for you, Madam."

"Thank you." She smiled at him and walked toward the small office.

I wanted her to take us inside. She did that with Omar two days before when she'd signed him up at the high school. "Please let us come with you," I begged.

"Wait here until I come back," she said.

We stood there, anxious and alert, as a boy, close to me in age, approached.

"What are your names?" he asked.

For the first time, I saw someone I could befriend. I marveled at this beautiful person. My plain, paper-thin lips paled in comparison to his full ones. Unlike mine, which looked like it didn't belong on my face, his nose fit perfectly. I stared at his flawless figure, his tight curls, and his well-toned muscles. "I am Idil, and this is Elmi," I responded.

He looked at me through enormous eyes that far outshone mine. "Welcome to our school," he said.

I was about to thank him, but the bell rang just then, and he left.

A few minutes later, Mother emerged, wearing a forced smile. "The principal will take you to your classes."

"Could we start tomorrow morning?" I asked her. "Please don't make us start in the middle of the day." It didn't matter whether I started at the beginning of the day or the middle or ten years from then. I didn't want to go to this school. I reminded her she didn't make Omar stay when she signed him up, but I had to follow the principal to my grade eight class. The head teacher took Elmi toward his seventh-grade room. I walked slowly, to delay the inevitable, but the principal's strong strides urged me on, and we reached my classroom much sooner than I'd hoped.

The teacher placed me in the second seat of the second row. "We are sitting in alphabetical order and that is your seat, Idil," he explained.

The boy who had welcomed us earlier was sitting two rows away from me. The class was quiet, and disciplined, but I knew, as the new student, every single eye in the room was on the back of my head. My skin prickled. I buried my head in the exercise book the teacher had placed on my desk and did more math problems than were assigned.

"My name is Sidow," my hero introduced himself at the start of the lunch recess. "Where did you come from?"

"We moved from Gaalmaran."

His eyes settled on my face. "That's far away from here. Why did you move?"

I averted my gaze, fearing he could read my thoughts. "The military transferred my father here." I had no intention of telling him the real reason.

He seemed satisfied with my answer. "Do you want to play?" Sidow's smooth skin glowed.

"Yes, I'd like that."

※

A month after we came to the school, I invited Sidow over. "You should come to my house next Thursday."

"I'll have to ask my father," he said, but he declined the invitation the next time I asked. "My father doesn't like the military. He says they bring nothing but horror."

I continued to ask Sidow until he finally agreed to come. The day he decided to walk home with us the gate opened, and the metal rings clanked, announcing our arrival. I turned around to welcome Sidow, but he was retreating from me.

"You live in there?" He pointed an accusatory finger at the huge house. "You never said your father was the commander."

"Does it matter?"

"Yes, it does."

It took more than five minutes to convince Sidow to come inside. "My father is not home," I said to encourage him.

"Will your mother mind that I am here?"

"No, she won't. She'll thank you for helping us at school. I told her how you let us join your game."

"If you're sure." Hesitant, Sidow entered the house. He examined his surroundings with careful attention. "Your father is the general?" He spoke as if it were a crime to hold such office. "I shouldn't be here."

"My parents are normal people, like any other parents. Don't worry." I walked between Elmi and Sidow. They had bonded over their shared love for art from the first day we played the Draw Your Answer game. In that game, one team member would make a statement and the others were expected to draw their answers in the dirt. The person with the best drawing won, and Sidow held a long-running winning streak.

Elmi leapt toward his room, and Sidow and I followed. "I'll show you what I am working on now. Tell me what you think, honestly." Elmi lifted the pad next to the box of his art supplies as soon as we made it into his room. "Well?"

Sidow took the sheet from Elmi. "It's a fantastic start. I love the color choice."

"Could you help me improve it?" Elmi appreciated the compliment.

"Of course. I'm not an expert, but I will teach you what I know."

I touched Sidow's elbow. "I want you to see Father's study."

Sidow was drawn to the artifacts as soon as we entered the office. "I didn't expect these here." His hand caressed the wooden frame around the photo on the wall. "I thought your father would use pieces from his own region, not from here."

I followed Sidow's gaze. "These were here when we arrived."

Sidow stood in front of the drawing on the wall over Father's chair and explained the images on the man's hair. "That is the name of the girl he likes, and next is the symbol of his tribe and her tribe merged together to show how much he loves her." Sidow went to the window on the opposite wall. He gasped at the sight of the wooden milk pitcher. "That dhiil is at least three hundred years old!"

I went over where Sidow stood and ran my hand along the seams. "It looks new."

Elmi did the same as I did.

Sidow inhaled. "I know, but it's very old." Sidow stopped me from lifting it up. "A long time ago, each tribe had one of these filled with milk. As a gesture of thanksgiving to the spirits, the villagers left it outside."

His knowledge of the culture intrigued me. "What happened to the milk?"

"The following morning, the tribal elders woke up and found the dhiil empty, clean, and newer than it had been the night before. It never aged," Sidow explained the legend.

"We lost the tradition when the colonial governments seized them as art pieces." He paused. "They were never meant to be artifacts."

Tiny soft butterflies filled my stomach. "You know so much."

We spent the hours that followed in the study, flipping through pages of books and newspaper articles. Mesmerized by Sidow's narrative, I didn't hear Mother come into the room. She hadn't been in the house when we got home.

She stood next to the door, resting her right hand on the doorknob, her shoulders squared against the frame. "What are you doing in here?" Mother's expression teetered between bewilderment and contempt.

Mother stared at the three of us around Father's desk, Sidow, reading from a book of poetry, and Elmi and me listening, entranced.

"Go play outside and don't be found in here again!" Mother shouted and startled me. "*Ever.*"

We left quickly, Mother's words chasing after us.

"Maybe I should go home." Sidow seemed nervous.

I picked up a stick to mark a game of hopscotch on the soft earth near the vegetable garden, between the main house and the service quarters. "No, please don't," I pleaded.

"Your mother is upset with me."

I'd never seen such hot anger on Mother's face before. Even Father's affairs didn't make her face contort like that, but I wasn't willing to admit it to Sidow. "No, she isn't. She just doesn't want Father to find us there."

We played for another hour, but there was no joy in the game.

Sidow stopped in the middle of the last square. "I should go now."

Elmi and I followed him to the main gate. "See you at school on Saturday," we said in unison and watched him until he disappeared out of sight.

Mother waved for me to come to her when I returned. "The nose on that boy, and those lips!" She spoke as if she were reminding herself of what Sidow looked like. "How could you?"

"How could I what? What are you talking about?"

She smiled. "His nose is so big you could build a village in there." She removed the bread from the tinaar. "How could you befriend the likes of him?"

"He is very kind to both Elmi and me. I told you how he helped us the first day." Of course, I wouldn't admit to the feeling of excitement that filled me each morning when I laid my eyes upon him. "Do you remember what I told you? How he'd let us join his team in the yard?" I threw questions at her instead of telling her about the deep well that opened inside my belly at the sight of his beautiful smile.

"I would never have imagined this was the boy you gave such a glorious description of," she said, and dismissed me without forbidding me to have Sidow visit again. I took liberty with that loophole.

# CHAPTER FIVE

ONE MORNING, six months after I started the new school, Sidow let me in on a secret. "We are going to the waterfall for a tournament this afternoon," he whispered in my ear as we lined up to submit our homework. "We leave at the lunch bell. No teachers; just a few of us."

The implication scared me. "You skip school?"

"Yes." Sidow dropped his math workbook in the basket. "We do it every month." He winked at me. "The half-hour break gives us enough time to get to the waterfall and avoid suspicion."

I nodded, but the uncertainty stayed with me all morning. Even when I told Elmi at morning recess, I doubted we'd go through with it, but we did. At the sound of the bell, eighteen students, including Elmi and me, left the yard but not as a group. We left through different points of exit and met up near the snack carts that lined up outside to sell to the students at recess and lunchtime.

The path to the waterfall snaked through two walls of thick evergreens bordering the farms on either side of the walkway. The narrow alley was wide enough for two people to walk side by side at first, but it gradually grew narrower. The borders of the farms seemed to be moving closer, forcing us to walk in a single file. We shouted words at each other, passing messages up and down the row. Halfway there, I noticed blooms of dust rising from under my feet and settling on my sneakers. The brown earth made the white fabric look like an overused dishrag. "Oh, my shoes! Mother will be so angry."

"She will be," Elmi agreed. "But don't think about her now. She might not be home when we get there. Just have fun."

Elmi was right, but Mother's reaction the last time I showed up covered in mud flashed through my mind. I'd played tug of war after school that day, after a light rain had coated the earth with a thin crust of mud. It covered my clothes.

One look at me and she burst into tears. "I am staying in a miserable marriage so you aren't raised by a stepmother, and you do this!" She wept as I changed. She snatched my pants and blouse off the floor before I could collect them and went to the laundry tub.

Her reaction wasn't normal. I had done similar or worse things before. She often chastised me and even punished me, but had never dissolved in a pool of tears like she did that day. "Sorry, Mother. I didn't mean it. Mother, let me do it. Let me wash them."

She moved away and dropped my clothes in the hot, soapy water and scrubbed. "It's only for you I stay." She spoke with a mournful tone. "The boys will survive. They have their father. A girl in her stepmother's home might as well die. It is no life. I should know."

"I promise never to get dirty again. I'll always listen to you and do what you say. Please stop. Please." I wrapped my arms around her.

"You've no idea what's waiting for you out there," she continued. "There's no love between your father and me. He has moved from one mistress's bed to another, without the decency to marry a second wife and stay put."

It was bad enough Mother suffered, but it hurt to hear that it was for me alone. She tolerated every insult, poured Father his drinks, even though she hated to, and endured him constantly sleeping with other women. I was awed by her commitment. I remember thinking there would be no love—not for a child or a husband—strong enough to keep me in such a relationship. That made adding to her pain an even a greater crime. From that day on I paid attention to where I sat, hesitated to play any game that required contact, and kept clean.

Sidow pointed at his rubber sandals made of the thin inner-layer of old tires. "This is what you should wear."

"I didn't know."

To avoid further destruction to my shoes, I stepped around the exposed section of the walkway onto the grass-covered parts. That slowed me down, and others, except Elmi, moved ahead.

Elmi took my hand. "Come. We have to catch up." He led me toward the waterfall where the children were gathering.

❧

The sound of the water rushing over the rocks and the excited voices of children from other schools reached us before we saw either of them. The sound came from behind a curtain of *booc-booc* bushes and a thick growth of *ghalab* trees.

On each side of the waterfall rows of mango and banana trees were protected by a wall of large evergreens.

Sidow approached the others. "It is your turn to get the fruit."

Three boys stepped forward. "We are ready," they said in unison.

"Get mangoes this time. We had bananas last month," Sidow instructed. "Only take what's fallen to the ground."

"We will." And with that, they disappeared.

Sidow took a seat on a rock cliff at the edge of a whirlpool under the waterfall. Elmi and I sat beneath Sidow's perch. Less than five minutes later, the three boys returned with armfuls of rich, ripe mangoes. They passed them around. The juice from the mango dripped down my hand and reached my elbow in sugary, golden-streaks. The sweet smell of the fruit remained in the air long after we'd washed our hands.

Children dared each other to dive underwater, deeper and longer every time. I turned to Sidow, who was keeping score of the competition. "This is so much fun. Thank you for inviting us." One of the swimmers stayed under water too long and others began to shout. "Maybe he's drowned!" I said, and got up and moved closer to the edge of the water.

Sidow came down from his seat and took my hand. "He'll be fine."

I didn't realize I was holding my breath until the swimmer surfaced. "He is alive!" I joined the excitement and victory dances that erupted with each child who emerged from the water.

Within seconds of one game ending, another began. A bout of wrestling led to a boxing match and then a skipping-rope contest. Each winner received an award—a rock, a piece of wood, a flower petal, or a military-style salute from the rest of us.

Sidow took center stage again. "This concludes another tournament. See you next month."

Children scattered as quickly as they had come together.

"I loved the victory dances. Did you see them jiggle their scrawny behinds?" I said, as we walked away. I laughed hard at the memory of their underwear, stuck to them like a second layer of skin.

Sidow joined me.

※

Elmi and I walked home from school, desperate for a plan to avoid Mother's wrath, but were unable to reach a solution. I opened the main door, and she wasn't there waiting for us. This was a perfect opportunity to go to my room and change into sandals, but her voice coming from the sitting room grounded me.

"I thought he'd learned," Mother said.

A figure wrapped in a white robe sat across from her. "This is bad, very bad. She controls him. You must act quickly—right now."

The implications were so obvious that my stomach lurched. *If we should move again, I'll die,* I thought. I forgot my shoes and stood next to the wall listening, with Elmi right behind me. *Could things get any worse than they had been with Ayan?* I prayed that was impossible.

The enshrouded being described Father's new love. "She is tall, has long dark hair and a slim build, somewhere between eighteen and twenty-five years old." She could have been one of many women.

"Add this to his soup, and throw away what's left over so no one else eats it. You will see a change right away."

"Where does he find them?" Mother asked.

"He's not to blame. The women do it. They throw themselves at the men. You'd have no trouble if they kept away." The being sighed as if exhausted by the explanation. "If they didn't seek him, he wouldn't look. It is time for me to go. May Allah be with you."

Mother saw us as she ushered the woman outside. "This is Halima, the village healer."

I nodded and they walked past us toward the main door.

When Mother returned, she told me why the healer had come. I pretended I hadn't been listening, and Mother showed me two different bottles. "She knew everything," Mother said. "She described the woman perfectly."

"What happens when the next one comes along?"

"There'll be no next one. This healer sealed his ears to their advances."

"Why is it always the woman's fault?"

"Because it is. Everyone knows. To think your husband is after other women is to accept that you couldn't keep him content. Surely you, at fourteen years of age, can see that's not true. I can keep a husband better than any other woman, so how do you explain what's happening? What is the reason for Father's desire to be in any bed but mine? If he could think for himself, he'd see that all his needs are met." She stopped, realizing she'd said more than was necessary. "Never mind. This healer will take care of it. You'll see."

I listened to Mother's reasoning, but I knew this, like the others, was an effort in futility. A few days later Father had a new mistress. He'd moved her into the apartment next to his office, and just like always, Mother returned to her search in the village for help and visited one healer after another. Often she sat in her room for hours sorting potions into groups, dumping the ones that had failed, while looking at new ones with overwhelming hope.

In the days that followed, Mother became oblivious to everything except finding a cure for Father's infidelity. Elmi and I were free to do as we wished. "Come over," I invited Sidow every Friday with confidence.

"Are you sure your mother won't mind?" he'd ask.

"Yes. I am." I was certain she wouldn't even notice he was there.

❧

In Father's study Elmi, Sidow, and I read books, articles from *The October Star*—the national daily newspaper—and even government documents and memos. The technical pieces were difficult to understand, others were boring, but from time to time we stumbled upon something interesting and spent hours looking and reading.

Sidow was very good at picking great poems. "Read this one," he said handing me a thin volume. It was a poem about a battle between two tribes written by a man named Abdulle Hasan. It was long, violent, and glorious.

Sidow's excitement bubbled up before I could finish the first stanza. "A great poem!" He stopped me several times. "Read it again," he said.

I read the last twenty lines that described the final battle. The sounds and images of the fast-moving swords and daggers seemed to fill the room. "How many people died, do you think?" I directed the question to Sidow without taking my eyes off the page.

He didn't respond. I looked up. Sidow was no longer across from Elmi and me on the floor. Instead, he was sitting in Father's chair, something he'd never done before. He had a piece of paper before him and as I approached the desk I followed his eyes to his cupped hand, drawing vigorously on the page. His brows scrunched together in a single line. Sidow drew the battle as though he were there, watching everything from above the clearing.

Bodies of the dead littered the page as the battle raged. Victorious clan members stood in the middle of the field, holding their weapons aloft. In the distance, on the side of the winning tribe, he drew a line of women advancing toward the men with open arms. On the losing side, women held white sheets, to prepare for the funerals.

The sketch was intricate and detailed—beyond something such a young person could normally create.

"Where did you learn to do this?"

"I don't know."

"You don't do this in art class."

"They tell me what to draw, and I can't do that. I have to see it in my head." Sidow watched my reaction. "Do you understand?"

I wasn't sure I did.

"What do you think?" he asked.

I searched for a fitting response. "I love it," I said. Indeed, I did.

"Here." He gave me the drawing.

I snatched the sheet of paper away from him, lest he change his mind. I was in awe of both my luck and his generosity.

Elmi reached for it. I held it up, so he could admire it but I didn't want anyone to touch it. Not even Elmi.

※

Sidow's gift formed a deeper connection between us. I loved discussing literature with him, but I loved even more to see Sidow through his drawings. Through the shades, the lines, and color on the page Sidow morphed into more than a classmate. He became bigger and more important to me than any other boy.

"Draw the waterfall tournament," I demanded the following week. As the words passed my lips, I noticed how demanding I sounded. I wanted to grab them and shove them back into my mouth. "If you don't mind," I added to soften my bossiness.

"I don't." He went to the box where Elmi kept his art supplies. "I'll do it right now."

We moved to the sitting room. I stood in front of the decorative bay window. Tall panes of stained glass covered a third of the wall, from floor to ceiling. "I'll tell you what I remember from the last month's waterfall tournament, and you draw."

"Ready."

I talked for a long time, swept away by the memory of my experience of the magnificent waterfall, and Sidow's drawing materialized across the surface of the paper. "Okay, let me see."

He lifted the page, holding it before me. "Here."

I gasped.

In the center of the drawing was a lone swimmer leaping out of the whirlpool, hands outstretched, smiling broadly. Water ran down his body in long streaks. His dark skin shone against the clear water, and the droplets on his tight curls glittered like diamond dust.

On the cliff overlooking the water, Sidow drew a line of children clapping to mark the victory of the first swimmer to reach the surface. Below that image, they watched another in mid-flight, a cannon ball, hurtling toward the whirlpool. The images, refined and innocent, filled me with joy.

He extended the pad toward me. "It's yours."

My hand shook as I reached for it. "This is the best gift I've ever had." I was still wrapped in the marvel of my beautiful gift, when Mother entered the room. She had made her way up the stairs and into the room without making a sound and was upon me before she spoke.

"What do you think you are doing?" She grabbed me by the elbow and dragged me away from Sidow. "This is what you spend your whole day doing? With *him* here, and your brother involved?"

Elmi was already retreating to his room.

Sidow moved toward the door, ready for a quick getaway, but he didn't leave.

Mother waved her hand encompassing the area. "You have everything and all you want is to bring *him* here." She took the drawing and held it away from her face. "What is this?" Saliva flew out of her mouth and spattered the page. "*He* needs to go home." Mother knew Sidow's name, but she refused to dignify him with it. "He is leaving right *now*."

Sidow slunk away, a wounded animal, without saying good-bye. I wanted to run after him and take back the pain, wipe the tears I knew were inside, even if his cheeks were dry. "Sorry," I called after him as a cheap substitute.

Mother clenched her fists. "I don't want to see you anywhere near that boy or the likes of him again."

"Why?"

"Ask why again, and I will send you to Timbuktu."

The first time Mother uttered that threat, I was four years old and believed Timbuktu was a place where young girls died. At fourteen, I would've gone to Timbuktu rather than sever my friendship with Sidow. I ran out of the room. Mother didn't stop me.

Later that night, when I was in bed, she came to me. "Idil," she pulled the chair from under my desk and sat. "I do what I do to protect *you* from you. A girl who follows her heart is a great danger to herself. Please use your head."

If seeing Sidow was dangerous, I didn't want to be saved. I told Mother that, but she only sighed and left.

❧

The next morning at school, a cloud of sadness surrounded me. At recess, I sat on the rock bench at the far corner of the yard. Even after I was invited to join the girls in a game of skipping, I remained, plucking the grass beneath my feet.

Sidow left the soccer game and stood next to me. "I know your mother doesn't want her precious daughter playing with a Boon."

"You are a Boon?" The revelation shook me. I believed Boon people to be slaves for those from my clan, the Bliss. Mother had explained more than once that they were ugly and their brains were smaller than ours.

"Yes."

Sidow was like other boys, if not better. He was very smart and his refined image contradicted the picture I had of the Boon people as hideous and backward. "But you are smart, handsome, and kind."

Sidow's gaze landed hard upon me, covering my whole body in a smothering stare. "What did you expect?"

I couldn't tell him about the Boon image imprinted on my mind from the time I could walk. I was told that Boon people have wide noses, large lips, and darker skin—that they are first cousins of African apes. Mother often explained to me how my grandfather owned Boon slaves. "But you're... you look so different," I sputtered. Sidow couldn't belong to any Boon tribe. He didn't fit Mother's account of how stupid and degenerate they were. I gathered my leftover lunch and went back to class.

# CHAPTER SIX

WHEN WE RETURNED from school, Mother called Elmi and me into the sitting room. "I have new rules," she announced in an important tone.

Omar was in Father's chair, so I braced myself for what was to follow.

She pointed at me. "*You* will walk to school and *dugsi*—religious school—with Omar."

I heard a swooshing sound in my ears. The joy of walking with Sidow to and from school and dugsi flew from my grasp.

Omar jumped to his feet, angry. "I don't want her with me. She is a girl!"

I could've hugged him for saying that. I wanted to plant a deep kiss upon his cheek for despising my company as much as I hated his.

Mother appealed to Omar's sense of duty. "That's why she must walk with you. She's your responsibility." She waited for a few seconds for the statement to sink in. "You must watch her to protect the family name."

Omar sat back in the chair with a huff. He couldn't argue with Mother because he understood his duty and where it lay.

She walked to where he sat and placed her hand on Omar's shoulder. "She can't be anywhere *near* that boy, *ever*."

"The Boon boy?"

Mother nodded and turned to Elmi. "I want you to play with Omar on Fridays."

"Damn it!" Omar forgot his decorum and cursed in Mother's presence. "You want Elmi to play with me, too?"

She must have sensed she was asking too much of Omar because she didn't chastise him for cursing. "He is a boy. Who else will he play with?"

"Mother," Omar spoke with no reservation, "you know he is nothing like a boy."

Silence filled the room, and I waited for her open hand to land of his cheek for the implication. Instead she said, "Then he needs to be among boys. You have to teach him proper behavior."

"I will do it, but I want you to know that it is not fair." Omar got up and left the room.

"You'll help Hawa in the kitchen on Fridays starting this week," Mother instructed and the next day, she set her tortuous plan in motion.

Just like Mother ordered, I joined Hawa in the kitchen that Friday. Mother remained in the sitting room and only glanced up from her knitting occasionally.

An hour before dinner was called Elmi came in upset. "I don't want to play with Omar."

Mother ran her fingers through Elmi's thick, sweat-matted curls. "What happened?"

"I don't want to be near Omar, or his friends, anymore."

Mother gently pulled Elmi close. "Why?"

"They are killing cats in front of me!"

She used the sleeve of her dress to wipe his tears. "Play on the field, away from them when they do that."

"I told them I don't want to see it, but they won't let me go. They hold me tight, and make me watch."

"Mother, you know how Omar is," I added to show her how difficult it was to be around my big brother and his followers.

She looked at me as if she understood, so I felt encouraged to say more. "It isn't easy for me, either. I can do nothing right. Everything, from the way I walk to the way I breathe, draws a criticism from him. I am too slow, too fast, or looking at a boy."

Still, Mother remained focused on Elmi. "I'll speak to him," she said.

"I can't. I can't," Elmi wailed.

Mother put a finger over Elmi's mouth at the sound of the main door opening. "Is that you, Omar?" she called aloud.

He barged into the room. "Is Elmi still crying?"

Mother stood up and extended her hand to Omar. "Come with me." She took him into the study and closed the door.

Elmi stopped sniveling and followed me to eavesdrop.

"I don't want him around me!" The walls couldn't contain Omar's fury.

Mother used measured words. "Is anyone forcing your brother to witness animals being killed?"

"He is upset because we threw a rock at an alley cat; a stupid, injured animal made him cry."

"He is young."

Omar's words flew out. "What man, no matter how old or young, is disturbed by seeing that? I am ashamed he is my brother."

With his next phrase, Omar dismissed my complaints altogether. "And Idil! Don't even get me started on her!"

"I'm sorry, but you are the eldest brother, the head of the house after Father. You must accept the challenge. I need your help."

It felt as though Mother's pleading with Omar went on and on for hours. My legs got tingly and numb from squatting in front of the door for so long, but I continued to listen until Mother opened it. Both Elmi and I toppled into the room. Omar laughed, and left.

"I expect the two of you to follow the rules and listen to your older brother," she scolded us. "He is in charge when Father is not here. Keep that in mind before you complain."

Mother swept past us. Lost and helpless, I looked at Elmi. "We need a plan," I whispered.

"We'll never win against Omar."

I knew he was right. We were no match for Omar and his power as the eldest son.

I had to keep walking with Omar to and from school and

dugsi, while Elmi continued to endure Omar's company for the whole of every Friday.

茶

Instead of waiting outside the dugsi window like he usually did—glaring and making hand gestures—Omar finished his Qur'an lesson and left. I was stunned he didn't motion for me to hurry up. I watched him until I lost sight of him and went back to my reading. About thirty minutes later, I collected everything and left, grateful for an Omar-free walk.

I was halfway home when Omar darted out from behind a tree, looking excited. "Idil, come here." He led me away from the trodden path and into the narrow alley between the village huts and the military compound. "I have something to show you." He was excited, and his words tumbled upon each other and came out jumbled.

I was afraid, but still I went with him. "What is it?"

"Just come." He pointed at something. "Look at this."

I jumped back, away from the remains of a dead cat. Its open eyes stared into endless nothingness. "What is this? Why are you showing me this?"

Omar's excitement crackled. "It didn't turn away or blink. It died staring."

I closed my eyes to erase the hideous image from my mind, but failed. The cat grew bigger, well-defined and vivid behind my closed lids. I had to open them.

Omar sat next to the cat's corpse. "If you hid everything but the face, you could pretend it's still alive."

He removed the grass covering its tiny lower body, and

broken bones protruded from skin. Fresh blood and stomach contents oozed out of each opening, matting its gray fur. One of the front paws, the only limb still intact, was outstretched, as though it had tried to reach for something beyond its grasp. It beckoned me to become a witness to the evil at hand.

Omar smiled at me. "It was the bravest creature I have ever seen."

Bile filled my mouth. "This is disgusting." My head spun and I staggered backward, gasping for air.

Omar paid no mind. His voice seemed to come from a far-off distance. "It could fetch so much money if you had the right technique to preserve it like an Egyptian mummy. What do you think?" he asked.

*Omar is overjoyed because he's killed a cat.* I wanted to cry, to hit him, to yell at him, and to run away from him. I did none of that. "You...should...bury it."

His grin was too hard to bear. "What's wrong with you? I'm going to keep it here for a long time and show it to everyone."

I backed out of the alley. "Let's go home. It's getting dark."

Omar ran back and forth collecting rocks. "Give me a minute."

"We're late. Mother will be angry."

"No, she won't." He was right. If I was with Omar, Mother would be happy.

Omar erected a rock wall around the cat as a shrine. "We can go now." He walked next to me, his mouth spread in a wide, bright smile.

I didn't sleep that night. Whenever I closed my eyes, the

cat's image rose before me. In the morning I was exhausted, but the cat stayed with me. I rubbed my eyes until the skin burned and my eyeballs reddened. Still the cat's dead stare haunted me.

On our way to dugsi the next afternoon, Omar stopped. It was the same spot where he'd met me the day before. The cat's remains were still visible in the distance. "I am not coming to dugsi with you today," he said.

I placed my fingers over my mouth to contain my happiness. "Should I go back and tell Mother?"

"She doesn't have to know," he said, his voice stern.

"I don't want her to be mad."

"I said, she doesn't need to know."

I nodded and ran, Omar-free and exhilarated.

# CHAPTER SEVEN

ANTICIPATION FILLED the schoolyard at the unscheduled assembly. Teachers walked between rows of students to silence their curiosity.

At the sight of the principal's determined stride, the teachers took their places at the front.

The principal stood at the podium for a long pause before beginning. "This is a very important assembly." He held a folder up and wiped his brow. "Today we are here to share a great news." He stared into the distance, above the lemon trees that lined the yard. "The country must come together on this particular issue. The government has just decreed that the practice of subjugating people based on their tribal origin is illegal and immoral."

Standing still, I marveled as the principal read parts of the legislation.

"Bliss and Boon are equal. One is not better than the

other." He stopped, giving his words a chance to sink in. "We are all Somali, one language, one religion under the same flag, government, and constitution." Another pause.

We were being ushered in to a new era. Despite the risk of being caught inattentive, I glanced around the schoolyard to see if others were as exuberant as I.

"Every Somali person, child and adult alike, must understand this as one nation with one goal—to be united with no tribal differences." The principal's words took me to a happy place beyond the restrictions I felt, due to my feeling for Sidow.

"The new law will erase the divide. After today, each person will marry, trade, and align with whomever they choose. Schools must teach children to reject tribal-based hate, and we'll be taking this directive very seriously." He placed the microphone on the podium and dismissed the students. The teachers gathered around him.

I knew this was Allah's way of legitimizing the friendship I'd developed with Sidow. "Did you hear?" I asked Sidow.

"This changes nothing."

His response was outrageous. "What do you mean? It is the law now."

"You will always be Bliss, and I will always be Boon."

Anger rose within me at Sidow's insistence that tribal differences would continue to exist among us. "That's illegal now and immoral. You heard the principal."

"Rules on paper mean nothing."

I swallowed several times to bring my heart into rhythm. "But that is the *law*," I repeated as we entered the classroom.

"Your mother will never accept me as your friend, let alone your husband."

*Do you like me enough to be my husband?* I wondered. "You don't know that," I said.

"Right." The word dripped with sarcasm. "This will cause nothing but trouble. You mark my words."

Sidow was smart, even wise, but he was wrong about this. He *had* to be wrong.

⁂

I went to the kitchen before I took my breakfast at the table. "Could Sidow come over after school?" I asked Mother to put his claim to the test, to prove him wrong.

She didn't respond, but continued to serve breakfast.

"Can he?" I asked again.

"No, he can't. Not Sidow or the likes of him."

"Why do you hate him so much? Because he is a Boon?"

She didn't get upset. Instead she gave me a reassuring smile. "When you are older, you'll understand that these people are not your equal. That's Allah's way."

My gaze locked with hers. "But the president said…" Mother cut me off with a shake of her head.

"That is politics. It has nothing to do with us."

I blinked fast to push away the tears. "Why? That is not fair."

Mother seemed to be struggling to explain a complex issue. "They lack the dignity and the intelligence."

"You don't know him. Sidow is the smartest boy at school—wiser than Omar."

"It doesn't matter. They're meant to clean your house, not claim your friendship. That's how it has always been. It's not

64

something you, I, or a piece of paper from the government can change. Not accepting that will destroy you."

My throat was tight with anger. With all hope of retaining Sidow's friendship with Mother's blessing lost, I fled from her venomous words.

Elmi stood up from his chair at the kitchen table and followed me to the door. "Idil! Wait up!" he called.

I didn't stop until the school gate clanked shut behind me.

※

Instead of sending students to their classrooms for the lessons of the day, the principal had placed junior grades in one corner of the yard and senior grades in another.

"It's each school's job to show the students the right way," the head master said, reading the handouts form the Ministry of Education aloud. "Each creation must show the evils of tribalism. Get the supplies from there." He pointed to a heap of discarded material in the center of the yard.

There were pieces of fabric, wooden logs, rolls of yarn, old shirts, blouses, pants, and women's cotton dresses. We spent the rest of that week on a group project to interpret the hideousness of tribalism.

"Ours will be the ugliest," several students from my grade shouted at the others. We shared the supplies while keeping our designs a secret, so no one would copy.

Teachers tried to relate the project to our curriculum. Even the religion teacher found verses from the Qur'an—"We created you as regions and tribes so you might know each other"—that condemned the way Somali people used their tribal affiliations. The principal promised us treats, work-free periods, longer recesses, and food for the grade that created the best presentation, in this case the ugliest presentation.

On Thursday of that week, five days after the start of the assignment, the school held a burning ceremony. As each grade presented their tribe replica, grotesque images of different shapes and sizes filled the yard. Extra limbs, eyes, and heads protruded from the bodies of the ghoulish creations. Different-colored paints mimicked blood and puss that oozed from small openings.

We were very proud of what we'd created. "We have the best! Ours is the best!" Each grade danced a jig around the ghastly effigies as slogan's echoed and reverberated across the field. "Damn the tribe," shouts rang. One grade after another claimed victory.

The principal inspected our work. "Great job, children." He went to the ninth-grade area and examined a figure with a hand sticking out of its mouth. "Magnificent!" He wiped his face. "No lessons this afternoon." He ordered dismissal. "Go ahead, play. You earned it." The principal set fire to all the creations, starting with the winning project and they burned bright, wiping tribal-based divisions away, but I knew the truth.

❦

Sidow approached Elmi and me when it was all over. "Hi." His elbow brushed against mine, sending pleasurable sensations up my arm.

"That was fun." I was still flying high from the day's events. "Did you see ours burn?"

Sidow didn't speak until we were outside the schoolyard. "My father received a letter yesterday."

I stared straight ahead. "About what?"

"Farmers are asked to share the land," he said.

"What does that mean?"

"Farmers can only keep five acres per family member. Any so-called excess land must be sold to the Ministry of Agriculture." Sidow's voice was laden with bitterness.

Sidow understood the government's political maneuvers better than many, but I couldn't imagine such a thing happening. "That can't be."

"It's true."

I stopped walking. "What will happen to the land?"

"My father says the officials will give it to their clansmen."

I couldn't accept that statement. There had to be a mistake. Our leaders wouldn't perpetuate injustice. Even though the tribal elimination hadn't changed Mother's mind, the president would be fair. At least, one had to appreciate the honor in the attempt. Father's stories of traitors arrested, convicted, and executed rushed to mind. "People are just spreading lies," I said with as much certainty as I could manage.

Sidow stopped. "I have to go home."

I reached for his forearm. "Do you believe it's true?"

Sidow straightened his shoulders. "I have to go home," he repeated and walked away.

I saw why Sidow was rushing to leave. Omar was coming our way. I waved good-bye. Could such action by the government be true?

❧

The aroma of the bread in the oven welcomed me into the house. Inside, Mother wasn't wearing her normal house dress. She was in a black and silver kaftan. A sapphire ring, beaded gold necklace, earrings, and bracelet added to her festive look.

"Are you going somewhere?"

She shook her head no, picked up the *birqabad*—a metal tong—and removed the first batch of bread from the tinaar. "We have visitors."

I took a piece of the bread and dropped it back on the tray as the heat singed my fingers. "My schoolmates are saying the government is taking their family farms by force."

Mother missed the oven wall with the fresh dough, which landed on top of the red-hot coals. The moisture hissed. "Idil, go get changed." Mother held her bottom lip tight between her front teeth.

"Do you think that's true?"

She bit her lip even harder until it turned red. "Go to your room."

I leaned against the cement counter. "Could they be forced to part with their land?" I asked again.

"They're getting paid, and you must stop speaking of issues that are none of your concern. Understand?" Father appeared at the kitchen doorway.

"It's their land. They shouldn't be made to sell it," I said.

"The whole country belongs to the government." Father pointed at me. "*We* belong to the government. These people are so selfish. They want to keep the entire country. What happened to sharing?"

I heard the warning in Father's tone, so I stood there, mouth agape, rigid with fear.

"Hawa, bring the food now," Father said and left.

Mother turned to me. "Be silent, Idil. I beg of you child, stop talking. I can save you from everything except that mouth of yours." She stopped for a few seconds. "Take this." She pushed a tray filled with rice into my hand.

I took it without a word. Close to a dozen men, including members of the Red Berets—the secret police—were in Father's study. I placed the food on the table and turned around but not fast enough to avoid hearing the whispers of how big and beautiful I was becoming.

"If I could only get you to stop asking questions," Mother continued when I returned, "I'd be sure to save you from a wrong turn."

"I know. I am sorry, but I must. I can't understand how you go on without asking and knowing."

"To not ask or know is a woman's only way to survive."

I appreciated her concerns, but for me, to do as she advised was impossible.

"Come take the beans and flat bread." She sent me back to the study along with Hawa several more times. "Make sure to bring the empty dishes back without looking around." Hawa and I served food and drinks intermittently until the grandfather clock in the sitting room chimed at 8:00 p.m.

Mother retired to her room and ordered Elmi and me to do the same. Omar was in the study with Father and his men. At nineteen, Omar was not in school anymore and was considered a grown man with a seat at the table.

I went to my room right away, but only until I couldn't hear Mother's quiet movements.

"You should've stayed in your room," Hawa stopped me on my way to the study. "Your father will be angry if he sees you about."

"I have to know if what my friends are saying is true."

"And do what with it? Even if you find out that every detail of what they said is true, what can you do?"

I considered the question and finding no answer, moved closer to the study and listened. Some of the discussions eluded me, but I understood enough to be horrified. "The farmers are planning a protest." Father sounded upset. "They have cancelled the harvest festival."

"At least pretend you are helping me clean the kitchen," Hawa said and handed me a mop dripping with soapy water.

I took it clumsily—just in time before Father and another man abruptly left the study and moved to the sitting room. I busied myself cleaning the floor. They didn't seem to notice or care about me.

The man stood next to Father. A column of cigarette smoke clouded his face. "How many officers do we need to achieve the result we want?"

"Not more than twenty or thirty. The farmers have no weapons, no power, nothing," Father responded.

The man took a drag and blew another puff of smoke. "They won't go without a fight."

"We can contain them," Father said. "Traitors are animals. They should be put down like sick animals."

Still mopping the floor, I shuddered and waited for more, but they returned to the study and issued quiet instructions to the others. Father used a military code as more men dressed in full army gear came and went.

"It is not safe to be found in here." Hawa insisted I go to my room before she left the main house and headed toward the servants' quarters.

I returned to the kitchen and hid behind the door as soon as I heard Hawa's steps fade into the night.

I listened as Father instructed the men, but understood very little. In the end, he left with the last two Red Berets. I waited for Father's return, but he didn't come. It was past midnight when I went to my room. I lay down and somehow fell asleep and dreamed of Father and his men attacking the farmers. I woke up shaking not long after and stayed awake until it was time to get ready for school.

Elmi and I arrived earlier than usual. There were very few children, and the air in the empty yard was still and heavy. For the first time since the day I arrived at this school four years ago, the principal cancelled the morning exercises and sent us to class. Each room had fewer than ten students. Still, their voices damp with sorrow, the teachers taught their lessons as if every pupil were present.

"No one was at school today," I complained to Mother that afternoon. Elmi, by my side, nodded in agreement.

Her sewing needle kept moving. "Maybe their parents need them to help at home."

"Mother! The school was almost empty."

She stopped embroidering. "It is harvest time."

"Harvest break is not for another eight weeks." I looked at her for a reaction, and saw fear. "Were Father and the others planning an attack?" I knew, but I asked anyway.

"Leave it be, Idil. No use in asking."

I opened my mouth to say something, but Mother stopped me. "Be quiet about it!" She picked up the tablecloth and went back to embroidering. "Please, Idil."

For the following week, no one mentioned the absent students. The principal conducted the daily assembly as if they were there. He gave awards to classmates who were not present—called names and pretended a student came up and collected the certificate. The rest of us clapped on cue.

# CHAPTER EIGHT

SIDOW RETURNED to school a week after the raid. He approached me by the tree stump that served as a goalpost. "How are you?" Sidow kicked the dirt and the dust flew high.

"Okay." I waited for a few seconds before I asked the question burning within. "Where have you been?"

Sidow gave our surroundings a quick check. "Red Berets arrested two of my brothers along with a dozen other farmers. They were taken to the Lugooy prison." Sidow's lips quivered.

"Why?"

Sidow sat down next to me. "For taking part in the protest. Farmers who agreed to sell their land are free, but not my brothers." He used a stick to draw on the dirt.

"Why not?"

Sidow sighed. "My father organized the farmers' protest." Sidow rested his head on his knee and took a deep breath. "Today is my last day at school."

"No! You can't quit."

"I must. My father's broken by sadness and can't work. There is too much for my mother to manage alone, and my brother Hasan is too young."

I'd never imagined Sidow leaving school. He was so smart. "The year is almost done and the harvest is not for another two months. You should stay to write the exams." I covered my mouth to hold the coming sobs.

Sidow took my hand between his. "What is the point? This is only grade eleven, and I won't return for grade twelve."

Indeed. Sidow had to become a man and a farmer overnight, and school was out of the question.

"Are you going to be okay?" I asked as an afterthought.

"My mother is trying to hold on, but my father is devastated. He feels responsible." Sidow didn't bother to hide his tears.

I hugged him and we remained in a tight embrace until the bell that signaled the start of the day rang. We got up, gathered our books and food jars, and went to class together for the last time.

✺

After Sidow dropped out, school turned into a dreadful place. The girls and I drifted apart. During recess and free periods, we remained cordial, but I felt cut adrift from the others, the connections lost forever. A few weeks later, I went to visit Sidow at his house instead of going to the waterfall with the rest of the students.

Sidow saw me as I approached their main house and

smiled. He shifted a jug of water he was carrying from one hand to the other. "It is so good to see you."

"It's good to see you too," I responded.

"Where is everybody else?" Sidow asked.

"At the waterfall."

His voice wavered. "You should've gone with them."

I had gone once after Sidow left school, but the place was full of haunting memories and the echo of his laughter rang in my ears. It wasn't his absence, as much as his constant ghostly presence that rattled my nerves. "I wanted to be here," I responded. I followed him into his house.

"You might be the only one who feels that way." Sidow motioned for me to sit in a chair by the door of a room with a mud floor. Sidow's father occupied a single bed covered by hand-woven sheets. On the floor was a folded prayer mat. Two books and an oil lamp sat on a small table surrounded by four metal chairs. From several pegs on the wall above the table, hung a water pitcher, and six carved wooden mugs. The room, with its unadorned simplicity, was cozy and peaceful.

Sidow sat on the edge of the bed. He took a small rag and washed his father's face, neck, and arms. "He took to his bed after seeing my brothers' bodies. Officers brought their remains, but Father didn't even go to their funeral service. He has been here ever since." At Sidow's touch, his father moaned like a dying creature. Sidow placed a wet cloth on his father's forehead and pressed it. "He has been like this for three weeks now. The medicine is not working."

"I am sorry," I said. "Where is your mother?"

"In the kitchen, cooking."

His mother appeared as if summoned by my question.

She cleared her throat. "How are you?" she asked, but didn't wait for a response. Untied work boots flapped around her ankles as she walked toward Sidow. She clutched the cowhide belt that held her *guntiino*—the long cloth tied over the shoulder and tight around the waist. "Those men are here, waiting."

Sidow stood over his father on the bed, arranged the thin blanket around him, and bent to kiss his forehead. Sidow's lips lingered, unwilling to part.

Sidow's mother took the vacated spot and massaged her husband's feet. "You should go before they start measuring," she said, without glancing up at her son.

"Do you want to join me?" Sidow asked me.

"Yes, I'd like that," I said and followed him outside.

I walked behind Sidow in the narrow space between rows of mature corn. Stalks, rich with growth, bowed against the wind. The ears, with their flowery crowns bent close to the ground as if in prayer, came back without breaking. Soft, billowy leaves rustled and brushed against my cheeks. Their touch felt like long fingers caressing my skin. The beauty of the place distracted me, and I neglected to watch my step. My sandal caught on a stump at the border between the corn and the grain fields, and I fell.

Sidow turned around with a start. "Oh!" He extended a hand to help me up. "The paths change quickly between sections. You must be careful."

My heart leapt at the tender touch of his fingers. I nodded.

Next to the grain silo, we heard advancing footsteps. Men approached. The older of the two gazed at Sidow. "We can't start work until Tuesday. We have other work to do."

"I will lose half the crops if I wait four more days."

"You should have called us sooner," one of the men said.

"You are aware of my situation." Sidow sounded exasperated.

"Pay us a kilo of grain, instead of half a kilo, for every sack we harvest and we'll start tomorrow."

Sidow shook the older man's hand. "See you in the morning."

The men left, and Sidow followed them to the main gate while I waited. Upon his return, Sidow led me through the grain field, away from the house. "Come with me."

The land spread before us in an endless blanket of green. "Where are we going?" I asked.

He didn't respond until we reached the lemon trees that marked the border of the property. Sidow pointed to a large, sprawling farm next to his own. "Your father took that land."

I dropped his hand and turned to face him. "What?"

"Your father owns the largest grain farm in the village, maybe in the country."

I gasped. "But the government bought the land to divide between the citizens."

"You don't believe that lie, do you?"

He reached for me, but I stepped away. "That's not true! My father owns no land."

"Let me show you." Sidow climbed up onto a wooden barrel sitting at the border of their property. Although I didn't want to, I climbed after Sidow and stood next to him.

"See? You are looking at your father's farm."

I followed his finger and saw the distinct *sigel* of my tribe—a crossbow and arrow. It was engraved on a wooden board at the main gate of the farm. I knew Sidow was right, but a wave of indescribable anger surged within me. I jumped down off the barrel. "I have to go home," I said.

He climbed down, too. "Wait!"

"I shouldn't have come." I strode away.

Sidow followed me. "Let me walk you home."

"Leave me be." I was running by then. His steps ceased at the gate, but his words played repeatedly in my ears. *Your father is the owner of the largest farm in the village, maybe in the country.*

❧

Elmi met me outside the house. "Mother has been looking for you."

Any other day, Elmi in a stiff suit would've been comical, but I wasn't in the mood to laugh. "Why? What is happening?"

"We are going to the capital."

"What's in the capital?"

"I don't know, but get changed before she catches you like that."

I looked down and saw streaks of dust on my school uniform. I ran into the house.

By the time Mother came out, I had changed into a dress with a large pink bow in the front. I hated the thing, but she loved it, so I wore it to appease her.

Mother didn't mention my absence. "You look nice. Excellent choice." She placed one of her bracelets on my wrist. "There."

I ran two fingers over the bracelet, resting my thumb and forefinger on the elephant charm that dangled from it. "Did Father buy a farm?" I tried to sound casual, but my heart raced.

"Who told you that?"

I tugged at the clasp. "Did he buy the farm next to…" I stopped before I uttered Sidow's name, but she knew.

"Have you visited that boy?" she asked.

I retreated from the anger in her voice, but her suspicion wouldn't be erased. "No," I uttered the lie in vain.

"I looked for you!" Her gaze seared into mine.

"I went to the *masjid*. You said I could." Another lie.

I caught a glimmer of doubt on her face. "Never mind. We'll discuss it later," Mother said. "We own no farm, purchased no property, but your brother, Omar, has been hired to distribute the land."

"Omar is nineteen. What does he know about farming?"

"He's going to Italy to train. It is important to accept, while you are young, that some questions have no answers and some answers have no questions. Your life will be much easier if you curb your curiosity."

Father's car pulled into the driveway, and Mother spoke in quick urgent words. "Don't mention any of this." She lifted my chin until our eyes met. "Understand?"

She turned away and noticed Elmi tugging at his tie. "Stop it!"

"I can't breathe. This is too tight." Elmi loosened the knot at his throat. "Why do I have to wear it in the car? I'll put it on later, at the hotel."

Mother's burning eyes landed on his exposed neck. "Stop it!" she repeated.

Father and Omar got out of the car and went straight into the house without a word of a greeting to us. We followed them inside.

Mother stood next to Father and said, "We want to come to the capital with you, the children and me."

Father rearranged his briefcase. "I am taking Omar to the airport."

Mother looked away, crestfallen. "The children and I want to come." She tried to be cheerful, but it was no use.

"This is not a vacation. It's business." Father snapped his briefcase shut and went outside. We trailed along behind them again.

Mother tried one last time. "We won't be in your way."

"I will return as soon as Omar leaves. You will stay home." By the time Father reached the car waiting in the driveway, Mother saw the real reason we couldn't go. The silhouette of a woman sitting in the backseat filled the space behind Father.

Mother turned to Elmi and me. "Get into the house!"

We went, grateful for the reprieve.

# CHAPTER NINE

FOR MONTHS Mother continued to exist in a desperation-fueled search for the next potion. The sight of her tear-stained cheeks saddened me. I stood by her door and watched her count and recount little jars with dark thick liquid, like I had done so many times before.

"Idil come here and read this," she called, as soon she noticed me.

Each potion was like the previous one, and the one before that. "This is the same as the last one, and it didn't work," I said, but it made no difference.

"This one will work. It is the answer to all my troubles," Mother declared.

"Forget it. He won't stop." I had given up on wishing for Father to return home by then. I'd stopped praying for it, too. Even if Allah did answer, I was incapable of wiping away the anger and resentment within me. It was better this way—Father rolling from one mistress's bed to another. If only I could convince Mother to stop the search and accept it as I'd done. But that was asking too much.

"You want me to give up on my husband? To let another woman enjoy what I've built and worked on for years?"

"It has nothing to do with other women. It has to do with him!" I shouted the last part as if being loud would convince her to accept the inevitable.

"You wouldn't say that if this were your husband." She began recounting the row of tiny jars under her breath. Mother's statement stunned me. Would I ever behave like this? I wouldn't. Never would I marry someone like Father, or chase after him if I did.

"May I go to the masjid?" I asked Mother, but she didn't respond. I left her staring at the jars, examining their contents very closely, and went to Sidow's house.

Sidow was fixing a broken doorpost in front of the kitchen when I arrived. He stopped working when he saw me, placed the nails and the tools in a metal bucket on the floor, and leaned the hammer against the wall. "I didn't think you'd visit again," he said smiling.

"Yet here I am."

"Thank you for coming. It's good to see you." He walked toward his father's room, and I followed. Sidow sat next to the bed. "Nothing helps. Even the herbs for his joints are making his stomach sick. It's so difficult for him to breathe." He lifted his father's head and fluffed the pillow.

"I am sorry." I didn't know what else to say. I stayed with Sidow for two hours. Our discussion revolved around his father's illness. I visited him every Friday after that, but

I couldn't offer Sidow much support. He spent our time watching his father and not socializing with me. The wall of silence between us grew thicker and taller. The visits did little to satisfy my yearning to be useful to Sidow. Each time on my way there, I would devise a conversation to lighten the mood—a joke to make him laugh or some memory to bring back the old days we'd shared. But once in the room, my words were forgotten. I'd seethe with anger at the injustice and Sidow's lost opportunity for what might have been. In the end, I would only accomplish asking after his father and the harvest. After the first five minutes, I sat there silent.

My once easy pace and light feet heading toward Sidow's house slowed to heavy strides. I dreaded going there as much as I hated the thought of staying away.

Sidow noticed my struggle. "You don't have to come every week," he said.

Regardless of his suggestion to come less often, I knew Sidow didn't want me to stop. A mug of hot tea always waited for me on the table, steam rising from it in long, thin columns. Clearly, he was counting on me, and because of that, I wanted to continue and be there for him, but the misery of the visits was exhausting. Three months after I started—at the beginning of grade twelve—the moans of Sidow's dying father filled me with such sadness that I stopped going.

I thought about Sidow and his father often, especially on Fridays, and I even had the urge to go once or twice. I laced my shoes one of those days and almost went, but the memory of the dark, death-saturated room squelched the desire as fast as it had come. I'd only reached our front gate before I turned around and went back.

❧

"Sidow's father died last night," a girl whispered in my ear during math class three weeks after my last visit.

I focused on my worksheets to avoid crying. At the sound of the morning bell, I skipped school and went to see Sidow. On the way, dark clouds gathered overhead, and heavy rain poured down, drenching me. I rehearsed lines of condolences, said the words out loud, and repeated them so I wouldn't forget, but by the time his gate came into view, my well-crafted speech had evaporated. In front of the kitchen, a burjiko blazed under a large pot and half a dozen women milled around, cooking and cleaning.

Sidow's mother saw me come in and left the others to greet me. "He refuses to leave the room. Maybe you could help." She took me to her husband's room and stepped aside to let me in.

Sidow sat on the bed, hugging his knees to his chest. He looked at me with dry eyes and a forced smile. The hopeful playfulness that I loved had disappeared from his face. "Thank you for coming," he said.

I reached for his hand and squeezed. "I'm sorry for your loss." I spoke meaningless words of condolence.

❧

A week after the seven-day mourning period ended, I went to Sidow's farm.

His mother greeted me by the kitchen. "He's in the field clearing for the planting." She stirred the pot on the fire. "Go get your brother," she told Sidow's younger brother who hurried out to the field. "It's all too much for the boys," she said when the sound of Hasan's retreating footsteps died. "Loss on top of loss."

"I know. It must be very hard for all of you." I moved closer to her. "Will Sidow ever return to school?"

She took the ladle out of the pot and placed it on a plate. "Sidow is a man now, not a child."

I was desperate. "Aunt Ulimo," I appealed to her as if she were family, "there's only eight months left. If he comes back now, he could still get his diploma."

Sidow's mother shook her head. "For what? School is not for my boy. Not after what's happened."

Sidow arrived in the kitchen. "Idil, how are you?"

"Come back to school, *please*," I begged.

Sidow drew near. "Idil, I wish I could, but I can't."

My ears burned from the sweet sound of my name on his lips. I inhaled to steady my nerves. "All you need is to finish this year." I spoke as if Sidow didn't know the facts.

He brushed his hand on my cheeks to wipe away the tears. "School is for children, and I am a man now, the only one my family has."

The urge to apologize for the wrong done to this family welled inside, but I failed to gather enough strength to express my regret.

He took leave of his mother and pointed to a room next to the kitchen. "Come, I have a gift for you."

"A gift?"

Once inside, he opened a wooden chest and held out a rectangular metal container. "This is for you." He hesitated for a few seconds before handing it to me.

I opened the box and took out a folded paper. On it was the image of a young boy sitting in the middle of a corn-field. The late afternoon shadow of his body extended to the edge of the page. His open left hand pointed at a girl his age, walking away from him. The boy stared at something, or someone, in the dark space behind her. I felt for the boy, alone and isolated, obviously devastated by the girl's leaving. "Did they have a fight?" I asked Sidow.

"That's for you to decide. I create, and you analyze." He rubbed his hands together. "I'll understand if you walk away and never come back."

"Why would I do that?"

"We can never be together…your parents…" Sidow took a deep breath and sighed. "They'd never allow it. And not just them—my mother, too. She wouldn't want us to be together because she knows what we don't want to believe."

The enormity of what he was saying was clear, but I couldn't accept it. "What do you mean?"

"If we decide to be together, we will be destroyed," Sidow said.

I wanted to make a case for our relationship, to tell him that if our love was strong, others would have to accept it. But Sidow had spoken the truth and no one could refute it. "Thank you for this," I said instead. I placed the paper back in the container.

"I am glad you like it," he said.

We listened to the wind howling outside the cabin for a few minutes before either of us said anything. "I should go," I said, finally breaking the oppressive silence.

I bade good-bye to his mother and brother. Sidow walked with me until the chain-link fence of the base came into view.

We parted.

※

The seasons marched on, and spring arrived with its promise of new growth, weddings, and graduations. I was in grade twelve and seventeen that year. My determination to continue seeing Sidow had grown deeper. We met briefly every day after school. Sidow would wait in an alley halfway between the school and the military base. The more I saw him, the more I needed to be with him. I couldn't do homework, focus in class, or interact with others; he was all I could think about. Everyone knew of, or at least suspected, the forbidden relationship, and one by one my teachers raised concern.

One afternoon, my math teacher left his desk and approached me. I could feel his irritation. "Idil, why are you not working?" he asked.

My empty notebook page glared up at me with nothing but the date printed on the top.

"You have done no seatwork. Why is that?" Mr. Qalim's words were heavy with condemnation.

I had no answer, so I kept quiet, my eyes fixed on the desk.

"Finish it tonight for homework, and see that it doesn't happen again. Return the textbook tomorrow." Mr. Qalim walked to his desk, shaking his head.

Whispers of my attraction to Sidow swirled around me at school. "Someone is in trouble," a few of the girls giggled as I walked to and from classes. Their condescending laughter was a warning I shouldn't have ignored. Ours was a forbidden match, but still, I couldn't stop seeing Sidow. I'd arrive at our meeting spot after school every day and fly into his arms. "Everyone at school knows about us, even the teachers," I told him one day.

Sidow held me tight. "Maybe we should see each other less," he said.

I nodded and, after that, even attempted to go home twice without stopping by the alley where we met. But I failed both times.

# CHAPTER TEN

HASAN WAITED for me one morning after assembly and slipped a small piece of paper into my hand. "This is from Sidow," he whispered and went to the junior section of the yard.

I opened the letter at my desk. Sidow's flawless script graced the page. *I must go to town with my mother. Come after Asr prayer if you can—the same place.*

*See you there*, I scribbled on the back of the same sheet and placed it in Hasan's waiting hand at recess. I would have to go home first after school and then find an excuse to leave again, but I was committed to seeing him.

Lately, Mother had been happier and not in search of a potion to cure Father's infidelity. His affair was over, and he was trying to trade his military uniform for a suit in the capital. A move to the cabinet required a faithful man, or at least one who didn't flaunt his exploits publicly. He was at home more often than he was out. The fact that he spent his time in his study didn't bother Mother. She walked about the house and did her work with a smile on her face and used her free time to watch me closely. I'd often found myself under her searing gaze as I did my schoolwork or read books with Elmi. That night was no different. She said nothing to me, but I could read suspicion on her face. I waited for the chance to slip away, but the opportunity to see Sidow at the agreed-upon time was passing me by.

"What's wrong? You're restless," Mother said, her embroidery needle continued to move.

"Nothing," I lied.

"Go and do your lessons."

"I don't have any homework. I finished it at school." Mr. Qalim's seatwork still sat in my book bag, but I didn't care. Unlike Omar, Elmi and I always received good grades, so it was easy to twist the truth occasionally.

"Then go to the garden and pick some flowers for the vase on the table."

"Flowers?" I asked.

"You heard me. Go on now," she said and went back to her handiwork.

I was squatting next to the lilies at the back of the house when Hawa approached from the servants' quarters.

"What are you doing?" she asked.

"Mother wants flowers for her table."

"What for?" she asked.

"She's suspicious," I said. "I want to see Sidow. I've waited all afternoon, but she is watching me."

"She'll know if you leave," Hawa warned.

"I have to see him. I only need half an hour. She won't even know I'm gone." I looked up at her, asking without asking.

"I'll get the flowers. You go, but be quick about it."

"Thank you!" I said. As I dashed away, the sun was slipping behind clouds just above the horizon, spreading a dark blanket over the landscape. I ran, only stopping once to catch my breath.

"What is wrong? You seem worried." Sidow was standing behind the soccer field goalpost.

I glanced at the road behind us. "Mother was watching me. I had to wait."

Sidow's lips brushed against my left cheek. "You'd better go back."

I leaned forward to encourage him to stay close. "Hawa agreed to do my chore. Mother won't notice."

"Are you sure?"

"Yes," I said, but I wasn't. Indeed, I wasn't.

Sidow smiled. "You look handsome wearing braids."

"Am I unattractive otherwise?" I teased. "Men are handsome, women are beautiful."

"I should find a new word for you because neither is fitting."

I snuggled up to Sidow. My ear rested on his chest, and the rhythmic beating of his heart, responded to mine. Cocooned within the shelter of his strong arms, nothing could touch me. "I love you so much," I confessed.

He pushed me abruptly away from him and turned me around.

"What's the matter?" I asked.

"Your mother is coming," he whispered in my ear.

My back resting on Sidow's front, I saw Mother through the mesh between the goalposts. I tried to run forward, so I could reach her before she came upon us. If she didn't see me so close to Sidow, perhaps I would be able to convince her that Sidow and I happened to end up in the same soccer field without planning to. But it was too late.

Mother descended upon us and pulled me away from Sidow. "Your wandering ways led to this!" She dragged me, cursing and crying.

We had no time for good-byes. I was left with only a fleeting glance at Sidow's sad face.

Mother pulled me all the way home with no regard for who might see or hear us. She took me straight to the sitting room and pushed me down to the floor. "Say something, now!" she ordered.

I curled up on the floor, my knees touching my chin.

Mother grabbed a handful of my hair and pulled me to a sitting position. "Have you lost your voice?"

I placed my hands over my ears to shield them from her shrill voice. Mother yanked them both away. "You listen to what I have to say!"

Father came out of his study. "What is the problem?" he asked.

Mother became hysterical at the sight of his imposing figure. "Ask Idil!" She hit her chest with clenched fists and wept. She continued striking her bosom violently as if to punish herself for my sin. "Ask her!" she repeated.

Father's gaze shifted to me. "What is the matter?"

I took a deep breath and spoke, forcing the words out.

Mother stopped crying and listened. Once I began, the whole story tumbled out. At the end of my tale of falling in love with a Boon, an eerie silence engulfed us. The weak light from the lone lamp on the corner table made Father appear ominous in the gloom.

I averted my gaze, afraid to see his face burning with rage. But after a long silence, I lifted my head to meet Father's eyes.

He approached and loomed over me. "Did you say his father's name is Moallim Ali?"

"Yes."

"You love a Boon man?"

Before I could answer, Father slapped me across the face. My skin burned from the impact and tears ran down my face and wet the front of my dress.

As if trying to avoid any more contact, Father walked away and leaned against the wall. "Is it true?"

"Is what true?" I held my palm to my burning cheek.

Mother's eyes flashed. "Answer, you ungrateful imbecile."

Father started speaking with measured tone. "Did you continue to see him after your mother forbade it? Did you?"

"Yes."

"This is your fault!" Father directed his fury at Mother. "If you weren't so busy watching where and with whom I went—*if* you'd paid attention to being a mother—none of this would've happened!"

Mother crumbled under the weight of the accusation. "I am so sorry," she sobbed.

I wanted to tell her it wasn't her fault. There was nothing she could've done to stop me, but it was obviously not wise for me to speak, so I kept quiet.

Mother collapsed onto a chair and placed her face between her hands. "I am so sorry," she cried afresh.

Father moved closer to her and shook a long finger over her head. "If this doesn't stop, you'll pay the price—both of you. Take Idil to her room and lock the door." Father took two steps toward the study, turned, and faced her again. "Fix this. Now!"

Mother took me to my room, but she didn't lock the door. Instead, she came inside and sat at the edge of my bed. "I knew you weren't like other girls. You asked questions that were none of your business and felt sorry for people you shouldn't have cared about. But I didn't think it would come to this."

"I love him." I attempted to make her understand.

"Love! What a foolish thought. How could you love a Boon man—ignore the ugliness, the backward stupidity, degenerate behavior? How is that possible?" She didn't wait for an answer. She had it all figured out. I, a proper Bliss girl, couldn't fall in love with a Boon, unless evil was at work. "I can't blame you for any of this. How can I?" She was much kinder now, her voice soft with melancholy. "Sidow's mother must have used something very strong. You would not have fallen in love with a Boon of your own free will."

Mother was certain that Sidow's mother must have used *sixir* and *saangudub*—witchcraft and sorcery. She traced her index finger around the mark Father had left on my cheek before she got up and left.

She returned a short while later with an *idin*—clay pot— filled with coal and incense. "This will help dispel the evil curse." Mother shoved it under my nose and clouds of smoke rose in my face. "This will rid the sixir and you'll be free. May Allah, the Almighty, protect you from their evil acts," she shouted loud and clear so Allah might hear her all the better.

"Stop!" I told her between coughing spasms. "I love Sidow. His mother did nothing to me because she doesn't want us to be together, either."

"She doesn't?" Mother asked incredulously. Whether she thought I was lying to her, or she was offended by the audacity of a Boon woman rejecting a Bliss girl, I couldn't tell. She held the burning incense away from my face for a moment. "She doesn't want you to marry her son?" she asked again, making sure she heard me right.

I shook my head, hoping she was satisfied and would stop with her mission to get rid of the evil curse that wasn't upon me. After a few seconds of silence-filled staring, Mother left, locking the door behind her. I thought I'd managed to get through to her, but she returned twice more that night and three times the following day. She tried different concoctions from different healers. "Soon you will be free from the shackles of their evildoing." After she'd finished suffocating me with the clouds of smoke, she would state, "You don't care for him. I know you don't."

It was so tempting to succumb to her suggestions, to say what she wanted to hear, but I couldn't. "I love him! You need to understand that," I said. Even then I knew this too, would fall on deaf ears just like my suggestion to forget about curbing Father's affairs had. It was difficult for Mother to admit she couldn't control her husband or her daughter. It was easier to blame other women for Father's infidelity and Sidow's mother for my misplaced love.

"Your love is doomed. The sooner you are rid of him the better."

To Mother's disappointment, I remained impervious to her repeated pleas to denounce my love for Sidow.

"The best thing I can do for you as your mother, the one who loves you beyond reason, is to help erase your feelings for the Boon. Nothing good will come of it. Nothing."

She was not altogether wrong. Even through love-blinded eyes, I could see that. In my society, loving Sidow was a treacherous path to take. Still, my skin hungered for his touch, and my heart throbbed from the pain of his absence. I thought about him constantly and conjured his image in my mind so I could keep the memory alive. Locked in my room, my only connection to Sidow was the tiny notes he gave to Hasan to pass to Elmi to pass to me. I'd read and tear them into small pieces and hide them at the bottom of my wastebasket.

※

After two months of a relentless effort, Mother gave up trying to rid me of my love for Sidow and shifted her attention to something far more practical. She set out to find me a suitable husband. She came to my room to inform me of her new approach. "If you need a husband, I'll find you a dozen of your own kind to choose from," Mother told me.

"I don't want a husband. I love Sidow."

She started listing the qualities of a fitting match as if I hadn't spoken. "Good tribal lineage is important. He must have a high rank, nothing below a lieutenant. I don't want you to start at the bottom like I did."

"I won't marry any of them." I spoke louder.

At the sound of the front door opening, she got up. "That must be your father. I need his help if I am going to find you a match." She left my room to elicit Father's help.

I followed her to hear what she would say and how he would react to it.

Father only half listened, like a child receiving a chore from a parent. He walked toward the study as she listed her expectations. "I'll consider it and let you know," he said, committing to nothing.

"Do not consider. I am sure there are proper young men in the force. Bring one home and leave the rest to me."

Father went into the study and closed the door behind him.

Mother saw me standing there and smiled. "He will bring a wonderful one. Your father is a man with a good eye for the best. He's never made a wrong choice."

I looked at her and almost asked if we were referring to the same person. Was he not the man who took his soldier's wife as a mistress and paid the price for it? Was he not the man replacing one mistress with another? There was no point in being impudent. Father had stopped for a while and Mother had chosen to forget about his previous transgressions.

After a whole week of her asking and inquiring after the matter, Father finally came through. "I am bringing a young man to meet Idil," he announced. "He's coming home with me tomorrow night."

Mother buzzed around the house the whole of the following day to prepare for the important guest. She knocked on my door three hours before Father was due home. "A fine young man is coming. You must look your best and welcome him."

I had confided in Elmi that morning before he left for school. As I handed him my note to Sidow, I told him I wanted no part of Mother's scheme.

"Go along with the plan," he advised.

My eyes grew wild when Elmi suggested that. "How can you say that? You know I love Sidow more than my own life!"

"Just for now—to buy time. Do what she says. It'll be easier for you that way."

Elmi always approached things calmly, no matter how serious the matter. He was right, of course. "I'll try," I promised.

Mother was beside herself by the time Father and the suitor arrived that evening. She sent me to the study with a tray of tea and biscuits instead of asking Hawa to bring the food in. "Take this. Be aloof, and not overly attentive. Look where I ended up, running after your father and making him feel important. Learn from my mistakes."

I did as I was told without wearing a smile as she suggested. She was waiting when I returned. "What did you think?"

"He is too old." I hadn't looked at him at all and didn't know his age, but I said the first thing that came to mind.

"What do you mean? Your father said he is twenty-two."

"I don't know what Father is thinking, but the man must be nearly forty."

"I'll go and check." She picked up a tray of fried fish and potatoes and went to the study. A few minutes later, she returned miraculously in agreement with me. "Idil, he is not forty, but he is not twenty-two either."

"See? I told you it wouldn't work."

The fact that Father didn't find a man that met her expectations, didn't deter Mother. "I'll discuss the age issue with your father before he brings the next suitor," she said and continued to coax him to find someone more fitting.

A stream of men followed the first one, but I returned from the study miserable each time. As the sixth matched failed, Mother's frustration mounted. "You can't just reject every single match. What is wrong with this one?" she asked impatiently.

"I don't…" I stammered. There was nothing wrong with the man. Not much older than twenty, he was handsome in his uniform. His smile was inviting and if I hadn't been so committed to Sidow, I would have seen promise in him. "Mother, I only want Sidow," I managed to answer.

"I know. You've said that how many times now? You love the Boon. I get it. If this was a perfect world, I would say marry him. But it's not, so I'm asking you to be practical because there's nothing rational about your love for the Boon." Mother placed her hand on my shoulder to stop me before I fled to my room. "If you must reject, which I hope you won't, next time have a better reason."

I left, and Elmi got up from the kitchen table where he was doing his schoolwork to follow me. "Don't tell her what she knows, but can't accept. Say Hawa told you she saw him with another girl. Give her something that makes sense to her."

This was a clever approach, something only Elmi could think of under the circumstances. Mother hated a man with wandering eyes. She wanted me to get married quickly so

I wouldn't bring shame to the family, but even that wasn't enough to saddle me with a man who strayed. She knew the humiliation that came with such a union. Just like Elmi suggested, I went along with her plan and spent hours with Mother, preparing for each visitor, even though the effort left me exhausted.

Every time we expected a visitor, she would coach me anew. "Move this way when you greet him." One time she'd scolded me for not smiling enough when I returned from taking the food to Father and the suitor. Her outrage had been palpable.

"How do you know I didn't smile?" I'd asked her.

"You returned with the same scowl you left with," she said. "Next time smile this way." Mother plastered a fake, bright smile across her face. *Effortless.*

Tears welled in my eyes and threatened to spill. "I can't do this." I darted out of the kitchen toward my bedroom.

"Be careful," Elmi warned me when he met me by my door where he waited during each of these events. "If you don't pretend to go along with this, she will marry you off without your consent."

The tears I'd been holding back while with Mother, gushed. "I can't. I won't," I wailed.

"You must try." Elmi's tone was kind but firm. "You have no other option."

I stopped crying and wiped my face. "I don't know how long I can pretend."

"As long as it takes."

"Then what?"

Elmi didn't have the opportunity to respond because Mother joined us in my room.

"Could you leave us alone?" Mother waited until Elmi closed the door behind him before she looked at me.

I felt exposed and wrapped my arms around my chest. "I *don't* like him, or any of them. You know I don't, so why are you making me do this?"

"Because I'm your mother and I love you." She wiped my face. "You must try, child. Give them a chance so you find a husband without destroying yourself. All I want is what's best for you."

I didn't think she was looking out for me as much as she was worried about the whispers that would come from her friends. Women from all the way in the village where she and Father were born would send her accusing comments about not being able to control her daughter. Others close by would stare at her when they saw her, confirming that she was less than capable of running her house. But I didn't say that to her. "How is marrying someone I don't want the best for me?" I asked instead.

Mother shook her head and left me. A week after the last failed attempt, she came into my room with great news. "I am sure you will fall for this one. I asked your father for him specifically."

"How do you know him?" I didn't care, but I asked anyway for something to say.

"I saw him at a gathering last week. Handsome, a lieutenant. This is the one. You must look your best tonight." Mother walked around the house nearly floating with excitement.

After two hours of preparation, and three changes of clothes, Mother led me to the sitting room. "Sit here and relax," she pointed to Father's lazy chair. "Read a book or the paper so it looks as though you just happened to be here."

I picked a book of poetry, but I was unable to focus on the words. My mind conjured Sidow's beautiful image and imposed it on the page.

 ﷼

Father walked in alone, much earlier than Mother had expected. "Where is the young man?" she asked as she took his jacket and hung it on the hallway hanger.

"I had to cancel," he responded casually.

"Cancel?" I asked, exuding happiness. Elmi's warning stare kept me from saying more.

"What do you mean? I prepared dinner, made Idil ready. Doesn't she look ravishing?" Mother asked.

Father looked at me for once and I am not sure if he saw me. "Omar is coming home tonight. I thought you'd prefer to welcome your son instead of doing this." He pointed at me.

I am not sure what Mother would have opted for, finding me a husband or seeing Omar, but she agreed. "You are right." She smiled at me. "Go and get changed."

I removed the jewelry with greater joy than I had experienced for a long time and got changed into a simple short-sleeved dress. I left my room and went to Elmi's. "I am so happy Omar is coming home," I told him, as we made our way back into the kitchen in search of food.

Father changed from his military uniform into khaki pants, a long-sleeved dress shirt, and a sports jacket. "I am going to pick up Omar from the mayor's palace, where he is being brought from the capital," he said.

Mother, Elmi, and I went into the sitting room after Father left and settled for the long wait that followed. I was grateful that she wasn't fixated on erasing my love for Sidow, if only for one night. I sat on the chair next to hers and laid my head on her shoulder. She wrapped her arm around my head and kissed me. "I know what you want my love. Something I can't offer."

I said nothing in response because I didn't want to break the spell of happiness that had descended upon us. We waited there, quiet and comfortable, until we heard Father's voice in the hallway.

"Your brother is here." Mother moved with quick steps.

Elmi and I got up and followed her to greet Omar.

# CHAPTER ELEVEN

MOTHER CALLED us to the table. Despite Omar and Father's assurances they had eaten, she insisted on serving the food. "After such an absence, you must eat your mother's cooking."

Omar smiled, but didn't serve himself.

I was happy to see Omar. For the first time in two months, attention shifted away from me, and I wanted to keep it that way. "Tell us about Italy," I suggested with a forced cheeriness.

Omar wasn't a great storyteller, so his descriptions of the country and its people were clumsy. "The buildings are large, I mean huge. Most are ancient." He didn't elaborate, produce postcards, or show pictures like Father had done when he returned from the Soviet Union. "The language is difficult to understand," he added.

"Did you enjoy your time there?"

He pushed food around the plate without eating. "Once

I hired guides and translators, I was able to enjoy it."

No one said anything for a few seconds. "Did you make any friends?" I asked in a desperate effort to fill in the silence.

He smiled as if he was happy I'd asked. "Yes, I did." Omar pulled a photo of a woman out of his jacket pocket and held it facing us. "This is Sheila."

The woman had a full head of blonde curls, ocean-blue eyes, and pale skin, so white that Elmi and I later nicknamed her Paper.

I reached for the photo, but Omar pulled it away. "Who is she?" I asked, eager to keep attention away from me.

Omar regarded Mother's expression for a long time before he spoke. "She is my wife." He extended the picture toward Mother.

"Get that away from me!" She pushed Omar's hand with such force the photo landed on the floor beneath my feet.

I picked it up and looked at it. Sheila was wearing a yellow sunflower dress that hugged her hips and ended at mid-thigh. She had leather sandals with matching flowers on them. She was stunningly beautiful, but by Somali standards, Sheila was stark naked. *Why did Omar bring this photo, knowing it would offend?* I passed it across to Elmi.

Mother pushed the chair back, and it clattered to the floor. "How dare you bring such an abomination here?" She walked to the large bay window in the sitting room. "We sent you to train, not to find a wife. And this one is *gaalo*—not even Muslim!"

Father joined her by the window.

Omar yanked the picture out of Elmi's hand and sat down. "She is my wife."

Mother bolted toward Omar, but stopped inches away from him. "Don't call her that! She is not that!"

Father said nothing.

Fascinated, Elmi and I watched the scene unfold.

Omar leaned over, put the photo down in front of him, and rested both elbows on the table. "Don't call her what?"

Mother walked away from Omar before she responded. "Don't call her your wife! She is not your wife! She will never be your wife!" Mother was sobbing by now.

Omar traced his forefinger around Sheila's profile on the picture. "You are right. She is *more* than a wife."

"How do you mean?" Mother asked.

Seconds on the clock ticked away, as Omar took his time in responding. "She is my partner, the backbone of the business."

Mother glared at Omar. "What business is that? What does that have to do with anything?"

Father and Omar acknowledged each other with simultaneous nods as long and uninterrupted silence filled the room.

Mother looked from one to the other. "Someone needs to explain what's happening."

"As Omar says, Sheila is very important to a business he is setting up. He didn't marry her to be his wife, but to establish an ally. For children and family, he'll marry a Somali wife, a girl of your choosing," Father said.

"He has to let her go!" Mother was adamant.

Father spoke in a consoling tone. "Never mind her. She's not important. He'll find a girl from a good Somali family." The statement sounded planned, rehearsed.

Omar's jaw tightened, and angry and hollow eyes gave his

face a strange look. He clenched his fists. "I will do no such thing."

"Stay out of it!" Father ordered. "Could you find him a wife?" he asked Mother.

"Who'll have their daughter be second to a gaalo woman?" Mother responded to Father's question with a question. "Would *you* marry your daughter to such a man?"

Father stepped away from Mother. "Who spoke of a second wife?"

Omar left the photo on the table, got up, and paced the floor. "I am not marrying another wife!" Omar yelled, but no one paid any attention.

Mother glared, stone-faced, at Father. "If a married man takes another wife, she would be the second."

Father gave an exasperated sigh. "This woman isn't here, and never will be. So, if you can't find him a wife, you will have only yourself to blame."

Mother must've realized her influence was waning because her tone changed. "You'll have to promise me she will be the *only* wife, not the second wife."

"Yes, I promise." Father agreed as quickly as she asked.

A bright smile—one I hadn't seen since Father's return from the Soviet Union—spread across Mother's face and lit up the whole room. "I'll find the perfect wife, ten times better than this gaalo woman."

Father winked at Omar, and they went into the study together.

I picked up the picture. At the sound of the door closing, I turned to Mother. "That's it?" I challenged. "He marries a gaalo woman and is rewarded with a second wife? I am pulled out of school and paraded before countless men I don't care for, and you promise him the perfect Somali wife? Why can't I marry Sidow?"

Mother's eyes darted between the study door and my face. "Omar is a man," she said, as if that justified everything.

"And?"

"If Sheila and Omar have children, which they won't, the children would have light skin and soft features, not ugly, large Boon noses, puffy lips, and kinky hair like the children Sidow and you would have."

"Sidow is a Muslim and a Somali, and Sheila is not Somali and is gaalo. There is no comparison."

"Idil, I didn't make the rules. I am trying to help you accept what you can't change."

The more I listened, the angrier I became. "What are you telling me? This is your doing. Father wouldn't have even found out anything if you'd left me alone."

Elmi pulled me out of the sitting room and into my bedroom. "Idil, you'll get nowhere arguing with Mother. She is just as helpless as you are." He sat on the foot of my bed, but said nothing more.

I finally gained control over my emotions. "Do you know what business Omar is in?" I asked.

"I heard Father tell his friend that he'd partnered with men who import *chat*. But since government employees are not allowed to own businesses, he'd appointed Omar to be his representative in the business," Elmi responded.

Chat—a plant from the cannabis family—was banned from Somalia a year after we moved to Bledley. Ever since, many people had been jailed for bringing it into the country through the black market. It surprised me to learn that Father, a top army general, was involved in such an illegal business, and I said as much.

"There is always a huge gap between what people seem to be and what they really are," Elmi said.

I agreed with him.

"The house is quiet. Do you think Father and Omar have left?"

"I didn't hear them go, but I think so." I got up and went to the door.

Elmi followed me out into the main corridor of the sleeping section of our house. "Listen," he said. The sound of Mother singing one of her songs from happier times reached us.

"I haven't heard that in ages," I said.

Elmi put a hand on my shoulder and smiled. "Now she will leave you alone. The focus will be on the search for Omar's new wife."

Elmi was right. Mother not only left me alone, she forgot I existed.

❦

"When is Omar leaving?" Mother asked Father two days later.

"Next week. He'll be returning in two months."

"I must have a wife for him, ready to wed by then," she said, giving herself a deadline. There was no shortage of girls wanting to marry the "Golden Boy," but Mother wasn't easily satisfied. She shared the name and age of each girl she considered with the village healer, but always returned with nothing of value and full of gossip. "That was not the one. She was not as pretty as I would've wanted, and the healer said she'll have no children."

"No girl will be good enough," I said to Elmi each time Mother came home.

"The longer she takes, the better it is for you," he reminded me.

"I know."

The hunt continued without producing the desired result. "I need to find a girl that steals his heart, so he forgets the gaalo woman." Mother was determined to have a bride ready when Omar returned.

Omar would take any girl because it didn't matter to him. But Mother wanted a girl so superior that she'd erase Sheila from Omar's memory.

Two weeks after Mother had set out to find an unequaled Somali wife for Omar, it became obvious that no one in Bledley would meet her standards. "I'll go back to Gaalmaran. I'll find the right one among my own people," she announced one evening.

Father listened. "What for? There are plenty of girls here."

Mother scoffed. "You would know."

Father didn't take the bait, but remained calm. "Give yourself more time. Look hard here before you go far."

"My son needs a splendid girl from an exceptional family," Mother replied and began to set her travel plans. She would leave the next morning. "These two are your responsibility, especially Idil," she reminded Father before she departed.

I shrank back into the book I was reading to avoid detection.

Father looked puzzled, as if he couldn't remember the restrictions he'd placed on me. "Don't worry. We'll be fine."

Two hours after the car carrying Mother drove away, Father left the house and didn't return until we were in bed. I stayed home for the first two days to make sure Father wasn't watching. He wasn't. From the third day on, I enjoyed unlimited freedom and, uninhibited, wandered the streets of the village. I grew bold and visited Sidow on the fourth day. He ran to me when he spotted me in front of his house. His smile made my heart leap.

"You have come!" Sidow's excited shout brought his mother and brother outside.

His mother's face creased. "You shouldn't have come here. We need no trouble."

Sidow frowned. "Mother, greet her. She is a guest."

She ignored him. "I've lost three men and I can't afford to sacrifice another," she said.

In her position, I'd have felt the same. "I am sorry, I mean no harm," I told her. "Only I missed him so much."

Sidow was glaring, somewhere between anger and fear. "*Mother!*"

Still, her focus was on me. "We're no match for your father, and we want no trouble with him. Please stay away from us." She rocked back and forth on her heels.

Sidow grabbed my hand. "Come! We are leaving."

His mother stepped toward Sidow as if to restrain him. "This is so dangerous. If not for your own safety, consider your brother and me. We're depending on you." Her words carried the sorrow in her heart. "Your father was as stubborn as you, and look what happened."

Sidow forged ahead. He didn't stop until we reached the

waterfall. We climbed the cliff overhanging the whirlpool and sat on the narrow boulder.

Sidow stared far into the horizon. "If I disappear, this is where you'll find me. I'll always be here, waiting."

"Don't talk like that. You frighten me."

He leaned over and touched my cheek. "I'm frightened too. My mother is against this as much as your parents are." Sidow rose to his feet and stripped to his underwear. He dove into the whirlpool and emerged a few seconds later. "Let's meet here every afternoon until your mother returns," he shouted.

I listened to the intermittent sound of barking dogs from the surrounding farms, and calls of the grazing cattle in the fields until Sidow had finished swimming and returned to sit next to me.

I touched his slick, wet back. "A relationship can't survive in hiding."

"Do you have a better idea?"

I gathered him in my arms and cradled him back and forth. We didn't speak after that, but we met at the cliff every afternoon for the next two weeks. I often arrived before him, climbed up, and listened to the water falling far below. When Sidow arrived, I pretended I hadn't heard his determined footsteps coming until he sat next to me and touched my cheek. Only then would I return his greeting with a smile.

❧

"Come to the harvest festival with me tomorrow night. Please," Sidow begged.

"I'd love to." I was ecstatic he'd asked.

The next day, we met early on the cliff and stayed there until it was dark to avoid others seeing us together. Perched on the rock, we watched the sun paint the sky with golden rays. Then, under the cover of the starless night, we walked to the market that had been converted into a festival plaza for the week. We didn't go inside for fear of being noticed, but skirted the perimeter, listening to the drumbeats and excited voices of children inside. I took Sidow's hand. "This is so much fun," I said.

He pulled me to him. "One day we'll dance together in there."

The statement was a promise and it was then I gave Sidow our first real kiss. Caught unaware, he took a couple seconds to respond. With our lips pressed hard together, our body heat rose. His tongue danced inside my mouth, slowly at first, then faster and faster, until blood rushed to my head and made me dizzy with pleasure. After a few fleeting minutes, we pulled apart, breathing heavily. The fear of clumsy first kisses that had haunted my imagination dissipated. "I have to get home before Father," I said reluctantly for I didn't want to break the spell of our first intimacy. "It's getting late."

"That was heaven," Sidow said, his words thick with joy.

We were quiet again for the rest of the way until we reached the fence of the military compound.

"Thank you. You have made me so very happy. See you tomorrow," Sidow said as he wished me goodnight.

I smiled, waved, and went inside, excited for the next day and more time alone with Sidow.

# CHAPTER TWELVE

"I AM GLAD you are here and safe. I was worried," I heard Father say.

I opened my eyes and the rays of midmorning sun streaked the floor between my bed and dresser. The memory of last night and the anticipation of the afternoon to come made me smile.

I sat up and stretched my limbs, extending the good feelings throughout my body until Mother's unmistakable voice pulled me to complete wakefulness.

"That driver made so many stops; I thought we'd never get home. We left Gaalmaran yesterday morning and drove the whole night without rest," she complained.

I lifted my palms skyward in thanks. Mother's early return had prevented the grave consequences of her discovering that I was visiting Sidow while she was away. I left my room as quickly as I could get dressed and went to Mother in the sitting room. "Mother, you are home." I feigned excitement and flew into her awaiting arms.

After a prolonged hug, she stepped aside. "This is Rhoda, the daughter of your father's first cousin, and Omar's bride-to-be."

"I am glad to meet you." I stepped forward and extended my hand to greet the young woman.

Rhoda hesitated for a few seconds before she let her hand meet mine. "You're Idil?" she asked, instead of greeting me in the usual manner.

Something was amiss with her handshake. "Yes," I responded.

Rhoda turned to Mother as if I wasn't there. "I want to get changed."

"Idil, show her Omar's room and the bathroom."

I led Rhoda across the living room and beyond the study before I spoke. "Have you met Omar?" I asked.

"No."

I asked Rhoda about her family, what school she went to—here I found out she'd left school after grade five because she found it a bore—and she was eighteen years old. To all my other questions, she gave only nods or one-word answers.

I tried to further engage Rhoda as she emptied her bags and moved items into Omar's empty dresser. "How could you marry my brother when you don't even know him?" I decided to get to the point.

"Because my parents agreed to it," she answered.

Rhoda's response bit me like the African red scorpion that had stung me at the waterfall a few months earlier. The fact that she could agree to leave home and marry a man she'd never seen because her parents wanted her to do it bothered me. It made me feel like an ungrateful child for rejecting all the men my mother had proposed. But more than that, I wanted the match to fail because if Rhoda married Omar, Mother's attention would return to me. I needed to interfere quickly. "You're nothing more than a blanket to cover his shame," I told Rhoda two days after she came.

Rhoda shrugged her shoulders, walked into the bathroom, and closed the door.

Still, I continued to whisper in her ears for the days that followed. I saw it as a mission against time. I needed to get to her before Omar came and their marriage arrangements were finalized. Every night, I thought of new ways to convince Rhoda to walk away from Omar.

"Leave her alone because it won't work," Elmi told me.

But I couldn't stop. One week after she'd arrived, I went into Omar's room to show Rhoda a family photo. "This is me, Elmi, Mother, and Father. The person standing by Elmi is Omar."

Rhoda offered nothing more than a single glance. "Do you know he has another wife?" I asked, but Rhoda didn't flinch. "Would you like to see her picture?" I held Sheila's photo—the one Omar had brought when he'd introduced her—tight in my grip.

Rhoda's gaze burned into mine. "He can't be married to her. She is gaalo." Her voice cracked, and the words shook. "*I'll* be his wife, not the gaalo whore. Your Mother promised that to my parents."

*She knew?* The realization stunned me. She *couldn't* have known. No woman would accept such an insult, no matter how fantastic the arrangement. Still, I was happy Rhoda had come down off her pedestal and spoken to me. I had finally gained her attention. "He can marry four wives. It says so in the scriptures. You can find it in there yourself if you want. You can read the Qur'an, can't you?" I remembered Rhoda saying she had left school early, and I threw the words at her as if they were weapons to shatter her façade. "Omar *is* married to her and she's the first wife. That makes you the second."

I wanted Rhoda to wilt under the weight of the revelation. I didn't care that my words were hurting her, even though Elmi told me I was being mean. And anyway, I was saving Rhoda from a miserable life because I knew how evil Omar could be.

Unfortunately, Rhoda didn't react the way I expected. Instead, she grabbed the picture out of my hand, ripped it in half, and gave it back to me. "Here! The whore deserves nothing more."

I folded the two halves together and held them close as if I would be able to mend the pieces back together. "You'll have to do more than destroy her picture."

Rhoda glared at me. "I must fulfill my father's promise. You just take care of your end of the bargain."

"What?"

"Oh! You didn't hear?" Rhoda peered into my eyes and found nothing but confusion in them. "No, you didn't. I can see that now." Rhoda stopped to enjoy my horror-stricken face. "It's too bad your father didn't tell you, and you have to hear it from me. You are marrying my brother, Jamac, in exchange for me accepting Omar with his gaalo whore."

"You lie! I made no such promise!"

Rhoda laughed, satisfied. "No, but your father did. A girl doesn't write the contract; she just carries out the transaction." Rhoda sat up on the chair, put her elbows on her knees, and rested her chin on the palms of her hands. "Jamac must be married. He is twenty-five, and the village girls are not exactly rushing in to claim their love, so my father made *you* the condition."

My skin burned with rage. "I *will not!*"

"You will."

"I'll die first." I got up and left Rhoda. Her mocking laughter followed me out.

Mother met me between Omar's room and the kitchen. "Idil, I am glad you are spending time with Rhoda." If Mother noticed my flushed face, it didn't show. "She could use some company until you brother returns and sees what a treasure she is."

Rhoda was stunning and could've married any man, but had to accept Omar. She did it because she felt it was her duty. Unlike her, I felt no obligation to worry about Omar's marriage. Besides, he already had a wife and had no need for Rhoda. But I knew, like she did, that we were the sacrificial lambs to protect our family names. "Rhoda said I am promised to marry her brother, Jamac!"

"Oh dear, your father didn't say anything?" Mother read the answer on my face. "He should've told you. I sent him a note while I was away to ask his permission for your hand. I asked him to tell you about it, and he said he did when he called us from his office. I had to agree to their demand, otherwise they wouldn't have let me bring Rhoda home with me."

"Well! He *forgot* to mention it, and I don't want to marry Jamac." Whether he told me or not, wouldn't have mattered.

"Jamac was in Italy with Omar, and he knows about Sheila. At first, they refused to accept my proposal unless Omar left the gaalo woman. It was not until Jamac asked for you that they gave their permission, provided you married Jamac."

"And I am an object to be traded? Did you think of me, what I want?"

"I thought about you the most. I know you want the Boon. I don't have to ask. But that cannot happen. To marry the Boon is as far from you as the moon and the stars. Jamac is the best choice for you. We know his family, and no harm will ever come to you from him. Your brother gets a wife, and you get a husband."

I took a deep breath to steady my voice. "I love Sidow."

"You'll learn to love Jamac. You have to, you must."

"I won't."

"What do you think Rhoda is doing? She hasn't seen Omar, but she agreed to marry him because a woman does what she must, not what she wants."

I opened my mouth to say something, but Mother left the kitchen before the I had the chance.

※

Two days after Rhoda's horrible revelation, I wrote a note to Sidow for Elmi to deliver. "Mother found me a husband," I scribbled. I stared at the page, trying to give details of the dreadful arrangement, but each time I lifted the pen to write, such sadness filled me that in the end, I gave up and sent the single sentence. I knew I would gain no comfort from Sidow's response, but still I waited with hope.

"Here." Elmi brought the response back the next day.

I unfolded the paper. Sidow had sketched a large teardrop in the middle of the page. He wrote the word *OH!* in the center of the drawing. "That's it?" I yelled, overwhelmed by the emptiness of the message, a split second before Mother entered my room. I crumpled the paper and held it tightly.

Mother pretended not to notice how upset I was. "Come see Rhoda in her outfit and tell us what you think."

I followed her out of my room and into Omar's, unsure of why Mother wanted me involved as I had no desire to give an opinion on the matter.

Mother held up an outfit for Rhoda. "Try this." She handed her a cream-colored guntiino. "What do you think? This one or the last one? Which of the two is the best?" Mother asked me.

"I don't know. It is for Rhoda to decide."

Mother held three more guntiinos. "Pick one of these. Which one do you want to wear to the meeting dinner? Think about it. Your family will be here, but most important of all, Omar will be here. You need something beautiful, but not overdone."

Rhoda tried them. By the time she unfastened the last *garxir*—the knot where the guntiino was fastened—her cheeks were flushed with joy. "I like this one for the dinner," she announced.

"Perfect choice, do you not agree, Idil?"

I did. The outfit looked gorgeous on Rhoda.

The clothing chosen, Mother's days were consumed by planning for the first meeting and the wedding reception, and Rhoda was happy to comply. Mother floated around the house in perpetual motion until Omar and Rhoda's family arrived. She worked on Rhoda for hours the day before and Rhoda went along without complaint. Rhoda's makeup and the henna designs on her hands and feet took on fantastic importance.

"Gorgeous," Mother pointed at Rhoda as if she were congratulating herself.

Mother was right. She had chosen well with both Rhoda and her outfit. Rhoda's parents showed an appreciation toward Mother for Rhoda's appearance and the festive dinner. Several times during that afternoon Rhoda's mother thanked Mother for taking care of her daughter. The invited guests and the family and Father's tribe elders were in awe of Rhoda. Everyone, except Omar. Omar didn't melt with desire—as Mother had hoped—when he saw Rhoda. He spent less than five minutes with her before he drifted into the study to chat with Father, Jamac, and his father-in-law to be. He gave no compliments to Rhoda during the meal, even after Mother practically asked him to offer her something. Omar stayed at the table out of duty, not desire, and went back to the study as soon as he could leave. Mother attempted to go after him, but Father discouraged her by closing the door as soon as they were inside. Elmi, Mother, Rhoda, her mother, and I moved from the table and into the sitting room. Hawa served tea and biscuits, but the tray and mugs remained on the coffee table, untouched.

An hour later, Omar emerged from the study followed

by Father and Rhoda's father. "I have an important meeting," Omar told us, and promptly left.

"What do you think?" Mother asked me after Rhoda's family retired to the compound apartment Father arranged for them during their stay.

"I don't think he liked her."

"What's not to like? Good family, looks, and manners—she has it all."

"I didn't say she isn't appealing, but that won't make Omar want Rhoda, just as much as a good tribal lineage won't make me want to marry Jamac." I thought the comparison was fitting.

"It is not the same. Omar agreed to it. He said he would take a Somali wife, one of my choosing, to keep his gaalo woman. Did you not hear him say so in this very room? Those were his very words," Mother spoke in an excited tone.

"He didn't say it. It was Father who agreed to it."

"But Omar didn't reject it. He must love her now, after all the trouble I went to."

"You can't demand that he love her." I had no desire to fight for Omar's freedom to choose, but I was using him to make a case for myself. "Maybe he loves Sheila."

"How could anyone love a gaalo woman? It makes no sense. Omar said he married her for the business." Mother dismissed my comment and settled in to wait for Omar's return. I stayed with her long after Rhoda and Elmi went to bed. Occasionally, she would raise one more reason why Omar should be smitten by Rhoda, but eventually she fell into a deep, contemplative silence. For my part, I was grateful to keep her company anytime she wasn't devising a plan to marry me off to Jamac. To her disappointment, close to midnight, Father came home without Omar. She jumped to her feet and rushed toward Father. "Where is Omar?" she shouted with enough panic to shake the house.

"He couldn't leave Sheila alone in the hotel."

Mother's anger increased when she learned that Omar had brought Sheila with him from Europe. "What is *she* doing here? I am planning a wedding in a week. What does he mean by this?"

Father's answer did nothing to soothe Mother's rage. "Sheila is here for a business meeting and she leaves the day after tomorrow. That is five days before the wedding." Father took two steps away from Mother and toward his room before he turned around quickly, as if he'd forgotten something very important. "She wants to come and meet the family in the morning."

"What?" Mother was so loud I feared she would wake half the house, but no one stirred. "You promised she'd never come here!"

"It's to meet the family, nothing more. Just pretend she's a friend."

"She isn't. She can't be here. I won't allow it. Sheila isn't welcome here!"

"It's only a breakfast."

"No breakfast, no lunch, no dinner. No Sheila!"

Father retired to his room. Mother continued to rant for another hour with me alone as her audience.

※

Although Mother hadn't wanted Sheila's visit, she woke up early in the morning and worked on an elaborate breakfast. The smell of cumin, garlic, and cilantro in poached eggs reached me in my room before the sun was up. I rubbed the sleep from my eyes and went to the kitchen. Several different pots and platters covered the counter next to the sink. Mother's determination to show Sheila proper Somali hospitality overtook her rejection of the meeting. "She must see that we are civilized. If she is coming, I want her to feel welcomed even if that is not in my heart."

On Omar's arm, Sheila joined us for breakfast the next morning. She wore a long, black skirt and silver heels. When she went to greet Mother, the slit of her skirt opened all the way to her mid-thigh and exposed her pale skin. She had on a white blouse with a flowery scarf under a long collar. Mother put on a bright smile when Sheila arrived.

Sitting at the kitchen table, Rhoda and her family among us, we passed the serving platters without speaking. Dishes moved from one hand to another in silence, as if we were communicating to each other telepathically.

We moved to the sitting room after the meal. Rhoda sat on the sofa next to her mother, her reaction measured. She'd learned about Omar's gaalo wife from Jamac, she'd heard Mother complain about this visit last night, and I had shown her Sheila's picture when she first came. Still, she acted like she didn't know who Sheila was and smiled pleasantly. She took it upon herself to serve the tray of coffee and dates Hawa had prepared and smiled as she offered a cup of coffee to Sheila. We all remained uncomfortable until Sheila, along with Omar and Father, left an hour after the meal.

# CHAPTER THIRTEEN

"THE BRAIDS must be balanced. Redo it now. If you think I'll pay you for this, think again," Mother chided the hairdresser. "Do you call this a wedding design?" She poked an aggressive forefinger right in the middle of Rhoda's head.

Rhoda submitted to pulling and tugging as the hairdresser braided and unbraided her hair. The henna lady drew and changed the pattern for Rhoda's hands and feet several times before Mother settled on one. "That works. Do it now."

Relieved, Mother smiled when Omar arrived with the groomsmen twenty minutes before we were to leave for the reception. "We are ready to go," she announced.

Omar and his groomsmen went in one car, while Rhoda and her bridesmaids took another. The rest of us piled into different cars for the short ride to the reception hall. The sound of the special music, intended to welcome the two families into the ceremony, spilled out of the building and met us in the parking lot upon our arrival.

Mother opened Rhoda's car door just a crack. "Stay there until Omar is seated. I'll send word for you to come in after him." She led the rest of us into the hall.

She took my hand in hers. "Come! I have a special place for you." She pulled me ahead and shoved me into a chair next to Jamac.

"Mother! I…"

She glared at me. "You must," she said, and left.

Jamac reached for my hand, but I withdrew it quickly. He plastered a nauseating smile on his face, his black teeth displaying obvious signs of chewing chat. He looked a decade older than he was.

Jamac didn't let my blatant rejection affect him. "You are more beautiful than your photo."

"My photo?"

"Your mother should have brought a better picture," Jamac responded.

I was wrong to think Mother had forgotten about me when she went in search of a wife for Omar. All along, I was part of her great plan.

Mother watched me from a distance. "Make conversation," she mouthed, but her attention drifted away from me when Rhoda entered the hall.

Rhoda was gorgeous, and guests whispered to each other about her beauty. Her hair, braided in thick, long cornrows, looped around her head. Large yellow beads, strung on silk ribbon, followed the braids and ended where they were gathered in a bun at the nape of her neck. She wore a yellow and red guntiino. Mother's bangles covered both of Rhoda's arms from the wrists to the elbows. A gold fan-shaped necklace rested on her neck draping Rhoda's exposed chest to the top of her breasts.

Four bridesmaids formed the wedding block around her. As tradition dictated, the four unmarried girls in the party were less attractive than the bride. From a distance, the four girls were like a flawless painting on canvas. They moved as one to the flute, the guitar, and the drums that played the wedding song—two steps to the left, one forward, two to the right, and one forward. Rhoda walked in their midst, elegant and stoic. In her right hand, she held a dhiil, carved for the occasion and filled with fresh camel milk. In her left hand, she held a wooden mug with her and Omar's initials carved in it.

The bridesmaids reached the end of their procession when Rhoda came to a stop in front of Omar and his four grooms-men at the head table. She opened the dhiil and poured the milk. She held the mug out to Omar and waited for him to accept it. He didn't move. He didn't take in Rhoda's promise to always nourish him. The guests rose to their feet, each pair of hands poised to clap as soon as Omar took the first sip. Rhoda's smile faltered, and her eyes lost their bright spark. The music that marked the wife's offer to her husband ceased and was replaced by the sound of dishes clattering in the kitchen. The four groomsmen stood up at once and hoisted Omar to his feet. Rhoda pushed the drink into his mouth, completing the symbolic task of a wife feeding her husband after a hard day's work. She kept the mug pressed against Omar's lips. "With this I promise to be your wife, bear your children, and build your home." Her voice was even as the vow spilled from her mouth.

Omar fumbled, and the milk splashed onto the white shawl draped over his shoulder, but the mug remained steady in Rhoda's hand. Omar drank the milk. "I accept you as the warden of my house, the mother of my children, and my wife."

I looked to see if Mother, standing behind the head table, had noticed that his acceptance was out of order. It should've been wife, children, home. I saw nothing.

A thunderous applause filled the air. Omar took the mug from Rhoda, placed it on the table and, eyes glued to her face, guided her to the empty chair next to him. The guests applauded so loudly that I covered my ears.

A bright smile split Mother's face as the union she'd planned came happily together. She walked to the center stage and announced the meal. A line of servants carrying large platters appeared. They placed a plate of rice, one with vegetables, and another with lamb and goat meat on every table.

The attention that had been on Rhoda for the last twenty minutes, returned to our table. "How do you live in this small village?" Jamac asked.

I pointed at my mouth to show I couldn't speak and gave my food undue attention.

"I'd go crazy if I had to live here. I am going to take you out of here as soon as we are married. Maybe we should move to the capital, or leave Somalia altogether. There is so much to see and do beyond the confines of this place." Jamac scanned the space as if this was a microcosm of the whole of Bledley.

I said nothing, and that seemed to discourage Jamac. He served himself food, and we ate in silence for the next half hour. Dessert followed the main meal, and tea continued to flow until the lyrics to the opening family dance started. At the sound of the first drumbeat, I darted toward the stage.

"You hate dancing," Elmi said, when I appeared in front of him. He was at Mother and Father's table.

"Not as much as I hate sitting next to Jamac."

"Be careful with the hate. You might be his wife." Elmi laughed.

"That's not funny."

I didn't like to dance and often avoided it but I was desperate. "If dancing would take me away from Jamac, I'd dance to eternity," I told Elmi. I remained on the stage for every dance after that and didn't leave until Mother pulled me away because it was the couple's last dance. I didn't even hear the announcement for everyone to leave the floor for the bride and groom. Omar and Rhoda came to the stage at the start of the *gelbis*—the song to mark the bride and groom's walk to their own house and embark on their life journey. As the singer reached the last verse of the song, Omar and Rhoda left the hall hand in hand. Both families and guests followed them into the parking lot.

Once outside, Omar lifted Rhoda's hand, kissed it, and released it. "I'll see you tomorrow," he said to her as one would when leaving a friend behind.

Mother rushed to Omar's side. "You *won't* see her tomorrow. She is coming with you—right now."

We all watched silently from a distance.

"Not tonight. It'll have to wait."

Mother grabbed Omar by elbow. "Everything can wait tonight, except for your bride. It is her wedding night. No woman should be left behind on her wedding night."

Omar pulled his arm away. "I am taking her on a month-long honeymoon tomorrow. I have business to take care of tonight."

"On your wedding night?" Mother was incredulous, but her question made no impression on Omar. She turned to Father. "Do something! Tell him this is not how to start a home."

Father jiggled his car keys in his hand. "I would if he didn't have a very important issue to tend to tonight. You know I would."

Despite Mother's determined stance to stop him with her stare, Omar got into the car with his groomsmen and left.

Rhoda lingered a few more seconds until one of her bridesmaids opened the car door and motioned her inside. Rhoda got in, still staring after the receding taillights of Omar's vehicle.

How Rhoda's family was quiet in the face of such humiliation was incomprehensible. They said nothing during the exchange or after Omar disappeared into the dark night, leaving behind a broken promise. As soon as Rhoda's car pulled away, they left. Mother, Elmi, and I went home with Father in his car.

❧

Father slipped into his study as soon as we were home, leaving Mother to stew in her disappointment. Unable to do anything else, she lashed out at us in short bursts. Mother wanted Elmi and me to stay awake and keep Rhoda company while she sorted out her thoughts. But then she complained every few seconds that we were being too loud. "Is it possible for you to stay in one place for a few minutes?" She didn't hide the sarcasm that dripped from her sentence. "An important issue? Who does business in the middle of their wedding night? I would like to know," she vented.

After an hour or so of Mother's rambling, Rhoda stood up. "Goodnight. I am exhausted. I'll see you in the morning." She went to Omar's bedroom.

Elmi stretched his arms and yawned. "I'm off, too," he said.

I expected Mother to send me to bed, but she didn't. She continued to complain. "I am trying to keep this family together and being thwarted all the time." She went on, listing her grievances well into the night.

Mother woke me up the next morning and sent me to Rhoda's room. "Sit with her, while I prepare breakfast. Poor thing. How humiliated and devastated she must be feeling right now."

I welcomed the prospect of seeing Rhoda realize how evil Omar was. *If she'd refused to marry Omar, I would have been free from having to wed Jamac.* I wanted to gloat and yell "I warned you," but Rhoda was still under the covers when I entered the room.

She sat up when she saw me and took something out

from under her pillow. "She will pay for this," she said, almost speaking to herself.

"Who?" I asked.

"Who else? The gaalo whore."

*Rhoda is more upset with Sheila, than she is with Omar.* "How is this Sheila's fault?" I asked.

"It just is! All night he was looking at this." She held a small key-chain sized picture of Sheila out to me.

I reached for it, but Rhoda closed her fingers, making the picture disappear within her hand. "Are you not angry with him?" I asked.

"I'll not give up my husband for her! Not for a white whore."

"But he was her husband first."

Rhoda looked me in the eye for a few seconds. "She was waiting for him at the hotel last night," she said.

"What?"

Mother arrived with breakfast before Rhoda had the opportunity to explain. Rhoda's face softened. The anger and determination that inhabited it seconds ago evaporated, and were replaced by sadness. The change was quick and believable, and Mother fell for it.

"I am very sorry." She placed the tray on the night table and hugged Rhoda. "I'll see to it you are taken care of, my dear. I promise." Rhoda melted into her embrace and wept.

As soon as Mother left, the real Rhoda emerged, angry and vengeful. "She doesn't know with whom she is dealing." Rhoda's voice carried an unmistakable threat.

An hour later, when Omar arrived to collect Rhoda, her face transformed again. The red, venom-filled eyes twinkled as she hugged Omar. She said nothing about him walking out on her, or going to the hotel to be with Sheila. On the surface, she was the happy bride. She even asked his permission to leave the sitting room. With an innocent-looking wave, Rhoda went to her room to get ready. Only a half hour after Omar came, they left on their honeymoon.

The month Rhoda and Omar were away passed uneventfully. Several times, I almost asked Mother to allow me to return to school and finish grade twelve but I didn't. I knew what she would say.

"And send you back to the Boon?"

She was right. Given the chance, I would have gone straight to him.

Since Mother didn't insist that I stay in my room during the day, I spent a great deal of time with Hawa. I followed her into the kitchen as soon she returned from the market. I helped her with the cleaning, washing the rice for dinner, and dicing the meat and vegetables for something to do and someone to talk to.

"You might learn to love him after the marriage," Hawa said after she listened to me complain about my impending marriage to Jamac.

She sounded so much like Mother that I had to look up to make sure it was Hawa. "How could I learn to love him when I love someone else?" It was easy for Hawa. She was getting married to Ilyaas, the boy she loved, with her parents' blessing.

"But how are you ever going to be with Sidow?"

"Maybe we could elope." I put the idea that had lingered in my mind for a while now into words, and that scared me.

"Elope? You mean to go to Cagaaran and marry him without your parents' permission?"

I had no idea how I would put such a plan into practice, but verbalizing it was a start. "Yes."

"Idil! I wouldn't consider it if I were you. You don't want to make your parents angry, especially your father." She stared at me and waited for my response.

"I won't," I lied. But I was turning the thought over in my mind. In fact, I shared my thoughts with Elmi that evening when he returned from school.

For the first time in weeks, Elmi came home that day without a note from Sidow. "Hasan didn't come to school," he explained.

"It doesn't matter anymore. I plan to elope with him soon anyway."

"Elope! Don't be absurd." His face creased with disapproval. "You are not eloping with Sidow. You can't, unless you want him dead, or in jail."

"Then what do you propose I do?" I was almost angry with Elmi for not being more understanding.

"I do not know, but eloping is not the solution," he said.

"It seems I have no choice." I fled to my room.

❧

Things remained at a standstill until the week after Omar and Rhoda returned from their honeymoon. Omar spent that night at home, but not with Rhoda. He was mostly in the study with Father. For the rest of that week, Omar came and went—to where, no one knew. Even Rhoda didn't seem bothered by his comings and goings and only shrugged when I asked her about it.

Jamac and his parents, along with a dozen other relatives, arrived at the end of that week. It was a Friday afternoon, and Elmi and I were in the sitting room, looking at his latest drawing.

"My parents are here," Rhoda announced and ran out the house. I wanted to go to my room, but stayed only long enough to hide my obvious displeasure. After I greeted them, I asked Mother if I could be excused. She tried to stop me from going.

Rhoda's father raised his hand. "Halima let her go. It is becoming for a young lady to be shy in front of her future in-laws and husband."

Rhoda followed me to my room. "My parents and yours will start planning your wedding as soon as your father gets home." A smirk spread over her face. "Wouldn't you like to know the details of your big day?"

The words lit an angry fire in my belly. "I'm not marrying him."

"Oh, you will," Rhoda taunted. "You will."

"I can't stand your brother," I said instead.

"You don't think I am in love with yours, do you?"

"I didn't ask you to love Omar. I'd sooner have you hate him."

Rhoda laughed so loud I was afraid Mother would hear. "We are more alike than different. We both are goods to be bought and sold."

"Speak for yourself," I said.

"If you want to delude yourself, you can do that. But I suggest you take control of the situation by becoming part of the process," she said and then promptly left.

All that night and the next day, I steeled myself to get through this one hour at a time. Meals were torturous sessions. I was forced to smile as I listened to plans for a future I wanted no part of. Where we were going to go for our honeymoon, the house we were going share with Jamac's parents in Mogadishu, and the furniture within it were discussed in detail. I nodded, pretending I was paying attention.

I took refuge in Elmi's room at the end of dinner the second night. "I have to do something." On Elmi's bed, I used his towel to wipe the tears.

Elmi handed me a folded sheet of paper, wrapped in plastic. "Here."

"What is it?"

Elmi opened his door and looked outside to make sure we would not be overheard. "Your parting gift."

"My parting gift?"

He took the paper back from me and unfurled it, exposing an exquisite but sad drawing. This was the first drawing Elmi had completed since we'd lost Sidow's company.

Elmi ran his fingers over the paper. "I started this the minute I realized you were leaving." He pointed at his drawing. "What do you think?"

The image of a girl on a long and narrow road filled the page. The end of the pavement disappeared under an ominous sky that reached to swallow the asphalt. It was dark around the girl, except for a bright light above her head. The sun, threatened by the approaching merger, struggled to peek through a small gap between the clouds. Her hands were outstretched toward a single ray that grew stronger as the road moved farther and farther away from her.

I turned from the vivid image that depicted my bleak situation only too well. "How did you know I was leaving? I haven't even decided yet!"

"You were right. You have no other option but to elope. I hate the idea, and it is very dangerous, but there is no other way."

"I'm scared," I confessed.

Elmi smiled. "When times are tough, hold this."

"I will, but I'm afraid I need more practical help."

"I know." Elmi refolded the paper and handed it back to me.

I rose from the bed, lightheaded and feeling the magnitude of the decision I was about to act upon.

# CHAPTER FOURTEEN

THE FOLLOWING NIGHT, I went to Hawa's room in the servants' quarters immediately after dinner.

Hawa stopped folding clothes and looked at me. "What are you doing here? You should be with the others, planning your wedding."

"I need you to help me elope." I told her quickly in case I lost the courage to ask.

She didn't seem as surprised as I thought she would be. "I know you have to do it, but I can't get involved. I'll lose my job."

I expected her to try and talk me out of the leaving, but like Elmi, she was resigned to the inevitable. "I'll ask Mother if I can come with you to the market to pick henna design samples. All I ask is that you stay at the market an hour or so longer than usual to give me enough time to reach Sidow's house."

"Will she let you come with me?"

"I think so, if I pretend to go along with her plan. When you come back, tell her I ran off and you spent the extra time looking for me. Be certain others hear you calling my name and they'll testify to it. Ask anyone you pass on your way home, if they've seen me."

"Does Sidow know?"

"Yes, I sent him a note with Elmi this morning. He didn't respond to it, but he knows."

Hawa nodded and went back to folding the laundry.

I kept in step with Hawa, holding on to one of the handles of the grocery basket. I rifled through a basket of fruit at one stall in the produce section of the market and surveyed the open displays just long enough for others to see me. "Look at this." I held a henna package out to Hawa. "This is a stunning design, is it not?"

Hawa nodded. Her eyes darted from the henna package to the aisle behind the vegetable stall. "We need to get to the butcher before all the good pieces are sold," she said.

I put the package of henna back into the box and moved to a stall with an array of costume jewelry. "Do you think Mother would let me wear this on my wedding night?" I asked the question loud enough for the vendor to hear, just in case Hawa needed witnesses.

"No! You are Idil Hussein Nuur, the general's daughter. Your mother would never allow you to wear anything but pure gold."

The vendor rolled her eyes and turned to the next customer.

"Come, let us get the meat." I walked alongside of Hawa.

As we drew closer to the canopy that housed the meat shops, Hawa walked a few steps ahead of me, allowing others to cut in. "Stay close," she said, but continued to speed up.

"I am right behind you," I called, but after I lost sight of Hawa, I turned around and hurried away from the market.

❦

On my way to Sidow's, I thought about the consequences of my actions. How long would it be until Hawa arrived home, carrying a half-full basket because, having lost me, she was too worried to do the rest of the shopping? I tried to imagine Father's reaction when Mother told him I was gone. How long would it take them to realize I had eloped with Sidow and they would have to deal with Jamac's family and the tribe elders? Drowning in frightening thoughts, I entered Sidow's farm from the side and went straight to the cornfield where I had instructed him to meet me.

"Hey," I whispered.

Sidow poked his head through the corn stalks. The leaves framed his face, making him look like the photo on one of the Wheat Board posters. "You are here!" Sidow hugged me. "I read your note, but I didn't think you would go through with it."

"You're surprised?" The possibility of Sidow rejecting the proposal to elope never occurred to me.

"No, just elated. Wait here. I'll be back in a few minutes."

Sidow hurried toward the shed at the other end of the corn-field where they kept the farm tools, and work clothes.

Lost in the fear and anticipation of what we were about to do, I didn't hear Sidow's returning footsteps. "Wear this," he said, holding a pair of work overalls and an old denim shirt. On our way to the bus depot, we kept a good distance between us so as not to appear to be together. I took a deep breath to expel the anxiety, but I couldn't dispel the dread. Sidow went up to the ticket counter and came back with the tickets. "The bus to Cagaaran is almost full and is scheduled to leave in ten minutes. These were the last two tickets."

The last call to board came as Sidow and I made it to our seats at the back of the bus. We sat down, and I put my head on his shoulder. Sidow caressed my back in small circu-lar motions. "I love you so," he said.

The drive southwest to Cagaaran—a town where those unable to gain their family's blessing could buy a *nikaax*— marriage ceremony—took much longer than I expected. The bus made several stops at villages along the way and each time a few travelers got off and others came on. I followed the movements of the oncoming passengers, afraid of a bounty hunter sent by my parents. The possibility of Father seeking revenge entered with each person who came on board. At every stop, I expected someone to grab me off the bus. "I am afraid of what Father might do," I said.

Sidow cupped my face between his gentle hands and kissed me in the forehead. "It is too late. We can't think about that now."

❧

The driver dropped us at a small market full of shoppers and gave us directions to the nikaax house. "It is not far from here," he said. "You should be there in five minutes."

We walked close to thirty minutes before we came upon the place. An old man met us near the gate. "Print your names here." He opened a notebook to a fresh page and handed it to Sidow. When we were finished, the man led us through a stone-walled garden. "You came at a good time. It is usually busy on Thursdays, but we don't have many customers yet." The man ushered Sidow and I into a tiny hut at the back of the large, sprawling property. "Go in there. I'll fetch you when it's time," he said and pointed at the opening in a dark gray curtain.

Sidow parted the fabric, and we entered. Inside were two other couples seated at small tables. Sidow and I sat at the last vacant table near the door. "I hope this doesn't take too long," I said.

An hour later, we were perched on two stools in front of an enormous man. The man shook Sidow's hand. "My name is Sheikh Deerow," he said as he leafed through the notebook and found our names. "Did you ask Idil's father for her hand in marriage?"

"Yes, but the father refused." That was only a half lie. Sidow didn't ask my father, but Father would have refused if he had.

"Do you have witnesses to confirm that?"

Sidow and I were surprised at the unexpected question.

"The children love each other, Deerow, and you are their only hope." The man who welcomed us earlier answered on our behalf.

Deerow shared a knowing glance with the man. "True. I am the last hope for many lovers." He responded as if the man's interjection gave him the proof he needed of my father's rejection. Deerow took Sidow's hand and held it. "Do you promise to be responsible for Idil, to house her, clothe her, and care for her?"

Sidow nodded.

"I must hear you say the words," Deerow insisted.

"Yes, I do." Sidow sat upright and faced him directly. "I do," he repeated.

"Beyond tribe and friends, outside work and play, only preceded by your parents?" Deerow rattled on.

"Yes, beyond all but my mother."

"Through illness, and whether she is barren or provides children."

"Yes, either way," Sidow confirmed.

"Should you decide to take a second wife, Idil has the right to ask for a divorce."

I jumped off the stool and was standing by the time I realized what I was doing. *Second wife.* The memory of Father's constant threat to Mother rushed back. Dazed and shaking, I sat back down.

"Could you change that so it says I won't take a second wife?" Sidow asked.

Deerow agreed. "How much is your dowry?" This question was directed at me. Confused, I turned to Sidow.

Sidow rested his hand around my shoulder before he spoke. "One thousand shillings,"

"Do you have the money to pay her now?"

Sidow pulled a bundle of broadleaf twenty-shilling bills out of his top shirt pocket. Here!"

Deerow wet his fingers and counted the money twice. "One thousand shillings," he announced and handed the money to me. "Please accept this as your nikaax sum," he said and turned to Sidow. "Sign here and here and here." Deerow traced a forefinger over the paper.

Sidow and I signed the document in three spots. When we were finished, Sidow paid Deerow the service fee and gave him a small tip.

"Here is your marriage license. Register it with the village and with both tribal elders."

Deerow gave the sheet of paper to Sidow.

Two hours later with the paper in hand, Sidow helped me to board the same bus we had come on back to Bledley.

It was a little after sunset when we arrived at Sidow's farm. Sidow's mother heard us coming before we passed the rooster guarding the gate. She ran toward us as we approached. "You are back safe!" She hugged her son, released him, and hugged him again. Then she took a step toward me, stopped, took another one, and hugged me.

We followed her to the house. She didn't say anything until we were inside. "Her father's soldiers came here this afternoon and tore the whole place a part. They looked under the beds, inside the grain silos, and in the shed. They threatened to shoot Hasan and me if we didn't tell them what we knew. Then one of them suggested you might have eloped, but the others laughed at him. 'A Boon eloping with the general's daughter?' they mocked. The chuckling died, as one by one, they came to the realization it was the only explanation for your disappearance. As quickly as the thought came to them, they boarded their truck and headed toward Cagaaran. I heard them say 'We will get them, dead or alive.' I prayed all day long for your safe return."

*What delayed the soldiers from reaching Cagaaran, or intercepting the bus on our way back?* Sidow's mother's words pulled me out of my thoughts and into the present.

"What have you done, my son? What possessed you to embark on such a dangerous course of action?"

"I had to, Mother. I had to!" Sidow responded.

"Her father will destroy us," she said as she took one of the stools next to the large wooden couch.

"I love Idil."

Sidow's mother wiped her face with the hem of her scarf. "This love will not flourish. It will kill everyone, even *her*."

"I tried to forget, to wipe Idil out of my mind, but I couldn't." Sidow squatted in front of her and rested both his hands on her knees.

"I am afraid for you, my son, for Idil, for all of us." She sighed and closed her eyes before she spoke again. "We must apologize for the elopement, take Idil back to her family, and ask for her hand in marriage, but I am afraid that won't fix it. Her father is a very powerful man, and his daughter eloping is bad enough. But eloping with a Boon is a great insult."

I moved closer to hold her attention, to make sure she'd hear. "You know what my father will say, how he feels. Please don't take me back there. I don't want to see them or deal with them. I can't bear to look at their faces after what I have done."

"You two have made a terrible mistake to be sure, but it must be corrected."

"It's useless to take me back when you know how he will answer."

"This is a marriage, a lifetime commitment. We must do it right. How he might answer doesn't change our responsibility. The elder will send a messenger to tell your parents that you are safe and request a meeting with them as soon as possible." She stood up from the stool. "Take Idil to your room and you sleep with Hasan. You mustn't bed her until we meet with her parents," she said and went to her room.

As custom dictated, it was her responsibility to make sure we had no opportunity to be intimate until Father's refusal was confirmed. It was only then that the nikaax, without Father's consent, could be accepted by Sidow's tribal elders.

I followed Sidow to his room and sat on the bed after he closed the door. I prayed as hard as I could for Father not to grant the meeting.

⋇

The day started slowly as we waited for the news of the meeting schedule from Father. I went to the kitchen when I awoke and forced the breakfast of bread and eggs down. Sidow lingered around the cooking area, only leaving for a few minutes at a time to check on the workers in the cornfield. His mother stayed with me, cooking and cleaning, but saying nothing. It was after we had finished eating the midday meal that a messenger arrived with word. The man took Sidow and his mother outside. A few minutes later the messenger left, and they returned.

Sidow gave me the news. "We're meeting your parents in an hour."

"Father agreed to a meeting?" I was shocked.

Sidow stood by the door and twisted the knob back and forth. "Yes, he did. I will check with the workers one more time and then we will leave."

I returned to the room until Sidow came to collect me. "Come. Everyone is here and ready to go and meet with your father."

Two elders from Sidow's tribe were waiting to introduce themselves and their wives to me when we entered the front room. One white-haired man, about Father's age, spoke to me. He looked at me with kind, regretful eyes. "We have to ask your father's permission. We know he won't grant it; no Bliss father would give his blessing to his child marrying a Boon. Still we must make the request for this union to count." He held up the marriage license we'd brought from Cagaaran.

The bright summer sun was hotter than it had been the day before. I had walked this route often, but today the landscape appeared more desolate than it had ever been. Seven of us, separated by our own thoughts of what was to come, moved in a funereal procession. Sidow and I walked in the middle, unable to connect with each other, while the two wives and Sidow's mother followed behind, whispering about wedding plans and dates. The two men led the procession chanting prayers and good wishes. The closer we came to the compound, the faster my heart beat. I had an impulse to run away when I saw the two lions guarding the metal gate. I took Sidow's hand in mine instead and forced my feet to move forward, one step at a time, slow and steady.

❦

Mother opened the door to the main house before we even knocked just like she used to do when Elmi and I returned from school. "Idil?" My name came as a question. Mother's face broke into an involuntary smile when she saw me, but corrected itself when Father called.

"Bring them in quickly," he yelled from inside.

"Come with me." She walked ahead of us.

We followed her into the main house. Father in full uniform, his gun visible in the holster on his belt, charged at us as we entered. "Why are you here?" he demanded.

"We're here to apologize for the children's action and to ask for Idil's hand in marriage like we should have done in the first place," the white-haired elder said.

Father stepped around the man, grabbed Sidow by the collar, and threw him back against the wall that divided the sitting room from the bedrooms. "Who do you think you are, eloping with my daughter and coming here now, expecting my blessing?"

I covered my ears against the sound of Sidow hitting the wall. It took him a few seconds to recover, but Sidow pulled himself up. The rest of the group, did nothing. I saw Rhoda standing between the study and her room, her feet apart as if getting ready to attack me. We locked eyes, and hers seethed with anger. *I gave myself to Omar and his whore, and you did this?* she seemed to ask without uttering a word. Jamac and his parents were not there. I surveyed the room in search of Elmi but didn't see him.

Father took a bowl filled with popcorn off the corner

table and threw it at Sidow. "How dare you disrespect me? As if taking my daughter without my consent was not enough, you come here asking for my *blessing?* Did you forget you are a Boon and you don't belong in my family?" Father's anger was palpable. "I received your messenger and agreed to meet you, thinking you'd know your place and send Idil home. I never imagined you'd come with your elders to ask for my permission as if you thought we were equal."

Mother turned to Sidow's mother seeking a woman-to-woman understanding. "My daughter wouldn't have married your son of her own free will. You played a part with your sixir and saangudub to make her fall in love with him. Please leave my child alone! Let her come back to her family."

Sidow's mother didn't say anything.

The meeting erupted into chaos, Mother begging them to lift their sorcery so I could think for myself and leave Sidow, and Father challenging their audacity.

It only stopped when a servant arrived with a note. "General, you have a visitor." The servant held small piece of paper. "He's from the capital and says he must see you right away."

The note stopped Father in his tracks. After reading it, he folded it in his hand. "Is he alone?"

"Yes, sir. He says it's important. He has a message from the president and he must see you now."

Father turned to me. "Denounce the Boon and stay home like a proper child, or go with him and cease to be my daughter."

I had expected such an ultimatum from Father, so his words didn't shock me as much as they might have. I noticed the expressions of others in the room: Rhoda's devilish smile seemed to indicate she thought I would fold; Mother's mouth hung open; the elder's kind eyes misted with tears. I didn't dare look at Sidow or his mother.

I knew that with my decision, all of our lives would be forever altered. "I want to be with my husband," I responded. Mother's mouth closed, Rhoda's face contorted with fury, and Father's mouth twitched. I turned to Sidow and saw him trying to keep the expression on his face neutral. A lone tear rolled down his mother's cheek.

"Go away! Get this filth out of my house. You are dead to me!" Father shouted and left the room.

# CHAPTER FIFTEEN

SIDOW'S MOTHER had started the wedding reception plans as soon as we returned from seeing my parents. She asked me questions to include me. "Do you want your reception in the daytime or at night?" she asked that first evening.

"Either is fine. It doesn't matter." I didn't want to appear ungrateful for her efforts, but all I could think about was Father. Six days had gone by and we'd heard and seen nothing. The silence and inaction terrified me.

"Which one do you want to wear?" Sidow's mother held one guntiino in each hand. "Traditional or modern?"

Sidow took the traditional outfit with their tribal symbol embroidered on it from his mother. "You should go with this. You'll look stunning in it," he said.

I nodded without any enthusiasm.

The week that followed the visit filled me with dread. I waited for Father to retaliate—send one of his soldiers to attack or intimidate us. I watched for a sign of one of the Red Berets coming into the house in the dead of the night. Each time Sidow was out, I worried he wouldn't return, but all was quiet. "Father doesn't let wrongdoings go unpunished," I reminded Sidow, as he came from the field into the common room.

Sidow didn't conceal his surprise. "Are you unhappy he has left us alone?"

Father's angry silhouette popped into my mind's eye. "No, I'm not, but I'm afraid he's planning something dreadful, something hideous."

"Maybe he has better things to do with his time and energy."

"I hope you're right." I dropped the subject when Sidow's mother entered the common room.

"I have a visitor for Idil," Sidow called out from outside his mother's room. It was eight days from when we'd eloped and seven days from when Father declared me dead. The reception was scheduled for that evening, and Sidow's mother and her lady friends were busy getting me ready. I still couldn't believe Father was allowing me to go through with the wedding.

I shouted with joy when I heard Elmi's voice. He was the last person I'd expected.

"You look beautiful," he said.

Without warning, tears ran my cheeks dissolving the kohl eyeliner in dark streaks. "How did you know to come today?"

"I have my ways, but crying wasn't the reaction I was

after. If I'd wanted to see tears, I would have stayed home."

"I'm sorry," I said. "Who?"

"Mother is crying over Father, Rhoda, Omar, me, and you, but most of all she's crying because she thinks she hasn't done enough to keep her family together. So, I came for your smile." He stepped behind me and tied a gold necklace with a heart-shaped pendant around my neck. "There you go."

I lifted the pendant and saw that on one side of the heart was the letter I and on the other was the letter S—initials for Idil and Sidow. It was beautiful and something only Elmi could concoct during such a difficult time.

I admired the gift. "How did you pay for this?" I asked, instead of saying "Thank you, I appreciate what you have done, and I am touched as this is the loveliest of presents."

"I gave Mother's jeweler—the one she hired to make the jewelry for your wedding to Jamac—a handsome tip and had him add the cost of this necklace to Mother's bill. I knew where he was because Mother sent me there with a note to cancel the order the day after you eloped."

"You shouldn't have done that."

"I think she noticed the charge on the bill because she asked me if I had purchased an item when I went to the jeweler, but she left the room before I could answer." Elmi traced the half-finished henna design on my hand. "I believe she wanted you to have it without having to admit it." Elmi hugged me tight and stepped away from me. "Don't forget to look at my drawing when you need to."

I pulled him closer. "Please, don't leave."

Elmi unfastened my hands from around his neck. "I have to. It's for the best."

He was right, but still, hot tears stung my cheeks. "I'll miss you so much."

He took both my hands and kissed them. "If you promise to smile, I'll come again and visit."

"I'd love that," I said and followed him out of the room. I waited until Elmi and I were outside and away from the others before I asked. "What happened with Jamac and his family?"

"They were angry with Mother and Father for not fulfilling their part of the deal, but they blamed Mother more. I heard Jamac's mother say 'A woman that can't keep her daughter in line is not worth the marriage she enjoys,' loud enough for Mother to hear after the news of your elopement came. As soon as Hawa returned without you, they packed their bags and left."

"And what about Hawa? Did she get into a lot of trouble when she came back?"

"Mother fired her and threatened to have her arrested if you weren't found safe, although she knew Hawa was leaving at the end of the month anyway, to get married."

"Was she angry with me? Did you ask her about me?"

"She told me she'd pray for your happiness." Elmi thought for a moment as if debating whether to say more. "I didn't come here to talk about Mother. I came to wish you joy. Have fun at the party," he kissed my hand and walked away.

I nodded and watched Elmi until he disappeared.

❧

By the time I finished with the henna decoration, the makeup, and the dress, the fear of Father's retribution ebbed. Sidow's mother and the ladies from her tribe adorned the Farmers' Hall with traditional artifacts. The decoration was simple and elegant, the food delicious and plentiful. The happy atmosphere was contagious. Sidow and I sat at the head of the wedding table. "Thank you for everything," I said to his mother when she brought a plate of dry, seasoned fruits to our table.

Young girls from other farm families of the same tribe served the food. The dinner started with black bean salad served in small wooden bowls. The main meal consisted of spiced rice, camel meat, and mixed vegetables on large oval platters, each large enough for four guests to share. Once the dishes were collected and the tables were cleared, the music started. The first dance was the traditional *Kaboobey* dance. "This looks complicated," I whispered to Sidow.

"We'll have to join in soon," he said.

"I don't know how."

"Follow me and do as I do." He stood up and extended his hand as soon as the second number began. "This is our song. I picked it myself. Come. I will teach you."

This reception was different from Omar's. People didn't take turns entering the stage, but came in together and left when they felt like it. There was no sharing of milk, no swearing to take care of each other forever. That had been done a day earlier in the privacy of our common room with only the tribe elders and the family.

"Dance with me," Sidow whispered.

We started our own circle and other larger ones formed

around us. At first, I couldn't replicate Sidow's elegant foot-work. I stopped several times to observe his movements. We pulled out of one circle and joined another. After a while, the sound of the music rang in my ears, and vibrated within. I followed the beats and moved despite my inability to under-stand the steps. We fell into rhythm. Sidow's arms hovering overhead as I followed his lead. My feet obeyed the beat of the drums, the singing of the flute, and whisper of the lyrics. I faced Sidow, and our eyes connected for a second or two before he turned around to guide me through the motions. We repeated the steps over and over.

"You are dancing like an angel." Sidow kissed me without missing a step.

The tension that had built inside me over the worry of what Father might do evaporated, and I danced without inhi-bition as if I could have gone on forever.

Sidow took my shawl and draped it over us. "This is the best night ever."

We danced under the shawl, and his smile grew bigger and brighter, until the music ceased. Hand in hand, Sidow and I went back to the head of the wedding table. Guests lined up for the formal well-wishing. Some hugged us, oth-ers shook our hands, and all wished us a prosperous future together.

We didn't leave the hall until all the guests were gone and the tables and decorations were stored away. A sense of happi-ness washed over me as we walked home openly as a couple. Alone in our bedroom, I kissed Sidow with passion, "I loved everything about our wedding party," I said.

"Everything?"

I nodded and kissed him again, long and deep. After our love-making, I fell asleep listening to the happy laughter of the guests and seeing the dancers in my head.

❧

I stayed in bed for a minute after I'd smelled the burning wood. "What is that?" I nudged Sidow.

He didn't move.

The smell grew stronger, and I jolted upright. "Sidow!" I yelled. He stirred, but didn't open his eyes. "Wake up!" I shook him hard.

Sidow awoke with a start. "What is it?"

"I think the house is on fire." By then, traces of smoke were seeping between the wooden logs.

When Sidow and I went outside, the kitchen was ablaze. Hasan and his mother stood next to us as long, hungry flames leapt from the roof of the kitchen and licked the sides of the house. The crescent moon blinked once then slipped behind a cloud as if it was hiding from the destruction.

The whole neighborhood came to our aid with buckets of water and sand, fighting a fire that was too big for their equipment. After a while, we could only stand helplessly and watch the flames move from one wall to the next with a vengeance. The fire trucks in the nearby military compound didn't arrive to help, nor did we expect them to. They never came to rescue the villagers.

The fire eventually burned itself out after it had taken all that it could. In the end, only Hasan's room was standing. Someone, I do not know who, brought stools and mats, and we sat under the big *qurac* tree, stunned by the destruction and grateful no one was hurt. Even the cows and goats in their shed survived. In the morning, the neighbors brought breakfast and tea. That afternoon, the white-haired elder walked with Sidow around the house so they could survey the damage together.

I saw Sidow spot the boot prints leading away from the house as he and the elder assessed the foundation for rebuilding. Sidow's body went rigid and his eyes grew large and scared.

"Those are military boot prints. Father did this," I said to Sidow when he came back to where we were sitting.

"Don't say that."

"We are lucky no one was hurt. This was a warning. He'll kill us next time. He'll come back to finish what he started. We should leave this village."

"I was born here and I'll die here." Sidow was adamant.

I urged him, along with his mother. "We have to go away. My father sent whoever set the house on fire." The thought of what else Father might do shook me.

Sidow walked away from me toward the house, and I followed him. He placed his hand on the charred remains of what had been a kitchen wall. "Let us hope they've accomplished their mission."

"They haven't. Not if you and I are alive," I said, but Sidow wouldn't listen.

"We'll place our trust in Allah," he said.

❧

The clearing of debris and the plan to rebuild began two days later. Men from the neighboring farms came to help with the cleanup before the builders could be hired and the supplies ordered. Their wives took turns making food and drinks. The white-haired elder organized the farmers into teams to take different shifts, so the rebuilding could go as quickly as possible.

Sidow's mother and I, along with other neighborhood women, kept water pitchers and teakettles full. To entertain the men, Sidow built a wooden stand and placed the battery-operated radio on it. They listened to the songs and swung their hammers in time with the music, only stopping to hear the hourly news report.

"The president announced his new cabinet earlier today," the news anchor began the broadcast. The president's latest attempt to quell internal unrest came three days after the fire.

The cabinet reshuffling of 1981, two years earlier, had done nothing to contain the problem that had started at the end of the Somali and Ethiopian war. The reporter proceeded to read the list of the new minsters. I dropped the hot kettle of tea and almost scalded my feet when my Father's name was announced among them.

Father had wanted to trade his military uniform for a civilian suit for a long time, but up to now he had been unsuccessful. He even took us with him to the capital once to meet with the president and his family. I remember the party at the presidential palace and how Father paraded us around to show others what a great husband and father he was. Father came back from the private meeting still wearing his uniform and the four-hour ride to Bledley was spent in silence. Now Father had received the appointment he'd been after for so long, and I couldn't have been happier.

Father's name and title, Hussein Nuur Minister of Finance, was third on the list as the reporter read through the new appointments.

"That's fantastic!" I couldn't contain my joy as everyone, including Sidow, looked on.

Sidow stopped hammering. "What does he know about finances?"

The yard was silent, and I heard the blood course through my veins. "Nothing. I'm glad he got it because it means they'll soon move away to the capital." I was certain Father's new assignment would save us from further assault at his hands. "Once out of the village, Father will have more important things to worry about."

It took a few minutes before the sound of the pounding hammers filled the air again, as men fell in time with the song that followed the news. No one mentioned Father or his cabinet position after that.

❦

"Your mother is here with Elmi." Hasan stood by the door. "Do you want me to show them in?"

It was a week after the fire, and Sidow and his mother had gone to the market to pick up supplies. With nothing to do, I stayed in the room after Sidow kissed me good-bye. It was one of the very few times we'd had physical contact since the fire. We were sharing a room with my mother-in-law and Hasan, and that left little chance for privacy. The room was bare except for three straw sleeping mats and one cloth prayer mat. Hasan's single bed, the only piece of furniture not destroyed, stood at the back. We convinced Sidow's mother to take the bed and three of us slept on the floor.

"No, I will come outside. Please take them to the sitting area," I told Hasan. Since we'd lost the front formal room along with all the furniture, we used six gembers under the large qurac tree. We received guests, ate our meals, and spent most of the evenings there. But mainly the men building the house used it to take breaks, eat, or socialize during the day.

I didn't know why Mother had decided to visit, but I wished she hadn't. "How are you?" I asked, as I motioned for them to sit. Neither she nor Elmi accepted the offer, so I remained standing, too.

"I am doing well," Elmi said.

"I know I needn't ask because I can see. But as your mother, I need to know how you are doing."

"I am not as bad as you and Father wanted me to be," I said.

"No Idil! Your father had nothing to do with it; I, certainly, had nothing to with it."

"Of course, Mother! The fire started all on its own." I took a deep breath to slow my racing heart. "If you have come to see the destruction, go ahead and enjoy the view. Unfortunately, we are still alive."

Elmi stepped from behind Mother and placed his hand on my elbow. "Idil, we came…"

"Let her be," Mother stopped Elmi before he said more. "She is angry. I understand."

"I am more than angry. I am devastated."

"I am sorry."

"Why? Because we are still alive?" I asked, my anger deepening.

"I had nothing to do with the fire, but I am still sorry it had to be this way," Mother replied, her voice heavy with sorrow.

"It didn't *have* to be this way. You could've stood by me, taken my side for once, and helped me marry the man I love."

"I was always with you. Why do you think I insisted on making you do what was expected of you? I could do nothing more than to guide you to the right path. I am only a woman after all, and not much different from you, except in age. Neither of us can go against the laws of society. I tried to make you follow what you can't change, only you wouldn't listen. Any woman that steps outside the line will be destroyed and you are already halfway there. I want to die before I witness the other half of your destruction."

Mother had come as close as she was ever going to come to admitting she knew Father was behind setting my house on fire. I didn't want to feel sorry for her, because I held her partly responsible for what had happened.

I let Mother hug me when she took me into her embrace. After a while, she released me and looked me in the eye. "Your father and Rhoda and Omar left yesterday for Father's swearing in ceremony. Elmi and I stayed so we could come and see you before we moved."

I knew my parents would move, but Elmi's leaving made me shudder. "I'll miss you," I told him.

Only an hour after they came, Elmi and Mother left. I stood by the rooster at the gate and watched them disappear into the alley and out of my life, perhaps for good.

# CHAPTER SIXTEEN

THE VILLAGERS joined us to celebrate the end of the rebuild. Their support got us through the tough times, and Sidow slaughtered a calf and held a great feast to show our appreciation. They ate and prayed for us and for better days to come, but it took me six months after my family moved to feel at peace with my surroundings. By then the laughter of family and friends filled the house, dispelling the sadness and dread that had lived with us since the day we eloped.

The focus turned to something personal. Friends and neighbors in the village inquired if I was pregnant. "Nothing yet?" they whispered as if I were not there. Still others asked aloud.

My mother-in-law gave the same answer after each doubt-filled question. "If Allah wills." That didn't stop people from asking. The inquiries came often and always to her even if I was in the room. She repeated the same answer, no matter who asked or how many times they did. "It's all in Allah's hands."

Even when I became pregnant, eight months after I was married, she said nothing. I gave her the news before I told Sidow, so she had the information next time the question arose. She only smiled, but never relayed the news.

"Tell them so they stop. Tell them I am having a baby." I didn't want the women in the village to think I was barren.

"Stop. Fadumo is coming." My mother-in-law stared at the door.

Our neighbor Fadumo, a childless widow, joined us most afternoons for tea. Fadumo took the stool next to mine and wrapped a white shawl around her. "Not ready to give us little ones?" For the first time, she directed the question at me.

The sharp edges of her accusation pierced my skin. "I am pregnant." I said it, very proud to show her I wasn't barren.

Fadumo blinked twice and took a long sip of the tea. "This is very sweet," she said, and drained the mug. She left quickly and without saying good-bye.

As soon as Fadumo disappeared behind the lemon trees, my mother-in-law turned to me. "Why did you tell her that?" It was the first time she'd ever been angry with me. "You don't announce a baby before it's time. You allow the baby to show when it's ready. A baby that is mentioned before time never reaches term."

I was taken aback by the absurdity of the statement. Surely saying you were pregnant did nothing to the fetus in the womb. "You should have told me!"

"I didn't think I needed to tell you. Everyone knows."

"I didn't! I have never heard anything like that before. My

mother's friends always discussed who was pregnant and who had a baby and they always had their babies alive and well."

My mother-in-law arched her brows to take in my naiveté. Clearly, she didn't believe in women speaking about their pregnancies without consequences. "I have to call on the healers. I'll be back soon," she said.

I hoped Sidow would come home from the market before she returned and reassure me all would be well, but he was still away when she came back. My mother-in-law took me inside the common room and pointed at a stool near the mat. "Sit here. We have men coming to read healing verses of the Qur'an over you." She covered me with a bedsheet and placed a metal bowl filled with water to my right.

Four men entered shortly after she left and formed a square around me. Each took one of the chairs she'd placed around the stool I was on. They read from the Qur'an. As each man read, the words calmed and soothed my worries.

I stayed in place even after the men left. I could hear their muffled voices on the other side of the closed door. My mother-in-law came in, took the sheet off, and handed me the bowl of water. "Here, take this into the shower and use the water to wash your whole body." She handed me a piece of paper. "Recite this as you wash. Throw the paper in with the water at the end of your shower to get rid of the evil eye."

I hesitated, not seeing the need to do it. Surely telling Fadumo I was pregnant would cause no damage.

"This will rid you of the curse." She nodded her head to reinforce her conviction.

I took the paper and the bowl and went to the bathroom

only to satisfy her. I recited the lines and washed with the water quickly.

"Done so soon?" she asked me when she saw me leaving the bathroom.

"Yes, I did as you said." I went to my room.

❧

The pain, harsh and biting came a week after I'd declared the pregnancy. I thought it was a normal stomachache at first and waited for it to pass, but the contractions radiated from my stomach to the lower back and legs. Half an hour later, I went to bed and asked Sidow to summon my mother-in-law for help.

She came and stood over me, wiping the sweat from my forehead. After a few minutes of comforting me, she sent Sidow for the midwife. "She'll be here soon," she assured me.

I sighed over the mention of the midwife. I didn't want to believe the implication, although I knew it to be true.

The midwife arrived and gave me a mug of thick and bitter bluish concoction. My stomach heaved at the smell, but I forced myself to finish it. We waited, but the contractions only moved closer together and I started bleeding.

The midwife tried her best to comfort me. "Lie still, don't move." She gathered the blanket and pushed it under my legs, lifting my lower body. "Don't push." She continued to peek behind the heap of fabric under me. She turned to my mother-in-law. "Too much blood. I have to stop this before she loses more."

After a long time of tugging and pulling, the midwife

verbalized what I suspected. "The baby is gone," she said, but continued to work. She cleaned me, placed an herbal remedy inside my womb and gave my mother-in-law some more to add to my tea and soup. "I'll return in a few hours to check on Idil." She left.

Sidow came in as soon as the midwife left and showered me with kisses. "Are you still in pain?" he asked.

"I caused the miscarriage." I sobbed.

"You don't believe that. My mother relies on old tales she's heard from her mother and her mother before. No one miscarries because they said they were pregnant."

I agreed with him, but it was difficult for me to ignore the closeness of my words to the lost fetus. I thought Sidow's mother would chastise me, but even she didn't seem angry. If anything, she felt sorry for me. She kept me clean and gave me traditional herbs and medications to protect me from pain and infection.

In the days that followed the miscarriage, I took one shower after another. I went to the bathroom with the intention to wash away the smell of blood. I rubbed the skin between my legs, over my belly, and feet, but upon leaving the bathroom, I felt no cleaner. No matter how hard I tried, I couldn't get rid of the stench of blood. The smell followed me everywhere I went. I inhaled the metallic odor with the food in my mouth and heaved and gagged after each meal. The physical pain lessened with time and finally disappeared. The pain of guilt remained. I replayed my mother-in-law's statement that I should've never told, no matter how many times Sidow said it was stupid to think I had induced the miscarriage.

He stroked the wrought-iron frame of the bed without making eye contact. "That's not true. The baby's time had come. It wasn't meant to get to full term and be born alive."

I was split between knowing he was right, and the feeling that if I hadn't said anything, it might have been different.

Sidow sat next to me and hugged me. I rested my head on his shoulder and cried. Still, the road back to Sidow's arms was long and difficult. "I can't," I said every time he made advances. After the miscarriage, I avoided him, I thought the curse was still inside and I shouldn't get pregnant again and lose another baby.

"There's nothing inside you." Desire boiled within Sidow as he worked hard to brush aside the pain of my rejection.

He faced the opposite wall, so I wouldn't see the tears I knew filled his eyes but I heard the disappointment in his voice.

The arrival of Elmi's letter dampened my spirits even more. As if he'd timed it, the letter arrived only three weeks after the miscarriage.

*Dear Idil,*

*I am sorry it has been over a month since I last wrote to you. I received your response, but waited until now for so much has happened since my last letter. Mother wants me to go to Canada for my schooling, and although I suspect she has other reasons for her crazy decision, I do not hate the idea. How she came up with the idea and the travel document I can't tell, but I appreciate her wanting me to leave home. I feel more and more isolated from both friends and family. Since leaving Bledley, I seem to have lost the desire to make friends and have kept to my books and art. Omar and Father all but ignore my existence, and that bothers Mother more than it troubles me. Omar's violent reaction to the news of your elopement might have frightened her for my safety, although she denies that when I ask her. Still, she doesn't want me to be alone in the house with Omar. Even when I asked her why she was sending me all the way to Canada, she just looked at me as if to say "I am sending you to the continent farthest away from Omar." I begged Mother to let me come and see you before I left Somalia, but she said no and wouldn't be persuaded, no matter how many times I tried. She is firm about keep-ing my journey a secret until I am safely away. 'No one, but you and I must know,' she said, and made me put my hand on the Qur'an, even though I'd given her my word I wouldn't tell. It took me more than a week to obtain her consent to this correspondence. She only agreed to it when I said she could post it herself. I am truly sorry I must go without taking my leave of you in person and I'm counting on your forgiveness. Please give my regard to Sidow and the rest of your family.*

*Until next time.*
*With all my love,*
*Elmi*

*P.S. Please do not respond to this letter, for I will leave this very night and will not be here to receive the mail. I prom-ise to write to you when I am able.*

After a whole day of reading and rereading it, I put Elmi's letter in the shoebox under the bed where I'd kept all his other correspondences since our parting after the great fire.

⁂

It took me more than two months to allow my love for Sidow to override the fear of the curse. Four months after the miscarriage, I was pregnant again. I'd missed two cycles before I even contemplated the possibility, let alone told anyone.

I threw myself into farm work to avoid thinking of the baby growing inside. In my free time I went to the post office hoping for a letter from Elmi. Finding nothing, I'd walk around the market aimlessly, as if looking for something I couldn't find. It was during one of those trips that I saw a woman making beaded jewelry. I stood by her stall and watched her work quietly. She placed one bead at a time in a yellow string and hummed a tune to herself. Other shopkeepers huddled together near their stalls when they didn't have customers, but this woman sat on a stool near her table and continued to create bracelets, earrings, and necklaces. I watched her three days in a row before I approached her. "How much are these?" I pointed at several bags filled with beads in one of her baskets.

"What do you want it for? Necklaces, bracelets, earrings?"

"How much are you selling one of those bags for?" I continued to stare at the basket mesmerized by the beauty of the beads.

"Buy one of the necklaces for only five shillings."

"How much is the bag of beads?" I asked again.

The woman looked disappointed. "It is not easy to make a necklace like this one." She rolled two necklaces in her hand and held them against the bright afternoon sunlight. "Buy one of these or even both. That's the cheaper way to go."

"Sell me the bag," I insisted.

"You farmers are so stingy." She lifted one of the bags up. "When I go to the big cities the women come and buy the items I make for twice the money." She waited for a few seconds to see if I would change my mind.

I didn't. "I want the beads because I don't know what I want to make yet." It was true, but the woman didn't believe me.

She looked at me quizzically. "It is three shillings for the bag and the roll of yarn to make it." She held out her hand for the money. "Buy the ready-made one. You won't be able to make one as beautiful as mine."

I paid her and left with the beads in my sack. That night, under the dim light of the oil lamp, I started a bracelet for my child. I labored over my gift to the baby every evening after that. I didn't want anyone to see it, so I only worked on it when I was alone in my room, or after Sidow was asleep.

Sidow often tried to engage me when he prepared for bed. "You are too quiet. What's going on?"

I'd touch the bracelet under my pillow pretending I was getting ready for sleep. "I am just tired," I'd say, and wait until I'd heard his rhythmic breathing. Then I'd pull the bag and yarn out and get to work. Every bead was different in color from the one before it and the one that followed it. Some nights, I'd work for hours and realize two of the beads were closer in color or were the same shade and unravel the whole thing to start over again. It was an obsession.

Four months later, I was ready to size the bracelet to fit the wrist of a newborn, while leaving enough room to add more as the child grew. I tried my big toe, the leg of a chair, a branch of the lemon tree in the yard, and the handle of a mallet, but nothing satisfied.

Sidow came upon me one of those sizing days. He peeked from behind the shed, smiling. "Does that mean…"

I shushed him. "It means nothing."

"Maybe you should leave the necklace untied until the baby is born so we can measure it against its neck," Sidow said, his eyes dancing with excitement.

Despite my determination to deny the pregnancy until the baby pushed out of the womb, I said, "It's not a necklace." By then the baby was making small moves, the gentlest kicks that came in unpredictable intervals. "Can't you see? It's a bracelet."

Sidow smiled. "I knew it, I knew it."

"Tell no one."

Sidow scoffed. "You are showing. My mother must know already." Arms open wide, he invited me for a hug.

"No, she doesn't. She would have said something." I didn't move to accept his embrace.

"You know my mother wouldn't mention a baby still inside the womb." He must have read the doubt in my face because he changed course. "Come to me. I promise I won't tell anyone. I can pretend I don't know. I'll be shocked when my mother finally decides to tell." He laughed.

❧

The labor pain wasn't much different from the miscarriage, except for its timing. It came too early in the morning and woke me from a pleasant sleep. I got out of bed, went to the bathroom, and walked about the room. I tried to lie down again, but I couldn't. Finally I nudged Sidow, and he sat up quickly, as if he'd expected me to give birth just like that.

"What is it?" he asked.

"Go get your mother."

"Is the baby coming?"

I stared at him, unsure whether to laugh or get angry at the stupid question. "Go get your mother," I repeated, gritting my teeth.

"Okay, I'm going." Sidow gathered his shawl about him and ran out of the room.

A few minutes later, his mother came with towels and a pail of water. "Sidow has gone to fetch the midwife," she said. She hadn't mentioned the pregnancy up to now—even after Sidow had asked her to go to the market with him so he could hire a carpenter to make the crib.

The whole process took less than two hours and it was not the nightmarish, never-ending experience Mother spoke about anytime she was unhappy with one of us. She'd often say how difficult it was to bring us into this world and how we didn't get any better now that we were outside of her.

"It is a girl." The midwife placed the newborn wrapped in a white towel on my chest and began the cleaning process.

Sidow came in as soon as the midwife left and kissed me all over. "She's beautiful like her mother." He traced his finger around the baby's face. "What should we name her?"

"Amina," I said. I had not thought about a name before

that moment. I think I had never expected to carry a baby to term. Between the supposed curse of announcing the first baby too soon and my mother's theory that no daughter who made her mother unhappy would have a fruitful life, I imagined I would lead a sad and barren existence. The name came to me as soon as Sidow asked, and I loved it.

"Amina," Sidow repeated the name to himself, as if he were trying to confirm he'd heard it correctly. "Perfect. It is beautiful," he said.

"Here, tie it on her wrist." I reached for the bracelet under the pillow and handed it to Sidow. The wrist was too small, so he put it on her ankle.

⁂

During the first month of my next pregnancy, sixteen months after Amina was born, I started a beaded bracelet for the new baby. I looked for the vendor I'd bought the beads from two years earlier, but when I failed to find her, I sent an order to the capital. The bag I received looked exactly like the one I'd bought before, but it cost twice as much. Still, I was grateful to have found it.

"What are we going to name him?" Sidow asked only two months after I got pregnant. My mother-in-law didn't complain about the early announcement this time, maybe because I'd only told Sidow, or perhaps because the ladies in the village weren't asking about it anymore.

"Adam," I responded.

"What if it is a girl?" he asked.

"You said 'him' and I gave you Adam. You should come up with a girl's name."

"If it is a girl we will name her after my mother or your mother," Sidow said.

"Okay." I didn't think we should ever name a baby after my mother. She would not appreciate a Boon child sharing her name, but I didn't say so to Sidow. The fact that he was including my mother in our life after all she had done was adorable.

Nine months later, when I went to labor, the pain was sharper, and the delivery took much longer than the first one. It started in the middle of the tomato patch. I dropped the basket of tomatoes right away and spent the next ten minutes getting from the vegetable garden to the common room. My mother-in-law saw me and sent for the midwife. The midwife came and examined me three times, each time declaring the need for more time. She ordered me to get out of bed and walk, only I couldn't move. I took a few steps around the room and went back to bed.

Sidow massaged my feet and held my hand, even after I squeezed it so hard, I almost crushed his fingers. He stayed with me until the midwife asked him to leave.

"This one liked it inside. He didn't want to come out," the midwife said as she placed the baby boy on my chest. "Here is your son."

I was exhausted but the wailing of the baby made me smile.

Sidow came in, Amina in his arms. "This is your brother, Adam," he said to her.

"Here," I handed Sidow Adam's bracelet. "Tie it on his foot."

Sidow pointed at the colorful bracelet. "Are you going to make him wear this?"

"I wouldn't have made it if I didn't intend to," I said.

"I thought it was in case we had another girl." I gave him a harsh look, so Sidow took the bracelet from me without another word and tied it around Adam's ankle. Both children wore their bracelets until they were old enough to complain about them. After that, the bracelets became family heirlooms.

# CHAPTER SEVENTEEN

WE SUFFERED through a year-long drought, two years after Adam was born. Sidow paid close attention to our farm, traveled far and wide to choose the right seed, and attended different meetings to discuss pricing and seed and crop-sharing. I appreciated the effort at first, and even told Elmi in two of my letters how hard Sidow was working, and how secure I felt. But after a while, his constant absences wore on me. We fought over his devotion to the land so much and so often that once I even threatened to leave him over it.

"So, you married a farmer and now you'd leave because he is farming?" Sidow asked with an unmistakable sarcasm I had never heard in his voice before.

"You are not a farmer. You are an *obsessed* farmer."

"Would you have been happier if I was in another woman's bed, instead of at the Farmers' Hall?"

That was a low blow, and he must have seen me recoil at

the question. "I'm sorry. That was not a fair thing to say," he said.

"You're right," I said and left the yard. Sidow's comment about a husband in another woman's bed triggered something deeply personal in me. Sidow and I had not only survived, but we were happy. The eight years that followed my parents' move away from Bledley had led me to a very different place than I was in when I married him. I had two beautiful children, now six and almost four, but Sidow's statement brought the memory of Father's infidelity to the forefront. From that day on, I watched my husband, waiting for the signs to show up. Perhaps the nightly meeting at the Farmers' Hall and the trips to other villages were about more than getting the best seeds. The notion had come to me and wouldn't leave. There was no rational reason for the feeling that lurked inside my head. I worked very hard to push it out of my mind. I reminded myself that Sidow loved me—he would never cheat on me—but that only lasted for a short time. Every time I thought about what I might do if I found out that Sidow was unfaithful my stomach heaved, and I had to run to the bathroom to empty it.

"You are not pregnant, are you?" Sidow asked when he saw me on my way back from one of those bathroom trips, tears running down my cheeks from the retching. "I thought we agreed we would stop until we recovered from the last drought."

Sidow's mother hated it when he spoke like that and had often reminded him that Allah provides for those he creates.

Still, he insisted that we have no more children until

things changed for the better. "Mother, I have six people to worry about. We can't add more to the load."

I don't think his mother liked the explanation any better than she had liked the reason that led to it, but she left it alone. Sidow was the man of the house, and it was up to him to make the final decision.

"I wish I were pregnant. That would make me feel more secure."

"What are you talking about?"

I told Sidow what I was worried about and how his comments had brought painful memories.

He laughed at me. "Idil, I was only making a point."

"I don't want to feel like my mother."

"Farmers have no time to be unfaithful. They have too much work to make time for that," Sidow said.

"But there are husbands with more than one wife." I pointed to two families in the neighborhood.

"That's not the same. They are not having affairs. They are married. That's legal." Sidow must have seen my eyes widen at hearing him justify men taking a second wife. "Also, they are not married to a beautiful woman like you." That was an attempt to placate me. He tried to kiss me, but I pulled away. He moved close and held my shoulders. "Idil, I am not your father and I am not looking for another woman. My father didn't take another wife and had no mistresses. You can ask Mother if you want. She'll tell you he never cheated."

I did that. I asked his mother.

She shook her head when I told her what my mother had gone through, trying to keep Father. "Women stay because they must, but men stay because they want to. If your father didn't want to stay, there was nothing your mother could've done to stop him. Healers don't change hearts, they mend them. Only Allah can do that. Sidow loves you and he is not going anywhere."

It was true. Sidow was faithful, but I was worried about what was yet to come. There had been a time before the Soviet Union, before Nadia, before Ayan, when Father was sweet and loving to Mother. He came home every night and called her pretty names. We ate dinner together as a family and they went to bed at the same time. Those days Mother scoffed at any women whose husbands strayed. All that was lost only weeks after Father returned from the Soviet Union. Mother spent the rest of her days trying to recapture the happier times in vain.

As it can do, time revealed to me that Sidow was not cheating, so the fear of finding him in another woman's bed diminished slowly and finally died on our eighth wedding anniversary.

Sidow hugged me close to him that night and said, "Can you believe it has been eight years from the day the two of us were on the bus trying to get married?"

I smiled at the memory and stayed in his embrace, not wanting to speak lest my words spoil the beautiful feeling between us. The happy days that started with the celebration of our long marriage were interrupted, not by another woman, but by the news of unrest in the northern region of the country.

❧

In the evenings, since the beginning of that year, after long days of work when the children were in bed, we sat around the fire. Others from the neighboring farms often joined us. We shared the news of the unrest in the north and our thoughts about it.

"The military planes have bombed two villages near Hiraay," Sidow brought word from the market one night.

"They are pounding the villagers into submission," another man said.

From both experience and upbringing, farmers were always suspicious of the government and its policies, but this was more than simple mistrust. "What would they get from destroying the country?" I asked, the first time I heard about the attack.

"They can instill fear. If a man is consumed by his need to protect or feed his family, he will be very unlikely to ask questions beyond safety and the price of grain and milk," Sidow explained to me.

Others nodded in agreement. We went on like that for months, discussing for hours each night what was happening in the north as fear in the south mounted. Yet, what was going on as we spoke remained distant until the trucks that were scheduled to pick up our crops weekly didn't arrive.

"Let us hope the shipment will be picked up next week," the white-haired elder said, as we gathered in our yard.

We had no discussion that night, and the farmers drifted, one by one, back to their homes.

The next week came and went without bringing any of the trucks with it, and the farmers worried about how they would keep the January crops in temporary silos if the previous crops hadn't been delivered to the Wheat Board for distribution. We waited and hoped for a pick-up, but two weeks became three, and three weeks turned into a month. Still no shipment left the village.

We gathered in our neighbor Dooyow's house when he returned from the capital after visiting his daughter. His news was alarming. "My son-in-law said the government is fighting with militia insurgents."

It was hard to believe the government that had ruled Somalia with such an iron fist for the last twenty-one years could be in such a trouble, but the crisis deepened.

"I was told the government has no power beyond army headquarters and the presidential palace. The city is in chaos," Dooyow said.

Every day from the end of January of 1991, Sidow, along with other farmers, went to the market to buy daily supplies for their families and to learn what they could about the goings-on in the capital. Fear about what to do with the crops and how to obtain necessities occupied our nightly discussions. We no longer spoke about the injustices the government might or might not have committed. We didn't question what we heard; we focused on how to survive.

After word of trouble in Mogadishu, the elders assembled at the Farmers' Hall and established a youth militia group to protect the village. The farmers' weapons were limited to a few hunting rifles, homemade bows and arrows, and daggers and knives.

Every night, along with the youth militia, the men from the villages waited at the truck depot for any information coming from the capital. Night after night, they came back with no news. The buses and trucks from Mogadishu hadn't come. Even the postal truck didn't come for weeks, taking with it my only contact with Elmi.

"A bus arrived this evening!" Sidow said when he came home late one night, five weeks after the news of trouble in the capital reached us. "It doesn't sound good. The bus was attacked along the way by gunmen who took money, jewelry, and three women." Sidow flinched. "Only two came back."

I had no intention of speaking, but the words tumbled out. "Did you see the women? Did you ask them what happened to the missing one? Were they raped?" I peppered Sidow with questions.

"I don't know. We asked the driver what happened to them, but he wouldn't say. He just locked up his bus and left."

We listened to the radio every day for any hope that all was well, and that the government had regained a control of the capital.

With the pompousness he had always possessed, the president gave his last weekly address just one day before he fled the capital. The fighting that had started at the end of December in 1990, the year that marked the country's final collapse, had been going on in the capital for six weeks by then. Still, listening to that radio address, no one would have known anything was the matter.

"It is every citizen's duty to reject rumors spread by the enemies of the nation." The president spoke with confidence. "You might hear that the militia has forced the president and his government from the capital, but that is not true. The government is leaving the capital for strategic reasons."

After the address, regular radio programming continued, but the story of the war in Mogadishu reached us all the same.

Tales of the horror continued to pour in, and the evidence of the government's fall arrived in Bledley soon after with convoys of military vehicles, filled with top government officials, including the president and his family. They were upon us before we realized we were under siege. Rows of cars, tanks, and emergency vehicles rolled into town, and the sound of gun salutes filled the night sky.

"What is happening?" I asked Sidow when he returned from the market.

"People are saying the president was pushed out of Mogadishu, and he is here with his military to plan how to take back the city."

"Do you think my father is with him?" I asked Sidow.

"Probably. Everyone from the president's tribe is coming this way. Your father knows the base and Bledley, so he must be with them."

Sidow was right. I said a quick prayer that Father would have more important things to worry about and leave us alone.

That night when we met at the Farmers' Hall, the discussion centered around what they might do next. All the following week the military stayed inside the base and didn't bother us. There were whispers about women of varying ages from several families having been taken into the compound. At first, we had no specifics, and it sounded as if the rumors were born out of fear, rather than fact. That all changed when the first actual name was announced at our weekly meeting.

"They took my daughter," a man named Enow told us. He attempted to stand in front of all the farmers and relay his loss, but collapsed onto his chair and sobbed.

Three days passed before she returned home. No one in her family—including the girl—spoke about what had happened to her. After that day, soldiers raided and looted one farm after another and took herds of sheep, goats, and cows to be slaughtered and cooked for their consumption. It was not *if* but *when* we would get hit. A month after the president and his soldiers came, it was our turn to suffer. Men in military uniforms showed up just before dawn. Guns aloft, they opened the gate to the sheep and goat barns. We left the children asleep inside, and the four of us stood against the kitchen wall with practiced silence.

"*You,* come here!" A soldier pointed his gun at us as they rounded up the animals.

I pointed a shaking finger at my chest to see if he was summoning me.

"No, you in the middle, come here." They wanted Hasan.

The man pushed Hasan with the butt of his revolver. "Walk ahead and lead the animals." They took Hasan, along with three sheep and four goats. They merged into the darkness of the dying night, minutes before dawn.

"I should have died long ago!" my mother-in-law wailed.

Sidow and I took her to her room and I stayed with her all day. She refused to eat or come outside until she heard Hasan's voice the following night. "I am so thankful you are home. Did they harm you?" My mother-in-law inspected Hasan.

Hasan stepped back. "I slaughtered and cooked."

My mother-in-law sighed. "If stolen livestock is the worst we suffer, we are lucky."

No one said anything more until Hasan spoke. "I saw your father."

"My father?" I asked to be certain of what Hasan said.

"He came out to the service quarters with two other men when I arrived. I didn't make eye contact, fearing he would recognize me, but he saw me anyway."

I watched Hasan intently, holding on to every word.

"He asked me if I had an older brother. When I shook my head no, your father called me a clever little Boon. One of the men asked him if he knew me since he'd lived in the village before. Your father denied it, saying 'I can't tell one ugly Boon face from another.' I have never been more grateful to be insulted."

"So, he didn't ask about me or Sidow or the children? Do you think he was thinking about us?"

"He didn't, and I don't know if he really recognized me. He came out three times while I was working, as if he was waiting for me to finish, so he could speak to me. But he never said another word. As soon as I finished, he pointed at two men standing by the gate and told them to take me home."

"Was my mother there?" I didn't want to ask, but I felt the need to know.

"I heard a woman speaking from within the main house, but I didn't see her."

"If Father was here, Mother is probably with him," I said. "Father set the house on fire with us inside, but now he has freed Hasan." I told Sidow, Hasan, and their mother that this made no sense to me. They agreed that the situation was odd, but were willing to take solace in the small gesture of good will.

"If your father recognized Hasan and set him free, then we must accept the gift."

# CHAPTER EIGHTEEN

UNDER THE CONSTANT scrutiny of the occupiers, life became tiresome. Walking, shopping, and making meager meals left me exhausted. The yard fires that marked the evening family time and the end of a hard day's work were left unlit. We no longer visited each other except to share our dwindling supplies of sugar, tea, and coffee beans. As if condemned by fate, neither the villagers nor the president and his troops could leave Bledley. I thought about Father often and wondered whether he thought about me as well. The fear of what he might do lingered, no matter how many times I reminded myself he had far more important things going on. I expected a soldier, sent by him, to arrive at my door anytime but I never anticipated Mother's visit.

She showed up one morning, seven weeks after the occupation began. "Idil!" She called my name in her unmistakable warmth that was now foreign to me.

At the sound of her voice, I dropped the blade I was using to dig potatoes and cried out. "Mother!" When I looked up, she was standing near me, a soldier with a large gun right behind her. For her to find me, she would have had to pass the house and the cooking area and encounter Sidow, Hasan, or their mother. "How did you get here?" I feared that the gun-toting soldier, standing at her order, might have harmed them on the way in.

"I saw Sidow and asked him to point me in your direction and let me come." Mother appeared haggard and unkempt.

"What are you doing here?"

"I had to see you before I left." Mother motioned to the soldier, who lowered his gun to the ground and moved a few feet away.

I had stayed at home, like others in the village, to avoid any possible run-ins with people from the base, but I never expected Mother to come all the way to the farm. I was both surprised and disturbed by her unexpected call. "What for?"

Mother shook her head. "Things are not right between us, and I don't know if I will ever see you again."

"You didn't worry about that when Father wished me dead."

Mother didn't respond to my statement. Instead, she whispered, "The president has ordered two other ministers along with your father to return to the capital and take care of things. But your father is thinking of deserting and carrying on with his business."

"Is the president staying here?"

"He can't go back because the capital is overrun by two different militias." Mother came closer. "Don't tell anyone this, but the president does not feel safe here or anywhere else in the country."

"Where will he go?" I didn't care to know where the president and his people went. All I needed to hear was that they were leaving Bledley.

"They'll continue to the south, away from here and out of the country. Your father, Omar, Rhoda, and I are going as soon as they leave."

"When are they leaving?"

"I'm not sure, but soon I expect."

"I wish you all the best, Mother!" If she noticed the sarcasm in my tone, she didn't admit it.

"I have made so many mistakes," she began as if speaking to herself. "Bringing Rhoda into my life, even when I knew Omar wasn't interested in her. You can't imagine how many times I ask myself why I, a woman who knows only too well the suffering that comes from being with a man who doesn't care for you, would put Rhoda in such a union." Mother stopped, took a deep breath and continued. "Everyone has suffered: Rhoda, Elmi, me, but most of all you." Here she hesitated. "Never mind. I can't help it now," she said.

"You can't, or you don't want to?" I asked, unwilling to let her off so easily.

"I am sorry, Idil." Mother looked at the soldier standing behind her, as if she were afraid she'd said too much already and he might report on her. His back was facing us, so she continued. "I pray things change before it is too late."

"It *is* too late, Mother. At least it is for my me and my family."

It was then that she hugged me, and I didn't pull away.

Instead, I rested my head on her chest and took in the scent—incense and homemade lotion—so preserved in my childhood memory. I held on, not wanting to let go.

After a few brief moments, Mother dropped her hands to her sides, ending our embrace. She kissed me on the forehead. "Good-bye, Idil. May Allah be with you."

I watched her walk by the main house, through the gate, and away from the farm. That night when we gathered in my mother-in-law's room to eat dinner, no one mentioned the visit. They didn't ask why Mother had come, or what she'd said. I was grateful for that. I told them about the president's plan to leave Bledley, but I said nothing regarding my parents deserting and traveling back to the capital.

A week after Mother's visit, the president and his troops left Bledley as quickly as they had come. The villagers emerged from their homes in daylight for the first time in weeks and waved and clapped at the departing convoy. For their part, the soldiers atop the tanks waved back victoriously and shot several rounds of gunfire into the air.

The joy that came with the departure of the president and his army didn't last long. Soon after, the fighting between the two militia groups that had pushed the president out of the capital spilled over and reached us in Bledley. Once united by their hatred of the dictatorship government that had ruled the country for the last twenty-one years, they couldn't agree on how to share power. Each faction wanted to govern in its own way, and that led to bitter fighting that engulfed the whole country.

Once in Bledley, the militiamen, unlike the president, didn't confine themselves to the military base, but roamed the village. They took homes among the residents and came to the market, looking for merchandise to loot amidst the empty stalls. In groups of four or five, they smiled often and asked questions about how and why certain things were done, who owned what land, and how much would it cost to buy. They visited farmers sowing seeds and wanted to know what each was for. The villagers gave responses only to the specific questions, without offering anything more.

One week after the militia arrived, the cry of a girl interrupted the dark night. My ears caught the bone-chilling sound. "Did you hear that?" I asked Sidow.

Sidow sat up in bed. "Do you think the children can hear?"

We both approached the children in their cot in our room. Since the start of the war, we had Amina and Adam sleeping with us. Sidow had fashioned a thick tarp over four wooden legs and placed it against the west wall. Amina resisted the idea at first. She believed she was too old to sleep near her baby brother, or in the same room with her parents. But we insisted on it, and after a while she reluctantly agreed. I placed my hands around Amina's ears, but she was awake and pushed them off, preferring to hide her head under her pillow. Adam continued to sleep under Sidow's protective hands.

I leaned toward Sidow. "That sounds like Owlio, Idow's fourteen-year-old." Their house backed into the west end of our yard. Often Sidow's mother and Idow's wife stood on either side of the lemon trees that divided the property and chatted or passed borrowed items to each other. I knew it was Owlio, because she was their only daughter. The girl's cry for help was loud and clear in the quietness of the lonely night. I could hear her, as if she were in the same room with us. Her father repeated verses from the Qur'an. Their fear filled me. I tasted their helplessness, and experienced their pain. The father begged the soldiers to take everything and leave his daughter alone. His wife prayed, but didn't speak directly to the men. I jumped at the sound of the blood-chilling shriek that came from the girl when a single gunshot split the night. The bullet silenced her father, but her mother's subdued wails and the Owlio's quiet sobs continued.

Under the rule of the militia, life in Bledley became even more difficult for all. Killing Idow and taking his daughter was a green light for them. From then on, the rebels and their followers took more and without consent. Men approached families telling them they were taking their daughters for wives, often more than one at a time.

"I have to marry a man named Ahmed," Hawa told me one day not long after the militia moved in.

Hawa's first husband, Ilyaas, had died two years before and left her childless. She had returned to the house of her parents, and we occasionally saw each other in passing, sometimes at the market, sometimes at town gatherings. We never talked about how she'd helped me elope, but I was always grateful for the part she'd played and the risk she took for my happiness.

"Do you want to marry him?" I asked, knowing very well she didn't from the way she said it.

"He is almost forty and I don't know him. He just came to my father and said 'I am marrying your daughter.'"

"What did your father say?"

"What could he say except to ask what day he wanted for the wedding."

I almost advised Hawa to refuse, to tell her father she didn't want a married man fifteen years her senior, a man she didn't even know. But I knew that was impossible to do unless Hawa wanted her family to be murdered. And even then, the man would marry her all the same. "I am sorry," I said.

Hawa was not alone. Although many of the rebels brought their wives with them, they were still taking girls much younger than Hawa and holding several weddings each day. Hawa and her family were not allowed to celebrate her marriage to Ahmed. "I am moving in with him and his first wife in a week," Hawa told me the last time I saw her.

❧

The news of Hawa's death came only three months after she'd married Ahmed.

"Ahmed says she died from cholera," Hawa's mother told us when we went to offer our condolences. "He didn't even tell us she was dead until after she was buried. We are right here in the village and we didn't even see her body," she sobbed.

"I am so sorry for your loss," I said, feeling the loss was also my own.

"I know he killed her."

"You don't know that for sure." One of the ladies said it to comfort her.

"He beat her more than he fed her because she wouldn't follow his rules. She told me herself. Last week was the worst. He'd beat her after she visited me. And now my daughter is dead, and he wouldn't even show me her body." Hawa's mother cried throughout the whole mourning week. Each time we saw her she repeated the same accusation, and all we could do was listen and sit beside her.

Losing Hawa in such a way brought the danger closer to us, but we had nowhere to go. The civil war continued to spread through the country as each tribe formed its own army and claimed authority over its own territory. And, as if punishing all of us for their wrongdoing, the sky above and the Allah who ruled it, sent rain begrudgingly in small sporadic droplets. For the two years that followed their arrival, one drought-ridden season led us to another. Finding drinking water and growing barely enough crops to feed our family became an accomplishment for us.

The militia leaders sent men to collect what they called crop yield tax. No farmer dared to resist or say anything aloud.

❧

"Two of the milking cows are sick," Sidow's mother returned from the cowshed with the milking pail half full. "I couldn't even get enough for us, let alone some to sell."

The sickness started with the one or two cows on each farm. At first, farmers slaughtered the sick animals, sold some of the meat, or shared it with others in exchange for grain or milk. But quickly the problem grew beyond one or two head of cattle.

"What do we do? Now we are losing herds of sheep, goats, and cows," someone shouted across the hall.

Soon the animals were too sick for us to eat, and carcasses remained on the streets and alleyways for days, rotting and emitting putrid smells that made people sick. It didn't take long for cholera to spread from infected ground water to humans. People died by the dozens, and Bledley earned the nickname the City of Death.

At first, we sold some of the crops to buy overpriced sugar, tea, and coffee, but even that came to an end. Two years after the start of the civil war, we were left without a single animal. Silos empty, all that remained were a few bushels of grain, maize, and sorghum.

"We have to leave. This is not home anymore. It's our burial place," Sidow said. "There are some international agencies helping refugees in the capital. If we can find a bus or cattle truck to take us there, we might get help. The roads are dangerous, but leaving can't be worse than staying here."

The following night we gathered what we could, some clothes, pieces of jewelry, a pair of shoes, and a pair of sandals for each of us.

Sidow's mother stared at the house next morning as we prepared to go. "I never thought it would end like this."

We allowed each other a moment to be alone with our thoughts and feelings about the place we called home. And then we left.

# CHAPTER NINETEEN

TIRED AND FRIGHTENED, we arrived in Mogadishu two days and one night after we'd left Bledley. We had very little money and some cheese and dried meat. The large tents that we had heard had been set up at the Ceelgaab Market by relief agencies were nowhere to be found. There was nothing except desperate people in a desperate hurry, coming and going.

"Where is the help people told us about?" I asked. We walked through the market in a daze. The vendors had their merchandise on gray blankets spread upon the ground. Mounds of corn, beans, and potatoes covered the area as far as the eye could see. Swarms of flies descended upon people and merchandise alike, creating a deafening buzzing sound. Barefoot children as young as six or seven wearing nothing but underpants, rushed past us, pushing wheelbarrows and calling out their wares.

Sidow's mother turned to him and said, "I know a friend

of your father's. He owns a business in this market." She led us toward Idris's Wheelbarrow Warehouse. "I haven't seen him for more than ten years, but this is his shop."

Idris, a tall muscular man, greeted us with a kind smile that felt out of place in this desolate setting. "I was devastated when I heard Moallim Ali died. I wanted to come, but couldn't." He encompassed us in his gaze. "I wasn't as lucky as he was, didn't have a son of my own, only girls, you see." He extended his hand to shake Sidow's. "Girls can't be left alone, not in this city, so I had to miss the funeral." He turned to my mother-in-law. "I am sorry for your loss," he said and waited for a few seconds before he resumed speaking. "I heard Bledley has become a large graveyard for our people. You've come for my help, I gather. I don't have much, but I'll take care of you." He turned around and picked up a small box from a desk behind him. He retrieved a little key and led us out of the office and to the back of the large warehouse that housed his wheelbarrows. "Come this way." We followed him to a shed at the back of the building. "It isn't big, but it'll shelter you." He handed my mother-in-law an American twenty-dollar bill. "Buy food for the children."

My mother-in-law turned the bill over examining the foreign currency. Since the collapse of the government, Somali shillings lost value quickly and American dollars became the common currency. "Thank you, Idris," she said.

The one-room shed was small and bare, but tucked behind the wheelbarrow warehouse and in the yard protected by Idris's security guards, it was safer than anywhere else in the city. We ate a few pieces of stale bread, slices of homemade cheese, and the dried meat we'd brought with us. My mother-in-law and I shared two small prayer mats with the children, and Sidow and Hasan slept on the bare floor.

The next morning Idris brought us three straw mattresses. "Use these for now." He leaned them against the door. "I have a job for your son. Work fitting a man. I loved your husband like a brother. He took care of me when I needed help."

Idris waited, but my mother-in-law didn't respond. She knew farmers relied on the land, not men, and she couldn't ask her son to work for another. Heavy quietness descended upon us and the few seconds that followed dragged.

"I'll take the job. It's very kind of you to offer," Sidow said.

He was up and out before dawn the next day.

"I counted wheelbarrows in the morning and counted them again at the end of the day when they were returned." Sidow's responsibility in Idris's yard was demanding. "For the rest of the time I worked on mending broken wheels and handles, and filling holes in the metal drums with no time for lunch or tea," he told us. "At least I am here close to you, and we are protected," Sidow added.

Each night, I rubbed his body with oil to relieve the pain that was mostly inside. "I am sorry you have to work at a market like a boy and not on your own land." My apology did nothing to reduce the sorrow that came home with him.

He moaned at the touch of my hand, but refused to admit he was hurting. The work here was nothing compared to hard farm labor. "I was on my feet the whole day is all." He sat up and rested his weight on his elbows, as a forced smile crept to his face. "Your lovely touch has cured me now," he said.

His words didn't match the actions that followed. He kept a thin line between us on the mattress as if avoiding the touch that might propel us into something we didn't have the privacy for. After a few nights of isolation, I had the courage to rest my arm on Sidow's shoulder. It had been two weeks since the last time our bare skin touched. I waited for him to push me away, but he didn't. He took a deep breath and I felt the rise and fall of his chest. After a while Sidow took my arm and wrapped it around his waist caressing it gently. He fell sleep after a few minutes.

※

"My nephew has come from the west." Idris visited us in our shack an hour after Sidow returned from work one evening. It had been six weeks since Sidow started working for him.

"He is a relation from the wife's side." Idris spoke haltingly. "My wife asked me to move him here, but I refused." Idris wiped his face with the back of his hand. "This room is yours. I won't take it from you, but I'm afraid I must give him your job. I tried to encourage him to get a delivery job, but my wife swore her nephew would not do boy's work."

We were grateful to Idris for keeping us in safety behind his business, but Sidow was losing both the income and the security of working in the yard, away from all the violence in the city.

"I understand," Sidow said.

Idris stood by the door. "You could deliver and still earn some money. I'm sorry. I know this is not good news for you, but I have no choice."

"I will take the delivery job," Sidow said.

❧

The mornings were difficult for Sidow. He'd pull me close to him an hour before he was due to leave for work as if begging me not to let him go. The first time he did that, I turned around and asked him what was the matter. He mumbled, "Nothing," got up, and went to work early. I learned that he needed me to stay still while his tears wet the back of my neck. He knew I was awake, but neither of us acknowledged it. Quiet and alone together, we remained intertwined until he was ready to release me and go to work. "See you tonight," he'd always say with a quick kiss to keep from lingering too long.

Sidow's journey through Mogadishu pushing a wheelbarrow filled with goods was not only hard, but it was scary. Explosions ripped apart one area of the city or another every day. The fear of daily attacks loomed over us each morning as he prepared to leave.

"I am afraid for you," I permitted myself to express the worry I kept contained the whole day. I washed and dressed his bruised hands, but it was to no avail. The wounds that started to heal overnight would open the next day under the wheelbarrow's handle.

"I'll be fine, Insha'Allah." He kissed my hands.

I prayed he was right.

❧

Sidow didn't come home at his usual time that night. It was dark outside, well past *Maghrib* prayer, and Mogadishu was not a city in which to be about after nightfall. Except for a few quick, fearful glances, my mother-in-law, Hasan, and I didn't acknowledge the dread that filled each of us. I boiled *kibili* fish and potatoes, fed the children, and put them to bed. The rest of the dinner sat untouched.

Hours after sunset, sitting by the dwindling fire across from Hasan and his mother, I heard a motor approach. Cars didn't usually come at night, so it was out of place. By the time we stepped outside, the engine had died and the lights dimmed, but shouts between Idris's security guards and the men in the car erupted.

"You must take him to his family," one man yelled before their discussion was reduced to a low murmur.

As soon as the vehicle pulled away and the taillights faded in the distance, the guards came through the yard, dragging Sidow by the arms. "They said he was attacked. He would've died if they hadn't come upon him and picked him up. That's what they said, but they didn't tell us anything else—not where he was or who hurt him."

Hasan and I took hold of Sidow, and the two guards walked off whispering to one another about how weird the whole thing was, and how lucky Sidow was to be saved by strangers.

Sidow was awake and groaned in pain at my touch. One of his eyes was swollen shut, and there were cuts in his left arm going up to the shoulder where his shirt was torn. We asked him repeatedly what had happened, what he remembered, what had become of his wheelbarrow. Still, Sidow said nothing.

❧

"I came as soon as I heard." Idris stood by our cooking fire early the next morning. "You should've called me immediately. How is he now?"

"Better than we feared last night," my mother-in-law answered. "Thank you for checking."

Idris walked back and forth, many questions written on his face. "Who brought him back?"

"Strangers. We never saw them, but your guards did."

"Strangers," he said and left. He returned several more times that day and the following evening, until he could speak to Sidow. "I am so glad you are safe," Idris smiled and sat next to Sidow on the prayer mat. "What happened yesterday? Do you remember anything? The men who attacked you?"

"I don't remember much."

"Was it before you delivered or after?" Idris asked.

"I think it was before." Sidow searched his mind. "I think it was when I knocked to deliver and someone opened the door and grabbed me by the shoulder."

"Don't think. You must know. I lost three hundred dollars' worth of merchandise and the wheelbarrow." He pressed his lips together. "The customers are angry."

Sidow's expression remained blank.

Idris looked to my mother-in-law. "Your husband was a good man. May Allah rest his soul." He raised his palms up in a practiced and automatic gesture of prayer. "Even he wouldn't suggest I lose my property."

"We are not suggesting that either, Idris."

Idris kept silent for a few seconds. "I'll walk away from

the cost of the wheelbarrow, but I must have the three hundred dollars."

Sidow's eyes widened and his jaws clenched. "I was robbed. You know I was! You know how dangerous that part of the city is. It isn't like I lost the money or did anything intentionally."

"I've done the best I can for you, but I can't walk away from so much money. You must understand I need to make up for the loss." Idris took his eyeglasses off his face and placed them on the top of his head. "I have receipts, ledgers outlining the inventory. I can show you everything."

"Don't worry. We will get the money and pay you back," my mother-in-law said.

"Mother," Sidow began. "It's my debt. I'll make the money. Idris, all I need is time to earn back the debt."

"How long will it take you? Months? Years? I wish I could wait that long, but I can't."

"I'll work hard…" Sidow was going to say more, but my mother-in-law's glare stopped him.

"Give us a day or two, and we'll have the money ready," my mother-in-law said.

"I knew you would see to it. You are a good woman." Idris turned around and left.

❧

Next day Sidow's mother and I went to the market and sold a pair of earrings that had belonged to her mother, a bracelet—Sidow's first gift to me—and the necklace Elmi had given me. With all the pieces, we raised six hundred and fifty dollars.

It was a fraction of what we could have received had we sold the jewelry to a proper certified jeweler, but it was more than enough to pay our debt.

"Where did you get the money?" Sidow asked, when my mother-in-law sent Hasan to summon Idris so we could make the payment.

I hesitated because it pained Sidow to not be able to support his family. "We sold pieces of jewelry," I said.

"Idil, you shouldn't have done that."

"We must pay Idris," my mother-in-law said. "We had no choice."

"I never should have left the farm. Death would have been better than having my mother and my wife pay for my debt." Sidow limped away like a wounded animal as Idris approached.

"Much sooner than I expected." Idris counted and recounted the money. "I didn't think you could get it this fast. I knew you'd do right. I only hope this didn't cause you undue harm." Idris smiled, his gaze firm on the money.

"What do we owe you for the room?" Sidow's mother was holding something tight in her hand. "For the rent?"

"Fifty dollars would do for the month," Idris said without a pause, as if he'd expected the question all along and knew she was holding that exact amount in her hand ready to go to him. "You didn't have to do this. I gave you the room for free until you could pay," Idris said, but all the same, he took the money. "I'll take this for the next month's rent."

"You can come and get another wheelbarrow when you are able to work," he said to Sidow, but his expression exuded doubt. "Only if you want to," he added.

Sidow only rested for three days. On the fourth day, he got up early in the morning and left. That day and for nine days to follow, Sidow returned with the same news. "I spent the day looking for work, going into shops and yards, but no one will offer me a job."

Then the offer came.

"Do you remember the men who saved me?" Sidow asked me the next night upon his return from the job search. "The ones who brought me to the yard, remember?"

"I didn't see anybody. Idris's guards brought you inside."

"Well, I saw one of them again, today."

"Really. I wish I could meet them and thank them, but we have no place to invite people."

"He offered me a job."

"A job!" These were even kinder people than I imagined them to be. "To do what?" I asked.

"He imports goods from overseas to sell: rice, flour, sugar, clothing, and other household items. He needs someone he can trust at the shipyard. All I have to do is keep an inventory of the merchandise and record everything that comes in." Excitement saturated Sidow's words. "He even gave me some money in advance, and I bought this." Sidow opened a bag and revealed a piece of meat, a few vegetables, and a small cake.

This man had saved Sidow—a total stranger—from the attack, brought him home, and now offered him a fantastic job, even paying him in advance? The suspicion of some ulterior motive came to me almost as quickly as Sidow's good news had. Did people who trusted others without a second thought still exist in Somalia? I didn't think so, but I decided to keep this to myself and be happy for Sidow. We shared the good news with his mother and brother and our children as we sat down to share the festive meal and the dream of better times ahead.

Sidow arose early next morning and came to me near the cooking fire. "I'll be home before sunset because I am done when the yard closes at four." He kissed me like he used to in Bledley—openly and passionately. Hasan and the children were still sleep, but my mother-in-law, sitting across from me, didn't even blink at the sight.

"Where are those bracelets? Did you see them when you washed my pants? I am sure they were in the pocket of one pair."

We called the children's beaded bracelets, the only items we had from the village, the family's lucky charms. "I didn't," I answered.

Sidow went back inside and came out clutching both bracelets in his raised hand. "I found them," he said and he put one in each pocket.

Sidow ate the *canjeero*—flatbread—and eggs and drank his tea very quickly. "I have to get going now. Pray for me, Mother." Sidow kissed his mother on the top of her head.

"May Allah be with you." She took his hand and blew on it.

The day that started with so much hope and promise turned into one filled with fear by sunset. I didn't worry until I heard the call of the Maghrib prayer coming from the masjid nearby. Sidow should've been home by then. He had said he would be done by four when the shipping yard closed, and it was well past six in the evening. I walked to the lane several times to check, but found no sign of Sidow. I put the children to bed, and once again, my mother-in-law, Hasan, and I stayed awake for most of that night. We waited and hoped for Sidow's return while fearing the worst. Hours passed without bringing the sound of his gentle footsteps. The anticipation of seeing him walk through the door, turned into an endless night of fear. The next morning dawned, still with no sign of Sidow.

# CHAPTER TWENTY

MY MOTHER-IN-LAW and I made several trips to the Mogadishu port looking for Sidow. Without the name of his employer, or the name of the company that hired him, it was hard to make an inquiry. Still, in desperation we asked about him. It was a delicate matter that needed to be done with care because Sidow, a Boon man, was not worth the effort for many people.

"One look at my face, and they'll not help." My mother-in-law reminded me that the physical features of the Boon people marked and condemned them. "It's better if you go alone." She stopped at the beginning of the rows and rows of metal containers lined up all the way to the beach. She adjusted her scarf around her face as if hiding from the accusatory stares.

I left her at the entrance of the shipyard each day for three days and walked through, hoping to find someone who might have seen Sidow.

I approached a man unloading boxes from one of the containers into a pickup truck. "I am looking for someone. He started working here three days ago, but he didn't come home."

"What tribe is he from?"

I knew the question had doomed me before I even answered. "Boon," I replied.

"Why would a beautiful Bliss woman like you be searching for a Boon man?" he asked.

"Because he's my husband," I said.

"What? He had the audacity to marry a Bliss woman and then leave her behind?"

"He didn't leave me. He went to work and never came home."

"Went to work you say." The man laughed and walked away.

His smug smile was disgusting, but I could do nothing about it. I stood there for a while staring after him and seething with anger.

Each day, I went home exhausted and hopeless. But at night, when we were alone in our shack, my mother-in-law, Hasan, and I asked each other what we would say or do if Sidow walked in just then. Would we be angry and yell at him for making us worry so much? Would we cry, or just look at him with joy because he was back among us again? I knew he would not be coming back as much as I was certain he wouldn't disappear for three days if he could help it. Still, I needed to keep the glimmer of hope that I would behold his beautiful face again.

❦

The fourth day after his disappearance, we didn't go looking for Sidow. My mother-in-law and I didn't discuss it or agree to stop. The morning of the fourth day dawned, and neither of us got dressed. I lit the fire much later than I ever did before and began making tea. She sat on the other side of it and said nothing. I made the canjeero and the bean soup and gave her some. She took it and ate quietly until Hasan and the two children joined us. I was offering a bowl of soup and some flatbread to Hasan for him and children to share when a woman came running toward me from behind the wheelbarrow shed. As she moved closer, I realized it was my mother. I hadn't seen her for two and half years, but there was no mistaking her. Her mouth opened, and her lips moved, but no words came out until she was standing next to me. "Idil, it's Sidow's body near Jalilow's jewelry store!" She gasped for breath.

I dropped the bowl of food and ran. My mother-in-law called after me to wait for her, but I kept running. I knew where the body would be, but I was still hoping she was wrong—that when I arrived, Sidow would be standing at the mouth of the alley, holding a big sack of food, and laughing at my foolishness for thinking harm had come to him. But in the middle of the alley, I came face to face with the horror of Sidow's beaten body. People walked to and fro, paying no attention to my dead husband lying there. Death and decay had become that common in our country.

Sidow was battered and broken with several long gashes on his cheeks, but he was wearing a clean short-sleeved shirt and khaki pants. Was that the same shirt he was wearing when he left? I wasn't sure. I took the large shawl I was wearing and draped it over Sidow.

Mother caught up with me.

"How did you know where I lived, and that Sidow was here?" I challenged her.

She lowered her gaze. "Sorry."

"For what? Do you know who did this to my husband? Do you know who killed him?" Using the word *killed* brought the dreadful reality closer.

"I was told he was here. I just needed to help…" She struggled to complete the sentence.

"Who told you?" I demanded, but she only responded with silence.

"I think you should leave now."

"I just wanted to help."

"You have helped enough."

Sidow's mother had arrived by now, and she raised her hand to stop me. "He is not coming back, Idil. No good will come of attacking your mother."

"I'll come back when you've had some time," Mother said and slipped away.

Sidow's mother waited for a long minute before she spoke. "I'll stay with my son. Go and see if you can find a way to get him home."

❧

"Is it Sidow?" Hasan asked when I returned. "Is he gone?"

When I said nothing, he knew. "I am sorry for the children, for my mother, for you, for me," he said.

Amina and Adam came running. "Mother!" Amina, eleven years old and a head taller than her nine-year-old brother, spoke for both. "Daddy is not coming back, is he?"

Oh, how I wanted to comfort her and tell her everything would be fine, but I couldn't. "No, he is not." I felt empty, bitter, and cold, but I did not cry. *My children! Boon, poor, and now fatherless*, I thought and hugged them both.

"Could you find out if Idris knows where we can get a truck to pick up Sidow?" I asked Hasan. I couldn't refer to my husband's remains as the body. I wasn't yet ready to let him go.

Twenty minutes later, Hasan, with the help of Idris and three other men, placed Sidow on the flatbed of the truck and brought him home.

As he was carried inside, I tried to avoid my mother-in-law's searing gaze, but still my dry eyes met her wet ones. I touched my eyes and squeezed them shut, but there were no tears, not even a hint of moisture.

An hour later, my mother returned. "I am so sorry for your loss. Is there anything I can do to help you?"

To an onlooker, it would have appeared as if Mother and I had a very close relationship. I wanted to push her away but I resisted the urge. She cried on my shoulder and offered me empty, comforting words. I was uncertain whether I was consoling her, or she was consoling me.

❦

Most of the visitors, including Mother, left by early evening, and our shack became quiet. The only sound that resonated with me that whole sleepless night came from the subdued waves of the ocean, slapping the huge boulders overlooking the beach, less than a mile away. I recalled Sidow's scent, his gentle hands upon my skin, his illuminating smile, his kind and encouraging words every time I complained that life was unfair. All night, I sat hoping those strong and positive memories would compel me to weep with pain, to appreciate the size of my loss, but they didn't. Daylight came and I had yet to shed a single tear for my Sidow.

"I need to see him," I told Hasan as he came out of the room Idris had given us in which to keep Sidow's body.

Hasan dropped his hands to the sides. "Don't."

"I need to see him," I repeated. "I must."

"Please..." Hasan begged, "it's no good. Don't."

"*Now!*" The tone of my voice silenced him. "*Before* you prepare him for burial."

Hasan tried to follow. "I want to be alone, please." I swallowed hard to calm my nerves.

Sidow's body lay on a straw mat, still wrapped in my shawl. I moved closer and, without thinking, bent to kiss him. The decay that encroached on Sidow filled the room and pushed me back. I ran to the door, gagging, but stopped before I opened it.

After a few seconds, I returned, sat on the floor next to the mat, and stroked Sidow's coarse hair, the only part of his body that was not ice cold and stiff. Ten minutes passed before I summoned enough courage to look upon his damaged face, but once there I couldn't turn away.

"You meant everything to me," I said with no sign of emotion, "so how is it that I am not able to cry?" I knew there would be no answer.

I emerged from the room without shedding a single tear.

❧

Hasan approached me after he'd finished getting Sidow ready for burial that afternoon. "I found this in his pants pocket." Hasan handed me a roll of American bills.

"Where is it from?"

"I don't know. It fell out of his pocket when I was washing him."

I counted the money—fifteen hundred dollars. "How could Sidow have this much money?" I asked.

"Maybe those who killed him left it for us," Hasan responded.

"You mean blood money? Why would they do that? It is not like we know who they are." The suspicion that Mother was somehow involved was building inside.

Hasan had no explanation for me. "Keep it for the children. We have to feed them somehow."

I held the money tight in my hands.

"Do you want to see him before he is taken?" Hasan changed the topic.

I hesitated.

"You don't have to."

"Yes, for a few minutes."

The room was different than it had been earlier that morning. The atmosphere was serene. The aroma coming from the incense burning in the four corners replaced the putrid odor of decaying flesh. Cedar incense mixed with sesame seed oil sat in small bowls all around the mat. For an instant, I wanted to lie next to Sidow and wrap my arms around his neck. Sidow's body was enshrouded in a white sheet, facing Mecca, the same direction he would face in his grave, his bare skin resting on black earth. *From dust to dust.*

Part of me wanted to see Sidow's face, but I fought the urge and sat next to him instead. Struggling to comprehend the finality of the situation, I remained there until I heard Hasan and my mother-in-law arguing outside the door.

I bent and kissed Sidow over the white sheet so as not to spoil his purity. "This is good-bye," I said and left the room with the weight of my lost love bearing down on me.

Once outside, I came upon my mother-in-law yelling at Hasan. "What do you mean, women cannot come? We are his wife and his mother. We are not 'women'."

"Mother, that is the rule," Hasan said.

"I do not care about your made-up modern rules. This would have never happened in the village. Tell the sheikh that Idil and I are going, or the body stays here."

We reached a compromise with the imam. He allowed my mother-in-law to go and asked me to stay. I agreed. The last thing I wanted to do was watch them cover Sidow with dirt. I stood by the door as the men came and picked up the wooden board with the body of my husband on it.

The four men, led by Hasan, walked away. I collapsed onto a gember near the door. Amina appeared, Adam right behind her.

"Daddy loved you," Amina whispered in my ear as if sharing a great secret.

"He loved all of us," I responded, and for the first time I cried. Amina and Adam joined me.

Mother came a few minutes after the funeral procession left. "I am sorry for your loss," she said again. She had been saying that since she had reported it.

"You don't have to be here." I didn't want her pity.

"I want to stay for the mourning period," Mother said.

"What has changed, Mother? Why are you so kind to me now when you weren't before?"

She flinched. "I sit at night, alone in my bed, and think about what I have done. I turned you out, sent Elmi away, and kept Rhoda as a daughter. She is angry with Omar, with Sheila, but mostly with me. I can't say I blame her. I condemned her to a life of unhappiness, and the sad part is I knew Omar had no desire for her. Still, I dressed her up and made her marry him." She took a deep breath to steady her shaky voice. "You asked what has changed, and I'd say nothing, except I am trying to get away from myself, from Rhoda, from Father and most of all, I want to be as far away from Omar as possible now."

"What did Omar do?" Something about the way she emphasized her distance from Omar alarmed me.

"Everything!" She started crying and would say no more.

The seven-day mourning period for Sidow's passing ended, and Mother lingered five more days. Her emotional side, the side that considered what was right and proper, told her to take me home—not to leave me in a land unforgiving to a woman found alone and unprotected. Her rational side, the side that understood the ramifications of such an action for the whole family, told her to leave me behind. In the end, she reached a logical decision, not hers entirely, and left me where I was.

# CHAPTER TWENTY-ONE

"HASAN FOUND this money in Sidow's pocket." I handed the cash to my mother-in-law. It was a day after the mourning period for Sidow's passing ended.

She turned it around without unfurling the bundle or counting it. "We should use it to set up some business to earn a living," she said, pushing the money back into my hand.

Whatever questions she had about the source of the money, she kept to herself. "I don't know where the money came from or who put it in his pocket," I said to see if she suspected anyone.

"It doesn't matter. My son is dead, and we have been left with some money. If the people who killed him decided to leave us a gift, let us take it." I was surprised by her practicality.

"I wish we didn't need this." I held the money up. "If it weren't for the children, I would have burned it."

She waited for almost a minute before she spoke. "Some

nights, ever since we left the village, I ask myself…what if the children weren't with us? Oh, dear God. What am I saying? I didn't mean…"

I waved to stop her from saying more. I knew exactly what she meant and suffered the same demons every night. Many nights I sat up gasping for air after one of those nightmares. In them, I saw myself childless and strolling happily through a beautiful meadow next to Elmi. In the morning, the feeling of joy that came from having no responsibility lingered and haunted my entire day. Only I never uttered it to a soul.

I held the wad of bills in my hand. "I don't want blood money from whoever killed Sidow, but I must take it."

"This is not a handout. It's rightfully yours. They robbed you of your husband and the father of your children."

I nodded and took the money back.

"I'll go out to work now," Hasan said when he heard my mother-in-law's plan for the money.

"We can't let you go. We've lost Sidow. We can't lose you, too," she said.

"Do you want Idil to work, while I sit here and do nothing?" Hasan asked.

"Yes," my mother-in-law and I said together.

Hasan didn't like the idea. As the only man in the family, he felt it was his duty to support us. But one look at his mother's stricken face, and he knew she wouldn't let him. Hasan reluctantly agreed, and two weeks after Sidow's funeral, I started selling breakfast and lunch to the merchants and their customers in the Bakaara market.

My mother-in law stayed in the shed the whole day along with Hasan, telling Amina and Adam the stories she used tell

Sidow when he was a boy. At the end of each day, she met me at the turn of the lane in front of the warehouse.

"How have you managed?" she'd ask, away from the children.

"Well enough," I'd respond.

"I am so sorry you have to work like this, alone in that market."

I avoided talking about the goings on at the market. "It's not too bad." I didn't want to tell her about the men who asked me to marry them, or the ones who placed their hands on my back even after I lied and told them I was married.

I tried hard to appear content, but obviously, I hadn't bargained for this. Marrying a farmer shouldn't have resulted in being reduced to beg or being at the mercy of men who hovered over me like vultures. "It's not terrible," I lied.

Raids and gun battles erupted at the market several times a day with little warning. With no peace officers or governmental agencies, people took the law into their own hands and crime was rampant throughout the city, especially in the Bakaara Market. The shop owners collected money from the merchants and hired a group of young boys to guard the market, but that effort did very little to lessen the constant threat.

I went to the market early every morning of the week under a blanket of darkness and returned home just before sunset with rice, a small piece of meat, a jar of milk, and a few wilted vegetables. Even Fridays were workdays, not the free and festive days they had been in Bledley. "It's getting easier now, and I have customers." I said it to partly reassure her, but it was somewhat true. It had been difficult for the first few weeks, but after a while I got used to the harsh daily grind and settled into a predictable routine. There was no future in the way we lived, but at least we were surviving.

❦

One morning, almost five months after I started working at the market, I noticed a girl of perhaps fifteen or sixteen, wearing all white, sitting on a small rock in front of my café.

Erect, shoulders squared, her back resting against the wooden wall, she wore a magnificent, radiant smile. "Is this place yours?" she asked.

"Yes." I opened the door and entered.

She followed me in and stood by the door letting the bright sun filter through her white garment. "I was just sitting here waiting for the time—for the morning to grow old and tired—but I didn't expect to see a woman here, working outdoors. This is a man's job."

The sheer purity of her outfit against the morning sun was almost blinding. I held a ladle over the large bowl to prepare the mixture for the canjeero.

"You're a grown woman. You must have a husband."

Sidow's image, heading for the lane, flashed before me and disappeared. "I do not have a husband," I replied firmly.

"I have one. We could share him."

"And be a second wife? Never."

"First, second, third—Allah gave men the hearts to care for more than one woman."

"That's not true." *If she'd seen how Father hurt Mother when he was going after his mistresses, she wouldn't have said that.*

The girl reached for a stool. "To be among strange men,

221

serve them, speak to them, take their money, and endure their stares is the greatest sin for a woman. Women should be protected and cared for in the home, but we walk around half naked."

Flames from the burjiko leapt as I poured the kerosene and lit it. I stepped back. "I haven't seen any naked women."

"Have you seen the clothing shops? Do you know what's sold there?"

"Clothes are not the problem. Behavior is to blame not garments in stores." I didn't know this woman, but I felt free to speak my mind.

"We could get rid of the sin. Cleanse it until we're as innocent as newborn babies." She waved her hands as if preforming a magical act.

"The entire Indian Ocean couldn't cleanse the sin in this country. It's in the soil, the blood, and bones of children and adults alike."

"Allah will say 'Be clean,' and it will be." She raised her palms. "Oh, Yaa Rabbi forgive our doubts," she said a quick prayer.

"Everyone would have to die for that to happen."

"Only some, not all. I am sixteen, but even I know you don't amputate the whole leg because of an infected toe. That wouldn't be right. In the same way, you don't want everyone to die because of a few. That would be foolish. You need only a few to go. That's all."

I cooked and cleaned as she prattled on. My customers will be here soon," I said, silently praying she wouldn't launch into another sermon.

She didn't, but she didn't leave right away, either. She

stayed for half an hour arranging and rearranging her scarf. She pulled a black veil from under her scarf and tied it on her face when my first customer entered. "I'm leaving, but remember there is no misery but that of our own making." She flashed a brilliant smile and left with a flourish.

※

Three hours later, an explosion ripped through the clothing shops. My store was close to the site of the attack, so the ground vibrated and shifted underfoot and the dishes on the table fell to the floor.

I ran outside, dropping my change purse along the way.

Jibril, the next-door merchant, called out to the other merchants. "We must help them!" He sprang into action. "Idil, bring water!" he shouted and raced ahead.

Thick, dark smoke poured from the site of the explosion. "Over here. Water, please. Water!" The pleading came from the wreckage. I darted toward the sound and stumbled over an old man.

"Water! Water." He lifted a hand and exposed his blood-covered chest. He took two big gulps from the cup I held to his lips. "She was angered by the women's dresses sold here." He held out his hand. "She had on her burial garment, all white. She came close and pulled a string at her waist." The effort to speak exhausted him and he motioned for more water. He took two more sips, laid back, and closed his eyes.

I held the water out to him again, but this time he didn't open his mouth. Some of the water ran over his sealed lips and pooled around his eyes.

"Idil, over there," Jibril called. "Take the water to that side."

I picked up the jug and left the man. From a distance, the outline of a head covered with a white scarf was visible. Thinking it was an injured person, I quickened my pace. The closer I got, the slower my steps became. Despite the smoke, I couldn't miss the whiteness of that scarf. I wanted to turn around and run but I didn't. I saw what I wanted to avoid. The severed head of the young woman, her lips parted in a frozen half-smile greeted me. What was she was thinking when she'd pulled the string and blew people to pieces?

Jibril found me standing there. "Idil, take the water back there. Please hurry!"

"The bomber, I met her this morning at my door," I told Jibril on our way back to our section of the market. Looking back now, the signs were there—the white garments, the anger about the clothing shops, the comments about removing body parts, and her fanaticism. "She was just a girl. I didn't think she was capable." *What could I have done to stop her?* "She said she was sixteen, but might have been younger."

Jibril gathered his shawl. "She killed four people."

"Including herself?"

"Five, counting her."

*You need only a few to go. That's all.*

Most of the stores were closed by the time I returned to my café from the site of the explosion. The market was eerily quiet.

My mother was standing in front of my shop, holding my change purse. "I came as soon as I heard," she said. "Can I help you with anything?"

I shook my head no.

"Let me drive you home. We will stop for groceries on the way."

Mother had visited me often ever since Sidow's passing, but her visits followed no specific pattern. Sometimes she came once a week, and other times I didn't see her for long periods before she showed up, unannounced. On some of her visits I could tell she'd been crying. I didn't ask her about it, and she gave no explanation. She did offer me some money, but only once, and I refused it. She never made the gesture again.

I sat in the back of Mother's Mercedes and wondered why things were getting worse by the day. Every time I took a step forward, circumstances pushed me three paces back.

Mother didn't ask me to come in with her when we stopped at a store in the Ceelgaab market, only telling the driver to wait for her.

"I hope this helps," she said, when she came back with a box filled with vegetables, meat, a sack of rice, and two cans of powdered milk.

"Thank you." It was as if she knew what I needed. The explosion had taken place before I could shop for dinner that night. When we arrived at the front of my place, Mother didn't ask if she could come in, and I didn't offer. Her driver picked up the box and followed me into the yard while she stayed in the car. Mother visited me with food once more after that before I went back to work.

# CHAPTER TWENTY-TWO

THE MARKET was closed for the following three days to tend to the dead and the cleanup. For the first time in five months, I could spend time with the children, my mother-in-law, and Hasan. The first day, I took my time getting out of bed and lighting the cooking fire, so it was midmorning before we finished eating breakfast.

"I have a request to put to both of you," my mother-in-law addressed Hasan and me after Amina and Adam went out in the yard to play.

"What is it, Mother?" Hasan asked.

"I want you to marry Idil."

I knew that custom encouraged a living brother to marry the wife of a dead one, to protect the land and the children—and in that order. I'd never imagined she'd propose such a thing in this case because there was no land to protect. Also, she knew I married Sidow for love, not for the size of his property. When a farm couple married, the size of the groom's property dictated the union.

"She is like my sister," Hasan sounded upset at his mother's suggestion.

"She is not your sister though. Idil is young and deserves a husband, just as much the children need a father. And you, Hasan, need a wife."

"I'll take a wife but not my brother's wife. As for the children, I can be their father without marrying Idil." Hasan got up and went outside after the children as if he were on a mission to show her that he was responsible for them already.

"Idil, you know better than he does," my mother-in-law turned to me for help. "This is the best option for both of you."

"I don't want a husband. All I want to do is take care of you and my children."

"Sidow is dead, and he isn't coming back. You can't tie yourself down to a dead husband."

She spoke as if I didn't live with the realization that Sidow was gone with every breath I took. Some nights, as I lay alone on the empty straw mattress, I'd tell myself that maybe if I closed my eyes long enough, I could summon him back next to me. Of all the horrible fantasies I had imagined since the start of the civil war, losing Sidow was never one of them. My nightmares consisted of dead children and desecrated families. Still, Sidow was never among the dead.

"I know, but I don't want to marry Hasan, or to anyone else."

"You married for love the first time, but you should do it for duty this time."

"I can't, but we will find a wife for Hasan."

"How? I have no farm, no house, no tribal elder, and no dowry. How do you imagine we would find him a wife?"

She'd raised valid points, and I had no counter for them. "We'll find a way," I said.

My empty promise didn't help her, but thankfully she dropped the topic. Still, many times I heard her murmuring in her sleep. The list of the losses she'd suffered and the pain she endured filled the night. In daylight, she stored all her worries for the following night and took care of the children in my stead. When the market reopened, I went back to work.

⁂

"Idil, Rhoda is here! She says there has been a car accident," my mother-in-law said as she entered the cooking area.

I blew into the charcoal to light the fire for breakfast. "What?" I asked and turned around to see Rhoda, standing right behind her.

"It happened outside Afgooye a few hours ago."

The relevance of the statement eluded me. "What are you talking about? What happened in Afgooye?"

"Your mother died in a car accident last night." There wasn't a shred of sadness in her voice.

"What was she doing there?" It was a stupid question, but I asked because I didn't want to acknowledge what Rhoda had said. Perhaps if I didn't, the words wouldn't become reality. But as soon as I stood up, the statement sank in. A wave of sorrow took over, and my knees gave way. I collapsed on the floor and cried.

Rhoda stood there, emotionless.

My mother-in-law gathered me into her embrace and stroked my hair. She consoled me, even though I was crying for Mother, while I hadn't for Sidow.

I had not seen Rhoda since the day Father threw me out of the house over twelve years ago, and yet her words were tinged with bitter resentment. "Your father wants you to get her ready for the burial. He's waiting in the car."

"Why me?"

"You are her daughter, and it's your responsibility. Don't expect me to do it, not after what she did to me." Rhoda stopped as if she'd remembered something. "Also, your father mentioned something about your mother wanting you to do it."

My mother-in-law touched my elbow. "You should go. It is your responsibility as the only daughter. It is expected."

I didn't move. "I have to go to work." I seized the first excuse that came to mind.

"Your mother just died. Take a day off. Who else will prepare her?" She held my face between her hands. "Like I said before, some things we do for love and others for duty." She led me outside to Father's waiting car.

I opened the door, got in, and sat next to Father in the backseat. Rhoda and a driver sat in front. I looked at Father and felt the urge to run away as the memory of the day he declared me dead flooded back.

"Thank you for coming so quickly," he said as the engine roared, and the car rolled out to the road.

"It's not like I had options." I should've been more careful because I knew that when challenged, Father could do great damage. Thankfully, he didn't respond.

The air in the car grew thick and oppressive with unspoken thoughts until the ringing of Father's phone shattered the silence. He took it out of the case on his belt. The caller's muffled voice came before the phone reached Father's ear. He listened and responded with nothing more than a nod here and an *uh-huh* there, before ending the call.

I gathered enough courage to ask, "Does Elmi know about Mother?"

Father sighed and nodded.

His calmness encouraged me. "Is Elmi coming?" I wanted to see my brother.

"No."

"Why not?"

"What would he come for?" Father shouted angrily. "The burial is set for today. It would take him over twenty hours to travel here and he wouldn't make it for the funeral."

"What about Omar?" I didn't want to see Omar, but wondered if Father was playing favorites.

Father glared at me. "That was Omar on the phone, asking me to wait for two days, so he could come." Father removed his glasses, placed them in their case, and set it in the space between us. "The body can't be outside the grave another night, let alone for two days."

Father was right. Burials were usually set within the first twenty-four hours of the deceased's passing. The families mourned afterward without fear of the body decomposing in the heat.

"And anyway, why does it matter? She didn't want to see Omar when she was alive. For months, she refused to speak, or even be in the same room with him."

"Why?" Suddenly, I remembered Mother's comment about wanting to be as far away from Omar as possible.

"She wouldn't say." Father sounded exasperated with the whole subject.

Rhoda turned and stared at him, her expression pained. "She didn't need to say anything. Obviously, she knew the truth about Omar. She knew how evil and self-serving he could be, only she realized it too late."

"What are you talking about? What did Omar do to Mother?" I demanded.

Father gave Rhoda a measured look under a knitted brow for a few seconds before he spoke. "Not another word," he warned.

Rhoda dropped her head low and faced the front.

Silence returned to the car, engulfing us once more. We drove under its heavy cloud until we came to a stop in front of a tall concrete wall surrounding a large house. Several men stood guard atop the roof, the barrels of their guns facing the main gate.

"Come." Father opened his door.

I followed him and Rhoda into the house.

Father led me to Mother's bedroom with Rhoda close behind. "There," he said. "I'll leave you to visit with her for a few minutes before you start the washing." He left, but Rhoda stayed by the door.

With one glance around the room, I saw that Mother had realized her love for luxury. The decor matched her taste, the furniture was handpicked and expensive. The bed, big and well-made, stood ready to receive its tired occupant in comfort. Lush sheets and pillows covered the bed and her happiness oozed from every corner. The room spoke her name, chorused her desire to have the best money could buy, while evoking the memory of the pain she'd endured to have it. Still, she often said she stayed not for herself, but for us. Most of all she suffered on my account. I knew, even in this magnificent room, she never rested, but this knowledge came too late, and a new sadness gripped me.

Mother's body was on a wooden table next to the bed. I kissed her face—the only part of her that was exposed. My tears wet the silk scarf covering her chest. "I'm sorry, Mother," I said. "I should have understood."

"The accident battered her body, broke every bone," Rhoda said.

I had forgotten Rhoda was there, and the sound of her voice startled me. I ignored her and draped my arms over Mother's remains.

Father reentered the room and stood between Rhoda and me. "The service will start soon."

I wept louder for the lost opportunity to make amends. I knew Mother understood my loss from the way she watched her words, how she looked at me when she thought I couldn't see. The sad expression on her face when I pulled away from her embrace, the help she'd offered especially when I didn't take it, spoke for her. Only I never made the same overtures. Now the chance to reconnect was lost forever.

"The force of the explosion flipped the car over and it landed on her." Rhoda was intent on inflicting more pain.

"Leave, now," Father told her.

"Idil might want to know what happened. I am just trying to help her understand." Her gaze bypassed Father and landed on me.

"Go, now!"

Rhoda's face burned with rage. "You are throwing me out?"

The question hung in the air for a few seconds before Father answered. "*Now.*"

Father ushered Rhoda out and returned shortly after with two ladies. "They will help you." He stepped aside. "The *kafan* is here." Father pointed to a large bag containing pieces of white cloth that would be used to enshroud the body.

We wheeled the wooden table Mother's body was on to the washing bay at the back of the room.

"My name is Haweya and this is Caliso. We will guide you in doing this," the elder one spoke for the two. "Start with the upper right," Haweya read from a book, as soon as the door latched behind Father.

Caliso held the pitcher of water over the body. "Wash the lower right before moving to the left." Haweya turned the page and continued reading. "Is the hair clean enough?" she asked, informing me that three washings were required.

"No, it's still matted."

"Wash twice more. It needs to be an odd number of times," Haweya instructed.

It was difficult at first, but after a while my hands moved on command. I obeyed the instructions and without much thought.

Caliso placed the pitcher on the nightstand. She took a white full-length dress with buttons to the ankles and three inexpensive sheets out of the bag Father had shown us. We spread the sheets out on the bed and put the dress on Mother. Together we lifted her clean body off the table and placed her on the bed.

"Use this to cover her hair." Haweya held a white scarf. "Rest her left hand on her chest below the right, as if in prayer." When we finished dressing Mother for her forever home, both women left.

The room became quiet until Father interrupted the stillness. "They're ready for her."

"No, not yet. They can't take her yet, not now." I wailed.

"It is time for her to go." Father took me to the back of the bedroom. "Stay here until I come back from the cemetery."

I cowered behind the headboard. Three men, along with Father, lifted Mother and placed her on a board. Each took one side and walked out, reciting the prayer of the parting.

❦

I stayed in Mother's room, trying to imagine how she'd existed in it. Was she happier than she'd been in Bledley or Gaalmaran?

I had lost track of time when Father returned from the cemetery. "She loved it here," he said when he joined me in the sitting area of her room. "She'd sit here for hours without saying a word." Father sat on the loveseat across from me. "Even when spoken to, she seldom said much in the last two years." Father stopped suddenly. Maybe he'd said too much. "Your Mother wanted you to have this." He held out an old rectangular metal canister.

I recognized it immediately. The lid was too large for the tin, but it was fastened with duct tape. I brushed an index finger against the side of the can, and the rust scraped my skin.

"She didn't know she was going to die, did she?" I asked.

"No, she didn't, but she was planning to give it to you when she returned. She said it used to be yours at one time. At least that's what she told me."

My mind traveled back through the years. Mother had caught me holding the canister that contained the drawing Sidow had given me after he'd dropped out of school. She yelled at me to take "the filth" out of her house. I ran to my room holding the can tightly. That afternoon I showed it to Elmi and then hid it under my bed, covering it with an old dress. I took it out each night to admire the image. The morning I eloped with Sidow, I wanted to take it with me, but the can along with the drawing had vanished.

"I can't believe she kept it all this time." I yanked at it. The tape gave, and the lid came off. My hand flew backward, and I gasped. There, in the center of a large roll of American bills held together by a rubber band, was one of the two beaded bracelets Sidow had with him that last morning when he left for his new job. The drawing, still folded the way I had left it, was tucked in at the side. I touched the bracelet to assure myself of its presence.

"Where did Mother find this?" *What happened to the other one?*

Father stood. "I have to go now."

"Where did she find it?" I pulled the bracelet out of the can and held it for Father to see. His reaction told me he was not surprised it was in there, but he pretended he didn't know what it was. A cold chill of fear crept up my back.

Father hesitated. "She didn't say. I only know she planned to give you this can, which was yours when you were young.

She said she wanted you to have it, since you didn't take anything when you ran off with the Boon. That is all I know." The way he enunciated every syllable so carefully told me that he knew more. "Does it mean something to you?" he asked.

"I lost the can when I was young." Admitting the significance of the bracelet could mean danger for me, so I didn't say anything about it or the drawing or the bundle of money inside.

"I have to go," Father repeated. "Rhoda has your ride ready," he said and left.

I unfolded the drawing and traced the sharp creases that interrupted the lines where Sidow's pencil had graced the page. I folded it again in the same pattern and placed it in the corner of the can. I turned to the bracelet and caressed it. The once-vibrant beads had lost their shine and looked tired and worn, but there it was. *How did Mother end up with this? Did she see Sidow alive after he left for work?* Suddenly, I felt unsafe in the house and wanted to leave.

Rhoda entered the room, and I slipped the bracelet back into the can. "I'm ready to go," I said.

Rhoda stared at the canister. "Your mother was so protective of that ugly thing from the minute Omar gave it to her. She carried it everywhere, even to the bathroom. I watched her for weeks, hoping she would leave it behind for a few minutes, so could I see what is in it, but she didn't. A month later, I asked Omar about it, but he only yelled at me to stay out of what was not my business."

"Omar gave this to her?"

"Yes, about six months ago. I know because it was about the time he tried to get on your mother's good side. I have never seen Omar work so hard at anything before, but she only moved farther away from him. What's in it?" Rhoda asked.

"Nothing. Just some trinkets and jewelry from when I was little."

Rhoda frowned. "It seemed more important than a child's stupid jewelry box. Your mother kept it so close as if it contained the most important life secret." She stopped as if waiting for me to confirm her assessment. When I didn't, she continued. "I know you're lying, but never mind. Come with me. The driver is ready to take you home."

I followed her to the door.

❧

Rhoda and I approached the car that had brought us earlier, and that same driver was in it. Only now, there was a second man sitting in the passenger seat. Rhoda handed the driver a folded piece of paper. "Come back as soon as everything is done."

As if he knew what instructions were written on the paper, he put it in his shirt pocket without reading it.

"Go ahead," Rhoda told me. "They are waiting for you." She pointed at the back door.

I opened it and got in.

Rhoda walked back to the house as we drove out of the gravel driveway. "You still look beautiful," the driver said, as he merged into the traffic on the main road. "Don't you agree, Ali?" he asked his passenger. The other man, holding a rifle, nodded.

The word *still* stood out. "Thanks," I said, not wanting to acknowledge him, but unable to ignore him altogether.

The car turned and sped in the wrong direction. "I live in the Ceelgaab market, near the wheelbarrow sheds," I said. Alarm bells sounded in my head. He knew where I lived because he'd picked me up that morning.

He winked at me through the rearview mirror. "Rhoda asked me to drop something off before I took you home. It won't take long." He drove farther and farther away from my home. Fifteen minutes later, he parked the car in front of a large metal gate. As if on cue, his phone rang. "Ali, I have to take this. Bring her in and take her to Omar's room."

Ali opened my door. "Come."

"I'll wait here until he is done."

"It's not safe for you to stay in the car alone without this." Ali held up his rifle. "Let's go."

We walked around the side of the house to a small side door. Ali rang the bell, and a guard opened the door.

"Follow me." Ali led me through large, immaculate sitting room and into a well-furnished bedroom. "Wait in here." He left me standing next to the bed and locked the door behind him.

Frightened, I walked around the room searching a way out. I put the canister Mother had left for me on the floor and twisted the doorknob several times, but it was locked. I tugged at the window latches in the room and in the bathroom, but metal bars blocked the openings. It soon became obvious that trying to escape was futile.

Framed pictures of Omar and Sheila sat on the night tables at each side of the bed. From one, Sheila smiled, her upturned face close to Omar's.

The bedroom door opened, and the driver appeared. "There you are," he said.

"Jamac!" I realized, only too late, I was staring at Rhoda's brother. Why had I not recognized him earlier? I walked backward, away from the bed.

He moved closer and stared at me with blood-red, wild eyes. "So, you do remember me!" Jamac sat on the bed and extended a hand "Come. Sit by me, my love."

"I have to go."

Jamac smiled pleasantly. "I fell in love with you the first time I saw you. Oh, how I have wished for this very moment."

"I need to get back to my children."

"You were supposed to be mine, but you left me and married a Boon man! How could you, Idil, *how?*" His voice cracked. "I was not only your husband to be, but your cousin. My sister married your brother. How could you humiliate me that way? You left me for a Boon! My mother tried one match after another after you rejected me, but I couldn't get you out of my mind just as much as I couldn't get away from others mocking me."

"It wasn't my fault. I never agreed to marry you, and I told Mother, but she wouldn't listen. I was already in love with Sidow when you asked for my hand. My parents knew that."

"Rhoda agreed to marry Omar because of me. She didn't care for Omar, and she liked another boy in our village. My parents made her because I had fallen in love with you when I saw your photo in Italy. Omar didn't care about Rhoda, but I was different. I *loved* you."

I moved closer to the door. "Take me home, please. Now."

"How could you ever say you loved a Boon man?" Jamac sounded sincere as if he couldn't comprehend my love for Sidow. Suddenly he got to his feet, grabbed me by the arm, and pulled me onto the bed. "I even contemplated killing the Boon." He pulled at my hijab.

I held the front part of the scarf around my face to stop him. He reached for the flap on the top of my head where the pin held. I pushed him. "Did *you* kill my husband?"

Jamac held both of my hands in one of his. "No one was supposed to get hurt. Omar was supposed to take you from the Boon and bring you back to me. He bungled the plan, like your mother did when she neglected to keep you at home until your wedding night. Omar failed to convince the Boon to divorce you and keep his children." Jamac kneeled on the bed and twisted my hands behind my back.

"Did Omar kill Sidow?" I asked, as a sharp pain shot from my wrist up to my shoulder. The scarf was tight around my neck, and I gasped for breath.

"The Boon is dead now, and his family can keep the children. You are mine. Everyone wins."

"I am *not* yours. Take me home!" I jerked away, and Jamac lost his grip momentarily. I took advantage of the sudden release, and pushed him hard. Jamac fell off the bed and onto the wooden floor with a thud. I ran for the door, but before I could open it, he grabbed me from behind and dragged me back to the bed.

"Not just yet." He ripped viciously at my dress.

I screamed, but Jamac covered my mouth with the scarf and muffled the sound. I yelled, kicked, and braced my feet, but despite my best efforts to resist, he moved me forward.

He threw me onto the bed, got on top of me, and kissed me. "You will enjoy this, I guarantee it," he said. "You'll see what it's like to have a real man of your own kind—how much better it is than bedding the Boon."

I tried to yell for help again, but Jamac took the opportunity to slip his tongue in my mouth. I bit it hard and held his flesh tight between my teeth. His blood, metallic and sour, seeped into my mouth until I retched and let him go.

He slapped me so hard my teeth punctured the inside of my cheek. "If you do that again, you'll die," Jamac smiled. "That's what happens when you don't listen." He glared at me, measuring my understanding.

I hated those eyes, dark and determined. They reminded me of the cat Omar had killed when we were young.

"Now, where were we?" He finished tearing off my clothes and threw them, reduced to shreds, on the floor.

I bent my knees to block his entry, but Jamac forced my legs straight. He reached for my underwear and tore it like paper. The clasps of my bra gave, and I broke under the weight of the humiliation. I watched him enter me—horrified, helpless—as if I was a witness to the rape of someone other than me.

He fell upon me after the excited flight of release and took a deep, satisfied breath. "That was good," he said, smiling. "You are the best." He held me tight against his chest.

My breathing grew heavy and labored, and rage surged within me. Mother was dead and no amount of "duty" could bring her back. My going with Rhoda, Father, and Jamac hadn't helped her and it brought me nothing but misery.

Jamac rolled off me. "What is the matter? Did I hurt

you?" He smiled and waited for my answer, as if we were two consenting people who had just made love together.

The smell of his sin nauseated me. I wanted to get up, to wash his filth from my body, but I couldn't move. My head ached, and I felt dizzy.

"I'll be in the house if you need me." He wished me a good night.

I stayed in bed long after he stumbled out of the room.

# CHAPTER TWENTY-THREE

A SUDDEN NOISE pulled me out of my stupor.

"What have you done?" Father's angry question caused me to sit up and pay attention.

Jamac mumbled a response I couldn't discern.

"Why?" Father's voice boomed over the silent house.

Jamac chuckled. "To make Idil mine, like you said I should."

"To *force* yourself upon her?"

"I did nothing she didn't enjoy."

Father must have slapped or kicked Jamac, because I heard a harsh bang, followed by a loud yelp.

Father's familiar, heavy strides filled the room as he paced the floor. "Never say that."

I could imagine the expression on his face; the deep lines around the mouth, large creases snaking up to his forehead. "I said make her agree to marry you, and you stand here, telling me you *raped* her! You're disgusting. Don't you realize I am her father—your uncle? How dare you do that without marrying her first? Don't you know that is a sin?"

"Is that much different from the mistresses you keep, or Omar's—" Father struck Jamac again before he could finish.

"Take care of this. Talk to her and convince her to marry you before I return with the sheikh in the morning. Rhoda! See to it that Idil is not violated again."

*Is he going to leave me here with Jamac still in the house?* New terror gripped me. I stood up and went to the door, wrapped in a bedsheet. My pain transformed into an unmatched energy as I turned the doorknob and found it unexpectedly open. Rhoda, Father, and Jamac stared at me, surprised, when I appeared in the sitting room. Father called my name several times, but I didn't respond. I took everything within reach—flower vases, table lamps, decorative pieces, photo frames—and hurled them. Within seconds, the room looked like a war zone. Still, I continued to find more objects.

Father and Jamac, took hold of me and pulled me back into the bedroom.

Father spoke to me as if he were reading from a note. "It wasn't supposed be this way. The plan was for you and Jamac and Rhoda to discuss how to finalize your wedding to Jamac. I am sorry this happened, but we can't change it now. We can only prepare for the future. Everything will be fine from here on, I promise you. You just wait here and listen to them."

"I want to go home to my children." I knew I was dead to Father. I knew he had set our house on fire. But I never dreamed he would participate in organizing my rape. That was low, even for him.

"You'll have nothing to do with those children. If you care for them and love them, you will pretend they do not exist. That is safer for them."

"You are telling me to abandon my children?"

"The children are with their family just like you are with yours. I could send them some money so the old lady can provide for them, or I could offer their uncle a job. But you are to have nothing to do with them from now on. You are not their mother, and they are not your children." Father turned around, and locked the door behind him.

A few minutes later, Rhoda entered the room. Her eyes landed on the framed pictures of Sheila and Omar on the night tables. "This whore's face is everywhere." Rhoda walked toward the bed and turned the photos face down with force. The lamps swayed and threatened to fall. She took a dress from under her arm and threw it at me. "Wear this. It should do."

I picked up the dress and traced my finger around the V-neckline. The sheen and luxurious softness of the fabric felt unfamiliar. The war that took everything from me—the love of my life, the glow of my skin, the shine of my hair, the meat of my bones, and, above all, my dignity—had not touched Rhoda. She existed in a bubble where no harm dared to go. "You knew what he was planning, and still, you sent me away with him." I choked on the words.

"I had nothing to do with this. I had no idea he would do this."

"You mean *rape* me. Say the word, you coward."

"I had no part in that. Like your father said, we were to discuss the wedding plans. The original idea was to do it when your mother returned from the cottage, but once she died we decided to go ahead with it anyway," Rhoda said.

"So, Mother was part of this?" Each revelation was worse than the one before.

"She was not part of it, but we intended to tell her and you at the same time. It would have been a pleasant surprise for both of you. She would've appreciated it, I am sure."

"My mother would've appreciated my being assaulted?"

"I told you, the attack wasn't part of the plan at all."

"If you keep saying that, you might even believe yourself after a while, but I never will," I said.

"Look, I stayed with your brother and his whore. You left Jamac for a Boon. No one—not your mother, Omar, or your father—did anything. They all watched as you eloped, built a relationship, and had children. Jamac and I were left to languish in our respective lonely beds. This plan was only a way to collect the debt owed."

"*I* owed nothing." I picked up Sheila's photo and flipped it upright to annoy Rhoda.

Rhoda focused on the frame. "A girl doesn't borrow, but always has to pay the debt—always." She walked back, picked up the two picture frames, and dropped them in the garbage bin by the door. "Still, unlike Omar, Jamac is willing to do right by you."

"And that was to rape me?"

"No. He was supposed to ask you to marry him."

"I don't want him anywhere near me or my children." The thought terrified me.

"The children are not yours anymore. Like your father said, they are where they belong, with their Boon relatives, and you'll leave them there."

"No." The very notion was unthinkable. "They *are* my children, and I'm not marrying the man who raped me! Not today, not tomorrow."

"Every night, when your brother gets into my bed after leaving the whore, I want to shriek 'Get away from me!' Still, I keep quiet, because I know my crying would do nothing, except add to the shouts of so many women to whom no one is paying attention." She cleared her throat. "I lie next to Omar after each violation, then I wash, dress, and smile. I suggest you do the same. You can't change what's happened, so why not get what you want—a husband and his protection. Think, Idil."

I fiddled with the hem of the fabric. "There's nothing to think about."

"There is a lot to think about." Rhoda glanced at me. "Let me know how the dress fits." She left and closed the door.

※

"You are coming with me until her father is ready to do the nikaax tomorrow." I couldn't see them, but I knew Rhoda was speaking to Jamac.

"I want to be here with Idil. I must keep an eye on her, so she doesn't slip away like she did before." Jamac was shouting by the time he finished speaking.

"You're not to be anywhere near her until she is your wife. Look what you did when she was left with you for one hour."

"It was your idea."

"I didn't say to rape her. I said get what is yours; make her marry you, even if by force." Rhoda pronounced the words with undo care.

"I did not rape her. I took what was mine and made love to her. And why should I need to force her into marrying me?"

Rhoda laughed. "You are not only twisted, but you are a fool. Can't you see you have nothing to offer her?"

"I can give her more than Omar gives you. I can promise to be in her bed every night, and she won't have to share my love with a gaalo whore."

"And you proved that by ripping the clothes off her before she had a chance to remove them herself?" Rhoda laughed aloud. "At least I am afforded the dignity to disrobe."

"Every time I trust others to keep her, I lose her," Jamac said. "This time I am not leaving it to anyone else."

"I will take care that she doesn't get away, but you have to come with me now."

"The same way you took care of her mother?"

Rhoda slammed something on a table. "Never say that! The woman died in a car accident, and I was not there."

"Sell that story to someone who would buy such a tale, dear sister."

I hoped Jamac would say more about Mother's death, but he didn't.

"Come with me now!" Rhoda ordered, and their footsteps retreated together.

❧

The house became very quiet, with no trace of Rhoda, Jamac, or Father. The only human contact I had for the rest of that evening was a kitchen girl who brought food and water to me. She didn't say much, but only watched from two large brown eyes. I asked her for Father or Rhoda, but she gave no response. "Here's food for you, madam," she placed the plate on a small table. "I'll return to collect the dishes." She rushed out.

Gradually, I became sleepy. I sat on the bed and rubbed the sleep out of my eyes because I didn't want to be caught off guard. The house remained quiet, and the gloomy darkness of night arrived with its shadows until the sound of heavy boots and men's voices took over.

"How long does he want us to keep her?" one man asked.

They were talking about me.

"Until morning," responded another. "Mr. Nuur is bringing the sheikh to perform the marriage ceremony for his daughter and Jamac after breakfast tomorrow."

That was it. They said nothing more about me. They drifted into casual talk of the latest tribal disagreements and what militia group they thought had the upper hand. After an hour or so, I heard a car pull into the driveway and the doorbell ring. The occupants of the car hurried inside the house and chaos ensued. "Let's go," someone said. "No time to collect anything. We must leave now, before they get here. The whole city is under siege and the battle is moving this way!" They stampeded out, as if the place was on fire.

As soon as the heavy footsteps died, I got off the bed,

put on my sandals, and went to the door. I turned the light on and saw my canister lying on it is side. I looked inside, and my heart thundered in my chest when I saw that the money, the drawing, and the bracelet were still there. It was lucky that Rhoda hadn't seen it. I picked it up, grateful it had escaped notice. I lifted the latch to the door gently, and to my great relief, it was unlocked. I hurried through the sitting room and out the side door. I walked quickly until the image of that dreaded place slipped into the darkness.

❦

The sound of heavy shelling followed me home. It was hard to tell in which direction the fighting was taking place. From east to west and south and north, one shelling responded to another. It was pitch-black when I arrived after hours of walking, terrified and alone, through the city. My mother-in-law cried with joy when she saw me.

"Oh, God! I haven't slept since you left. I felt so guilty for encouraging you to go the funeral. I'm glad you are back, safe."

"What happened?" Hasan asked.

"They kidnapped me after the funeral and tried to force me to marry Jamac."

"How did you get away?" My mother-in-law's eyes opened wide.

"Those who were guarding me deserted the house." Neither Hasan nor my mother-in-law asked any other details. They didn't inquire how I went from getting Mother ready for burial to becoming a captive.

I went inside and kissed my sleeping children, resisting the urge to wake them and hold them tight. I shook my head to dispel the thought of how close I'd come to losing them forever and went back to the cooking area to sit with Hasan and my mother-in-law.

# CHAPTER TWENTY-FOUR

IT WAS WELL past midnight, but Hasan lit the fire and the three of us sat around it. I waited until the heat from the flames warmed my body before I spoke. "We have to get away soon. We must take the children and leave." Father's warning that my children would be safer if I stayed away, flooded back. "I had to escape, and I have defied them again. They know where we live and they will harm us unless we go now."

The sound of heavy fighting in the distance increased my fear. Each explosion, louder than the last, shook the ground beneath us.

My mother-in-law got up and wrapped her shawl around her head and face. "I'll go to Idris and see if he can help us find a way out," she said.

"This late?" Hasan asked.

"With this raging battle, only innocent children are sleeping tonight," she said as she left.

Hasan and I sat by the fire, waiting and listening, as one loud explosion followed another.

Half an hour later, my mother-in-law returned with good news. "Idris and some other merchants have hired a truck to take their families to Bledley. We can travel with them but we must pay a hundred dollars for each adult and fifty dollars per child. I told him I would sell a piece of land and give him the money when we get to Bledley. He agreed."

"You don't have to sell anything. I have money." I untied the end of my scarf and exposed the American bills that had survived Jamac's attack and my flight afterward.

Hasan extended a hand toward the money, but stopped before he touched it. "Where did you get all of this?"

"It was a gift from my mother." I looked at my mother-in-law for a reaction, but all I saw was gratitude.

"The truck will leave soon, before sunrise," she said. "We should get ready."

We discussed how to hide the money. Putting it in Hasan's belt sack was too obvious a choice. Women's under-garments—bras and panties—were usual hiding places for valuables, so we avoided them. In the end, we tied it in my mother-in-law's scarf and hoped no one would check there.

I shook Amina awake. "We have to go home to Bledley."

She seemed to understand the seriousness of the situation as soon as she opened her eyes. She peered at me for less than two seconds, got up, pulled her sandals on, and stood next to me. "I am ready."

I did the same with Adam. "Wake up, my love. We have to leave right away." He awoke, opened his mouth to say something, changed his mind, and got out of bed. "I am ready to go." He stood next to Amina.

My mother-in-law, following the directions Idris had given her, led us through the back alleys of the market to a cattle truck parked behind a large warehouse. A gun-toting boy of about fourteen shouted, "Idris begged me to wait! Two more minutes and we'd have left!" The deafening thunder of firearms roared in the distance. "Put the children on your lap!"

We climbed the ladder into the packed truck as quickly as we could. Inside were four families—twenty-eight people, plus the driver and four armed guards on the roof.

"You move—no, not that way, this way." The boy paced the flatbed of the truck, stepping over or on people, determined to find space, though none existed. He pushed one passenger with the butt of a revolver. "You, sit here." He moved ahead. "You there, yes you. Move! Do you not hear?" The tirade continued. "You are taking up too much room! This is not your house!" He pointed at two spaces not big enough for a two-year-old, let alone for an adult. "You sit there and you here." He directed us and stretched out his hand for the payment. "Four hundred dollars for the family!"

Hasan gave him the money.

He counted and walked away.

Hasan sat in a tight-fitting nook. "Amina," he called, "come here with me."

Amina's eyes lit up, and she flew into his arms.

With his sister beaming in her uncle's lap, Adam felt left out and unsure of where to go.

My mother-in-law called. "Adam come to Grandmother."

"I'll sit with my mother." Adam's steps coincided with the truck pulling out, and he staggered but steadied himself and sat on my lap.

❧

The tires bounced over boulder-sized gashes in the road. I held on to the metal bars to keep from falling forward, only to return to a sitting position with a thump. To free my mind from worries of what Father, Jamac, and Rhoda might do once they found out I had escaped, I turned to the woman to my left. "How old is your daughter?"

"Fourteen. I lost four children and my husband in a mortar shelling two days ago." She looked away. "Why did I survive, and they didn't?"

"I am so sorry for your loss," I offered. "What is your daughter's name?"

"Aisha."

"She is a beautiful girl," I said.

I waited for her to say more, but she only leaned against the metal side and closed her eyes. Desperate to escape the encroaching fear, I turned to the woman on my right. She had four young children, the youngest asleep on her lap. "How old is he?"

She shielded the baby with her scarf as though I might hurt it. "It is a girl. He wanted a girl so much." She tilted her head to the side.

"Who?"

"My husband. He was so thrilled to have a daughter. The last two months were the happiest of his life."

"Where is he now? Is he in the village?"

No answer.

The child squirmed and whimpered. "You should give her something to eat."

The woman lifted the baby up to her breast, and it nursed. "He was so excited he couldn't sleep when I was in labor."

"Where is your husband now?"

She didn't answer, but closed her eyes and hummed a children's lullaby.

I gave in to the rocking motion of the truck.

❧

After what felt like an eternity, we stopped in the village of Diifow.

The boy who had loaded the truck earlier removed the tarp, and the sun poured down on us with vigor. "We'll rest here until dark," he announced and jumped from the rafters to the ground.

We took to the ladder as fast as we could. The women pooled all the food they had together: bread, cheese, butter, rolls of dried meat, and bottles of buttermilk. Idris and another man lit a fire and we made tea. Soon we had set up a modest feast.

My mother-in-law noticed the woman with the baby still inside. "What is she doing in there? Idil, could you please go and check on her?"

I climbed the ladder. "You should come and get something to eat," I said to her.

With the baby in her arms, and her other three children

unattended outside, she looked at me as if she'd woken up from a deep sleep.

"Let me help you." I guided her out of the truck and she followed me without resistance. She held the bundle in her arms like a drowning person holding a life preserver. She sat on ground next to her children, but made no attempt to serve them or herself. I gave her two slices of bread, a piece of cheese, and a mug of buttermilk.

She took two bites of the bread and cheese and drank half of the milk. She pushed the rest of the food into my hands, as if she were running out of time to eat. "Thank you," she said, and went back in the truck without checking to see if her other three children had eaten.

⁂

Our freedom came to an end when, a few minutes before sunset, we boarded again. The truck pulled out of its hiding place behind a large tree and reached the main road.

An hour later, under the darkness of the night, Adam grew restless. "It's too crowded. I don't have enough room."

My mother-in-law called to him. "Adam come sit with Grandmother."

"I can't. I am too heavy for you."

"You could sit next to me. I have enough space for both of us."

He hesitated, but I encouraged him. "Go to your grandmother."

Adam went.

No more than five minutes after Adam moved, a loud

bang overhead shattered the fragile peace. The men on the top of our truck returned fire, and a full-fledged gun battle erupted above our heads. The firing back and forth merged, making it hard to tell our defensive bullets from the enemy shots, until the truck came to a full stop.

Attackers ran up the ladder, yelling, "Get down, get down, now! All of you!"

We obeyed and moved to the ladder. They continued to shout even after all of us were on the ground, except for the woman with the baby.

Six men with AK-47 rifles surrounded us. "Empty your pockets! Hide nothing. Do you think we are blind? Dig deeper. Yes, give us everything." Three of them gathered the loot while the other three stood guard.

A man approached me. "Don't make me wait." He ran his hands under the band of my bra and shoved his fingers inside my underwear. "You're hiding money in here. Lift both your breasts, now."

I did, but nothing fell out.

He pushed me with the butt of the rifle. "Take your scarf off."

I hesitated, trying appeal to his sense of modesty.

"I said take it off."

I did as I was told and prayed they didn't do the same with my mother-in-law. What we thought was the best place for the money at first, now seemed the worst idea.

Luckily, he noticed the woman inside with the baby in her lap before moving on to my mother-in-law. "Hey, you up there! Come here!"

She didn't move.

"Don't make me come up there!" he yelled.

"Why are you begging her?" Another man, perhaps the leader, climbed up the ladder, two steps at a time. The woman did not resist when he pulled her to her feet. She followed him without a fuss. Standing next to the truck, he tried to take the bundle from her, but she wouldn't let go.

A tug of war ensued. Her oldest son, perhaps eight years old, threw himself at the man. "Stop! Leave my mother alone!" He buried his teeth in the man's thigh. The man yelped and hit the boy over the head with his fist. He continued to tug at the blanket with his other hand. The boy, once latched on, wouldn't let go, but cried. His mother, hearing her son's cry, released the bundle and sent the man flying backward. He landed on his behind with a thud.

She gathered her son in her arms and ran her hand through his hair. His dark curls glistened with the wet, shiny blood from her hand.

The man opened the bundle he had fought for. "Ya'Allah!" He shrieked so loud that other men from his group came running to him. "It's bleeding!" He came face-to-face with the blood-soaked body of the infant girl.

"The shrapnel must have hit her," I whispered to my mother-in-law.

"What is it?" The leader grabbed the bundle.

Blood seeped from the blanket and stained the white robe he was wearing. He looked at the woman sitting at his feet holding her son, noticed the solemn faces watching him, dropped the bundle, and ran. His men saw his blood-covered hands and followed him into the night with their loot.

The woman picked the baby up, wrapped her as though

she was getting her ready for bed, and rocked back and forth. Her son rubbed her hand to console her.

Idris squatted next to her. "We must bury the baby here, before we leave," he spoke to her in a gentle tone.

"No, no, no. Not without a proper funeral." She was adamant.

Another man joined Idris to convince her not to take the body with her. They reminded her she could do the mourning when she reached her family. Keeping the body would only prolong her sorrow and distract her from her living children, but she wouldn't listen. No matter what they said and how many verses from the Qur'an and prophet Mohamed's— peace be upon him—hadiths they referred to, she refused.

She held the child's remains close to her chest, the fresh crimson blood streaking her dress. "I did not see my husband's body." Her voice cracked with raw emotion. "Do you know what they told me when I asked? They said the explosion was so strong they couldn't tell what body part belonged to what person. I will take my baby in one piece and bury her properly." She got up, went to the truck, and resumed her seat. No one could argue against her.

"I cannot sit next to her." I lingered outside with my mother-in-law when others boarded.

"You could have my place," she offered.

It didn't matter where I sat because death had tainted the whole truck. Its scent, taste, and texture filled the air around us. "That could have been Adam," I said.

"Don't say that."

"Her little feet were inches away from my hip."

"Stop."

"Adam was sitting there only minutes before." I shivered as the words left my lips. "That could have been Adam," I repeated.

"Everyone goes in their own time," she said.

It was hard for me to accept it was this baby's time to go—and in such a fashion. "She was an infant." I sobbed for a child I didn't even know.

"Please stop...the children." She pointed at Adam and Amina, standing next to her, tears brimming in their eyes.

I took a deep breath, collected myself, and sat in the truck next to the dead baby. Once inside, I shook so hard, I had to sit on my hands.

"My husband came back to take her," the child's mother said. "He loved her so much, more than one human being should love another."

"People don't return from the dead." Again, the image of Sidow striding in my direction, warm and alive, came to me. What I wouldn't have given up to see that bright smile one more time!

She laughed, and others turned in her direction. "He adored her so much, it made me jealous!"

I pointed at her son, stroking her hand trying to gain her attention. "Your son is very kind," I said. I just wanted her to stop speaking, but I couldn't distract her.

She glanced at her boy for a quick second and laughed even louder. "Do you know what he said when she was one week old?"

"What?" I asked even though I didn't want to know the troubling details.

"He said, 'I'd die if something ever happened to her.' Oh,

I was so angry with him then!" She sighed. "At least he died before witnessing this." She lifted her hand and examined the blood. "In a way, he got his wish. They are together now."

⁂

We arrived at the outskirts of Bledley before dawn the following day.

That same boy who loaded us before, lifted the tarp off the truck. "Here we are. The village is not far now. You can see it from here," he announced. He was much less energetic than he was before the attack.

The driver whistled for our attention. "We'll send a messenger to the militia with money for permission to enter. When he returns, we'll go in groups."

Two hours later, the man came back with a letter of consent from the militia leader who had ruled Bledley since the president's departure.

I pointed at the woman with the baby. "She should go first." Nods of assent followed.

# CHAPTER TWENTY-FIVE

IT WAS JUST after the midday meal when we arrived at our farm. A boy, not much older than twelve, stood at the front gate. A rifle, twice his size, was slung over his right shoulder, and he approached as we walked toward him. "Who are you?" the boy asked.

"We are the owners of this farm," Hasan responded.

"You arrive just now, and you claim this here is your farm? You are telling me you own this land?" He chuckled.

"This farm belonged to us for hundreds of years, son." My mother-in-law tried to appeal to his respect for elders.

The boy took the rifle off his shoulder and leaned it against the wooden post. "I am not your son, and this here isn't your farm. You better leave before it is too late."

"We are not going anywhere," Hasan said.

"We'll see." The boy gave us a serious look and walked away.

I nudged Hasan's elbow. "Let's go before he returns. There will be trouble. I know there will be. I can feel it."

"We're not leaving." Hasan wouldn't budge.

"Please," I begged my mother-in-law.

She was staring at the house, lost in memory. "I had my children here, buried my husband, and he buried his parents. Now a mere boy tells me it is not mine, and I should leave?"

"Please," I repeated. "We have to go, now!" The children clung to me.

Hasan's face burned with rage. "This is our home."

"Not anymore," I said. It was too late. A man, accompanied by the same boy, came toward us from the house.

"The boy tells me you claim this is your farm," the man said.

I took charge before Hasan could say anything. "Sorry for the trouble. We were just leaving. The boy must have misunderstood. We were looking for a friend who used to live here, so we could spend the night." The man's eyes were fixed on Amina, and my heart beat against my chest. I took Amina and Adam, one in each hand, and began walking away, hoping Hasan and his mother would follow. I didn't dare turn back.

"What is your relationship to the women?" The question was for Hasan.

Hasan, frozen with anger, didn't respond. I turned around and answered instead. "This is my husband, that is his mother, and these are our children."

The man stared at me with contempt. "Ha! I see the wife is the head of this family."

Hasan realized the danger because he reacted by chastising

me for the man's benefit. "What did I tell you about answering when you are not spoken to?" He turned on me, violence in his gaze.

I played the part of the intimidated wife. "Sorry, it won't happen again." I bowed my head and looked contrite.

"It better not happen again," Hasan said and then spoke to the man. "Don't mind my wife."

"My name is Ahmed, and I must say, I admire a man who's in control of his wife. You may stay for the night, if you have nowhere else to go."

"We don't want to bother you. Thank you, but we'll find our friend," Hasan said.

"It is no bother at all. I'll send someone to help you get settled," Ahmed said, and left without waiting for an answer.

After he was gone, Hasan cupped my face in his hands. "I wasn't going to hit you."

"I know that."

"The way you looked at me—your eyes—were you scared?" Hasan focused on the empty field.

"I was acting for Ahmed."

Hasan stood close. "I didn't mean it. You know I wouldn't hurt you." He wrapped his arm around my waist.

"Don't do that," my-mother-in-law cautioned.

"Don't do what?"

"Touch her. They don't like public displays of affection, even if you are married." She turned back to door to her old bedroom, where Ahmed had gone in.

Hasan dropped his hands to his sides and grew quiet.

Amina stood before me. "Why did you say Uncle Hasan was your husband?"

"They won't like if we're together and not married."

"We've always been together."

"They think we shouldn't be."

"Who are these people? You've just met them, and they tell you how to be?"

Hasan turned to Amina. "We're not married, but we can't admit that. They won't accept us being together unless your mother and I are married." Hasan stopped for a few seconds as if waiting for Amina to absorb the information. "Do you understand?" he asked.

Amina nodded, but it was obvious the answer didn't satisfy her.

❧

Soon after Ahmed left us standing by the gate, twelve boys came from behind the house marching in a military style. Not one was older than fourteen. Each boy was wearing an old tattered T-shirt, and a macawis wrapped around the waist with a narrow, black belt. Their feet were bare and cracked like the dry earth they walked on. They were very thin—so thin you could count their ribs. Each boy had a rifle slung over his shoulder. Their eyes, large and wild, didn't appear to see us, but seemed to peer through us. Their cheeks bulged with wads of chat. High and on edge, the boys seemed to guard the place against imminent attack, although we could see no immediate threat.

The tallest boy said something that excited the others. They broke into fits of giggles, and the devilish sound sent chills up my spine. They laughed like the cackling hyenas before a feast. As quickly as it started, the laughter died, and twelve pairs of eyes, hungry and thirsty, rested upon Amina. She shrank from the heat of their stares.

The boy we'd met at the gate, left the group and came close. "How old is the girl?" He spoke to Hasan, but was staring expectantly at Amina and toying with his gun.

"Nine years old," my mother-in-law lied to place Amina below the age considered old enough to marry.

Hasan squeezed Amina's arm, warning her not to say she was eleven. The boy turned to the others. "They say she is nine. That is a lie." He laughed as though he'd heard the funniest joke in the world. The rest of the group joined him, holding their bellies in exaggerated hilarity. "She is a grown woman. Surely, we can see that."

Another boy from the group joined the first. "How stupid to lie like that when it is obvious she is much older."

There was no correct response in front of the rifles, so we didn't protest. After a while they sauntered away.

My eyes followed the retreating boys, and I saw the fallen lemon trees that once marked the property lines. Without the markers, our farm merged into the other properties on both the northern and southern boundaries. The uprooted trees lay rotting on the ground. Rain, like peace, had deserted Bledley, leaving the land forsaken, mutilated, and bare.

The boys disappeared behind the main cabin, and a while later a woman appeared. A black *cabaaya*—loose robe—covered her whole body. The outfit rotated around her, creating a cascading motion as she walked. A piece of sheer fabric covered her face except for the eyes, which darted back and forth. Her steps were light, hesitant, as if afraid of disturbing something sacred and fragile. She handed one straw mat and one cloth prayer mat to Hasan. "These are for you and the boy. The women will come with me."

The woman glanced toward the main gate before she lifted her face cover and placed a forefinger to her lips in a gesture of warning. "Come. My name is Layla, and I was told to bring the three of you inside."

My throat tightened at the sight of her sad, innocent-looking face. "And I am Idil," I told her.

She lowered her veil. "Ahmed wants the girl to be prepared."

"Prepared for what?"

"He thinks she is old enough, and he wants to take her as a wife," Layla said.

Hasan pulled Amina close. "He will have to kill me first."

Layla stared at Hasan. "He'll take her just the same," she said in an emotionless voice. "We have to go."

The boys emerged from behind the cabin again with the same intimidating glares. "Get inside," the oldest one hissed at Layla.

Adam reached for my hand. "We must stay together. We're a family."

"I don't want to go inside," Amina added.

"You must. Don't make this harder than it is," Layla's hollow voice was tinged by the hell and desperation around us.

"Adam, stay with your father. Amina, come with me," I said.

Adam stood back as Amina stepped out of Hasan's protective shadow. My mother-in-law, Amina, and I followed Layla to the main cabin.

Layla fished a large rectangular piece of fabric out of her waist bag. "Here, cover." She threw it at Amina.

"I'm not wearing this," Amina said.

Layla kept her eyes on the boy near the gate. "It is not what you want, but what you must do that matters."

The guard must have noticed Layla staring at him and strode closer. "What's taking so long?" He was the same boy who was at the gate when we first arrived.

"Nothing. I had a stone in my sandal," Layla said.

"Get moving, now." The boy, satisfied with the answer, walked back to his post.

Amina, threatened by the danger, cocooned herself in the cloth and walked between her grandmother and me.

The call for the *Duhr*—the midday—prayer coming from the masjid in the Farmers' Hall welcomed us into the main house.

As soon as Layla opened the door, a woman charged at us from the inner room. "What did you do?"

"I brought them in like Ahmed said. What else was I to do?" Layla turned to us. "This is Maryan, Ahmed's first wife."

Maryan looked at Amina with curious contempt. "What does he want with her?"

Layla took rolled up mats leaning against the wall and spread them on the floor. "You know the answer. No need to ask."

Maryan sighed. "Each one gets younger. There was Hawa, you, and now her."

My chest heaved. "She is only eleven years old."

"I'm nine," Amina corrected, "and I don't want to marry an old man."

"Never mind, Amina. It won't happen, I won't allow it," I said, unsure of how I would keep such a promise.

"He said you were the last." Maryan was speaking to Layla. "There would never be another. He promised me."

"He doesn't know the meaning of the word *promise*," Layla said.

"He can shoot us in the middle of the yard, but I won't allow this to pass. She is a child." I paced the floor.

Amina panicked. "No one gets shot. No one dies. I'll do what they want. Please, no one dies!"

"Stop! No one is dying," I shouted back to silence Amina and to quell my fear of what Ahmed might do if I opposed him. No one spoke after that. We settled on the mats that Layla placed on the floor of our old common room.

Maryan left as soon as we sat down and returned a few minutes later. "Ahmed is with your husband outside. He wants you there," she told me.

She took her scarf off exposing dark, wavy hair that fell to the middle of her back. She surveyed the room, searching for something, but didn't find it. She turned back to me. "Please go before he gets upset."

"Did Ahmed say what he wants with Idil?" Layla asked.

Maryan shook her head. "No. He just said to tell her to come out and then looked at his watch to time me. Please go. If you are slow, I'll be the first one punished. I'll have to endure his foul mood because it is my day to be with him."

Layla beckoned her. "Maryan, come sit. Idil will go soon."

Maryan's anxiety was palpable. "I can't. Please go! Why are you not leaving yet?"

"I'm going," I said, and stepped out of the room. Once

outside, I saw Hasan and Ahmed standing near the cowshed.

I stared at the ground beneath my feet and didn't look up until I was standing next to Hasan. "*Assalamu Alikum*," I greeted them.

Ahmed nodded. "Your husband has accepted my request for Amina's hand. May Allah guide us to the right path. I know the family has a long journey ahead, and I don't wish to delay your departure, so the nikaax will be tomorrow. We called you so you could tell us what is needed for the bride and help us get her ready."

"We weren't planning on a wedding and we have nothing for the girl." The idea to trick Ahmed into letting us leave came to me as fast as I could speak it. "I need to go to the market and shop for her—henna, dresses, and shoes." I listed everything that came to mind. "I'll need the whole day tomorrow if you are willing to wait one more day."

"Thank you for your help. May Allah reward you for your obedience." Ahmed was all smiles. "The day after tomorrow is agreeable."

Hasan didn't interject, and Ahmed didn't seem to mind that I—the wife—was leading the discussion this time. "Is it all right if Maryan and Layla come with me to help find outfits for Amina?" I asked. "They will know the best shops."

"If you wish."

"Could my husband come to see to it that his daughter gets all she needs?" I asked as gently as I could manage.

Ahmed smiled again. "Yes, that is a good idea. I will have my guards escort you all safely to the market and back."

Ahmed shook hands with Hasan to seal the agreement and sauntered off.

Hasan waited until Ahmed was in the house and couldn't hear us. "What are you doing? I didn't agree. I'll never agree," he said.

The thought of Amina in Ahmed's arms made me shudder. "We'll get away somehow. We will," I said without believing my words and went back inside the house.

Layla closed the door behind me as soon as I came in. "What are you going to do?"

I didn't realize I had been holding my breath until the latch clicked. I exhaled, tilted my head back, and closed my eyes. "We agreed to have Amina ready for a nikaax the day after tomorrow." I explained. "That way, I have some time to plan our escape."

"You can't lie, not to Ahmed. He will see right through you. He always does when I try to lie to him," Maryan said.

"We are not lying. We are telling him what he wants to hear."

After a long and involved debate, we decided to leave early in the morning and use the day to hire a truck that would take us out of Somalia.

"What are we going to do about the guards Ahmed is sending with us?" I asked Layla as the fear of Ahmed's retribution filled me.

"If we had money, we could pay off the guards and convince them not to come back," Layla said.

"We have money," I told her. Mother's parting gift might be our salvation, and I was willing to risk everything to save my daughter.

With that plan in place, we made the decision to take a chance on escaping.

# CHAPTER TWENTY-SIX

I LEFT the mat I was lying on before dawn and pressed my face against a space between two logs on the common-room wall. The farm was quiet and deserted. Memories of all the activities that had filled it before the war, slipped into the gray background of the drought-ridden landscape. The wind whipped rolls of dry hay back and forth, along with dust and dirt. The stools and chairs we had left in the room were gone, replaced by sleeping mats on the floor and cushions that lined up against the back wall. Amina and Layla were asleep on the same mat on one side of the room and my mother-in-law was across from them.

Maryan had left after supper last night because it was her turn to sleep with Ahmed in my in-laws' old bedroom. She had changed her outfit twice before settling on a yellow kaftan under a black robe. She rubbed perfume behind her ears and over her chest, but wiped it off mumbling that Ahmed wouldn't like it if she went past the guards smelling fragrant.

At the first light of morning, Maryan entered the room a great deal more somber than when she'd left. "Ahmed sent me from his bed as soon as I opened my eyes. He is so excited about tomorrow," she said and went outside to the cooking fire. The smell of burning wood reminded me of the beautiful memories this house held, but not for long. One glance at the desolation outside, and I was back in our present horror.

Maryan returned, holding a bowl of cornmeal and buttermilk out to me.

I took the food and set it on the floor. As I ate, I was confronted by the signs of neglect on Amina's body. She was still asleep on the mat, her chest rising and falling in even, rhythmic breaths. Her three-day-old braids had unraveled, leaving the loose hair tangled at the base of her neck. Rubber sandals, old and raggedy, rested against her small feet, and her thin legs stretched across the floor. For a fleeting moment, I envied Sidow, because death had sheltered him from this destruction.

Layla opened her eyes and nudged Amina, who was lying next to her. "Wake up."

Amina turned to her with a sleepy smile. "Can't I rest a little longer?"

"No. It is time to eat." Maryan handed a bowl of cornmeal to both Amina and Layla. She filled her own bowl and sat near my mother-in-law to eat. She finished her food and put the bowl and spoon away before she spoke. "I didn't sleep at all last night. A nightmare about our plan woke me. It was so vivid and frightening, I tremble even now to think about it."

"It was just a nightmare," I said.

"Yes, but you should have seen it. We were in hell, all of us, clamoring to get out, but it was hopeless."

"Is this not a living hell?" Layla interjected.

"Not compared to my nightmare. Fire was burning all around us, but it wasn't hot. It was ice-cold, and we were freezing." Maryan glared sharply at Layla. "That dream was a message for me—for us. You know as well as I do that disobeying your husband is a sin," she scolded.

"In that case, we should've gone to hell sooner," Layla said with a bitter laugh.

"It is no laughing matter. I want to leave as much as you, perhaps more, but this is a sign not to be ignored." Maryan turned on me. "You have brought conflict into this house. We were fine before you came." She pointed a finger at me.

"Were we?" Layla asked.

Maryan hesitated before continuing. "If she hadn't come here parading the girl, naked and wanton, he wouldn't have seen her. Women should cover up so as not to arouse men's desire."

"She is a child, and you hold her responsible for his wantonness?" I was stunned by the accusation.

"She's is a woman, grown and developed. He sees and he's attracted. Men wouldn't want, if it wasn't our doing."

"So, he'll want any woman in sight."

"He can marry four. You can't deny what's his by right. He's doing nothing wrong. He asked her father, and her father agreed."

"He didn't," I said.

"He must have. Ahmed is a righteous man; he'll do no wrong."

"Do you think your Mr. Righteous married me with my father's permission?" Layla was seething with anger.

"Well! With your long hair and small waist, which you refused to cover, what else could Ahmed conclude, except that you wanted him? The way you walked by the house every day going to the water well, even after I told your mother to keep you inside and make sure you were covered. You still did it and now you are in his bed more nights than I ever was."

"You're jealous of those nights? Pinned under him, all I can think is, how long until he's done?" Layla's voice cracked.

Maryan gave Layla a measured look. "All of you are committing a sin. I won't—I can't—go along with it."

I stood before Maryan to keep the situation from getting any more heated. "You don't have to come. But please, don't tell Ahmed. I have to save my daughter."

"I'd come if I could, only I know it's wrong—we all do. The dream last night was a warning, and all of you are going to a special hell reserved for those who don't listen to warnings."

"Please! I need to save my daughter," I repeated.

"If you wanted to protect her, you should have covered her long before you brought her here. You're going to hell if you...if you go through with this." She finished with an effort and ran out of the room.

"It will be a well-earned hell," Layla called after her.

"Layla, please leave it alone." I stared at the door where Maryan disappeared. "Will she tell on us?" I asked her.

"No, she won't. With us gone, she won't have to share Ahmed." Layla giggled. "But she'll only have him until the next twelve-year-old comes along."

"Or the next nine-year-old," Amina added.

⁂

One alley led to another through a Bledley much different from the one we left. The log cabin inns along the road to the market were deserted. The dry, dark landscape made it hard to recognize the town so ravaged by war, hunger, and drought. The buildings that housed the jewelry and clothing stores and cattle and grain merchant offices appeared as dry and ashen as the people within them. We arrived at the market an hour after we'd left the farm.

Layla nudged me. "The money," she whispered.

I extended my hand with the thousand dollars clutched in it. That was the agreed-upon fee for helping us escape. Layla had arranged it with the two men who guarded the women's sleeping quarters. The thought that others might know of our plan terrified me, but there were no other options. Layla told me the guards would take the money and go to another village. She took the cash from me and passed it to the guard on her right.

He dropped the money into his shoulder sack. "May Allah, reward you," he said, stepping aside along with his partner. They spoke in hushed voices for a minute, and then the one with the money turned to us. "I'll check to see if the truck is leaving soon." He pointed to a vehicle parked a few feet away. He approached the driver standing near the cab. After a few minutes, the guard returned. "He's going to Bledhawa, and they'll start loading soon. Come with me."

We followed him.

"This is my brother and his family," the guard said, pointing at Hasan.

The driver of the truck nodded. "Get inside now. We will leave soon."

We did as we were told.

※

Before long, a young man ushered other passengers in, collecting fares by the door. "Go in, go, go. Pay here and go inside. We have to leave soon." Close to forty adults and children, filled the seats by the time he came inside and closed the door.

He extended his hand to collect even more money. "This is for the militia roadside checkpoints," he told a man sitting next to us.

"I paid my family's fare at the door, just now. You counted it and put it in the box."

"Did you not hear me say just now that it is for the checkpoints on the road? That's extra. Twenty dollars per person."

"It was only ten dollars yesterday. Why more today?"

"Is this yesterday?"

"It is not fair for the price to double in one day. Are you not afraid of Allah?"

The young man became angry. "If Allah gets rid of the road checks, then you'll get your money back. I suggest you pay now and pray hard." The last part, I am certain, elicited many silent prayers.

"You are taking half my money. How will I feed my family for the rest of the journey?"

"That's your problem. Stop wasting time and pay now, or get off."

Having no option, the old man paid.

The youth snatched the money. "Do not make challenging me a habit," he said and moved on to us.

Hasan readied our fee. "Here."

The boy's hungry hand took it unceremoniously. The rest of the passengers paid the surcharge without delay.

About forty minutes after we boarded, the truck pulled out of the yard and drove off.

※

I peered through the gaps between the glass panels on the back of the driver's cab as the vehicle slowed. The glass partition allowed the view of a village ahead. I saw a man come out from behind a tree and slip back in again. He was there for only an instant, and he disappeared just as quickly. "Did you see that?" I asked Layla.

She hadn't.

The slowdown was momentary, and the truck soon returned to its usual speed. For a second, I thought I'd imagined the whole thing. If a person wanted to stop a truck to loot it, he wouldn't duck behind the trees. He'd block the road and make his demands. I looked again, and that *same* man emerged from behind a bush, lifted his arm, and threw a large, round object at us. A white light followed by a loud, screeching noise came at us, and a dark cloud of smoke filled the air. Then everything went black.

※

When I regained consciousness, I was lying on the floor of the truck. The deafening silence reminded me of something Mother told me when I was young. "When other organs and functions fail, the hearing continues. You can hear the mourners leaving your grave. You won't be able to think or feel, but hear, you will." Mother always wagged her finger after such a statement. I shuddered at the memory, but I knew I was not dead because I couldn't hear and I could still think. I climbed down and looked around for the rest of my family. It took a few minutes to locate them amidst the chaos, but even then, the relief of seeing Amina, Adam, and my mother-in-law, alive was short-lived. My head cleared. "Where's Hasan?" I shouted in a panic.

My mother-in-law threw her arms around me. "He went into the village to get some help," she cried, her voice sounding hollow and distant in my ears.

"Where's Layla?" I asked and hurried back inside the truck.

I found Layla, leaning against the driver's seat. A few pieces of glass and some metal shards had entered the passenger cabin through small openings in the wall, but it seemed that no one had suffered major injuries, except Layla and the old man who had argued about the fee when we first boarded. Layla appeared to be just sitting there, waiting for me to come and collect her. Her face was serene and happy, so her injuries couldn't be serious—or so I thought. She waved her right hand, but her eyes closed against her will. I climbed in next to her and saw what was wrong. Layla, pinned under the twisted metal of the cabin floor, could not move. The blast had lifted the floorboard under her and folded it around her thighs. A trace of blood ran from her knees to her feet. I took Layla's hand. She opened her eyes again and smiled. Her lips moved, but I couldn't hear, so I put my ear next to her mouth.

"Thank you for taking me out of that house so I could die in peace. For two years, I never smiled as much as I have smiled since you came." She took a deep breath and closed her eyes. They never opened again, and I knew she was gone.

I sat there for a long time, unable to move away from her.

Hasan eventually came back and found me. "Idil, you can't help her."

I continued to sit, holding Layla's lifeless hand and staring into the distance.

"Idil." Hasan came even closer. "Let her go, Idil."

I lifted Layla's hand, kissed it, and placed it in her lap.

"Here." Hasan extended a white sheet one of the villagers had brought. "Cover her."

I did, and then slipped out of the seat to join my family.

Amina emitted an ear-splitting cry when she saw me leave the truck alone. Adam wept so hard he gasped for air between sobs.

❦

Hasan, with the help of villagers, hastily prepared funeral plans for Layla and the old man and then returned to us. "It is time," he said. "The service will start soon." Covered in blood, dirt, and oil stains, he led us a short distance along the road to a nearby masjid.

The crowd was much thinner than it had been by the truck after we were first attacked. During the brief funeral, the imam encouraged us to pray for the dead and for their return to their Creator, a peaceful sleep in their grave, and an easy reckoning on the Day of Judgment. We stood beside those who didn't know Layla or the man. Later that night, we sat around a fire in an open field that served as a temporary camp for the passengers of the lost truck.

I didn't know Layla well, but the story she'd told me about her family came back to me. "They drowned in a boat on the Red Sea near Yemen," she'd told me as we sat in the truck just that afternoon. "Ahmed refused to let me leave with them, even after my father offered him money. I didn't cry when the news of their deaths came for I had lost them long before that. It was then I stopped crying." Layla had closed her eyes and stopped talking. I didn't ask her any more about it. Now as I sat at the campfire, her loss hit me like a wave and I wept hours after the others went to sleep.

❧

"I found someone who can take us tonight for five hundred dollars." Hasan brought the good news and the man seven days after the attack. "But he says there are no guarantees."

"No guarantees?" I asked.

"The Kenyan border guards are on high alert, so we might not be able to cross. He wants to be paid even if we don't cross."

The man limped in our direction. "This is your family? I didn't know there were so many. Five hundred dollars isn't enough. It's dangerous work for so little money."

Hasan spoke in a calm and measured tone. "Barre, you

agreed to a family of five for five hundred to take us to the camp. That was the deal we made at the market."

Barre's mouth twitched. "I didn't know children were included. Two children and three adults. Five hundred dollars isn't enough. I only want what's fair." Barre's eyes darted like a dragonfly in search of a place to land.

"How much are you asking?"

Barre's face brightened. He swayed back and forth in an exaggerated motion. "I'm a reasonable man. I'll take you for two hundred per adult and a hundred dollars for each child. That's a fair price to get you all the way to Ifo camp. Cheaper than most."

Hasan looked at me for confirmation.

I nodded.

"We'll pay," he said.

"Deal." Barre shook hands with Hasan.

"I'll be back in an hour, so have the money ready," Barre said, and left without waiting for a response.

Barre came back two hours later, driving a battered old car. He lurched back and forth as if his feet were threatening to slip from under him. Green crust from the chat he'd been chewing formed crisscross lines on his lips. His tongue, pink and raw, came out in slow motion, licked his lips, and darted back inside. He brushed his right hand over his eyes as if to rub the sleep away. The words were heavy in his mouth. "Is the money ready?" He labored over each syllable.

Hasan handed him some cash. "We'll give you four hundred dollars now and four hundred when we arrive."

Barre counted the bills with practiced hands. "Thank you. Get in. We have to leave soon because it is going to take five hours to get there." Barre inspected under the hood of the car, turned the key in the ignition, and started driving. He hummed a tune when he reached the main road.

We listened quietly as Barre continued to serenade us. "I should have been a singer. My mother said so herself from the time I was a boy." He tapped a finger on the steering wheel to keep with the beat.

I fell into a deep sleep, soothed by Barre's songs, and when he nudged me awake, I didn't know where I was. It took me a minute to realize I was in Barre's truck. "Are we at the camp?"

"We are almost there. You need to be awake in case they ask any questions. They usually don't once I bribe them, but you never know. Let the children sleep. If the guards see them, they probably won't wake them."

"Okay."

Barre started driving again, until we came upon six men sitting around a fire in front of a border outpost. Four of them stood up when they saw us and pointed their rifles in our direction.

Barre stopped the car and turned the engine off, but he took his time getting out, deliberately avoiding quick movements. He raised his hands before he walked to where the guards stood, and they in turn lowered their weapons. Barre and the men greeted each other like old acquaintances. They shook hands and chatted for a minute. Their smiles brightened when Barre gave some money to one of them. Barre walked back to his vehicle at a leisurely pace. He glanced back twice to assure himself of his accomplishment. "The magic of money," he said when he came to us.

I couldn't believe it was that easy to cross into another

country until the image of the men sitting by their fire grew smaller and receded into the distance. The fifty-miles between the border and Ifo refugee camp was the easiest trip of my life. The fear of not getting out of Somalia and away from Jamac, Father, Rhoda, and Omar fell away and I found myself imagining a future with challenges that I could overcome. The car left the main road and headed toward the camp, and the bright red sandy landscape confirmed that I was far away from the bleak outlook of my former life.

"Here we are," Barre announced at the sight of the endless shacks that littered the place. "I think you line up there." He pointed at the only brick structure. "I could take you to the market if you want to eat something before you start," Barre suggested. We took him up on his offer. Barre waved us a cheerful good-bye at the front of small eatery. "I must visit a friend before I go." He walked toward the west section of the camp, carefully counting the second half of his payment.

# CHAPTER TWENTY-SEVEN

BY THE TIME we had eaten and walked back to the registration site, the line at the office of the United Nations High Commissioner for Refugees in the Ifo Camp looped around the huts surrounding the brick office. I had left the children with their grandmother under a tree to rest while Hasan and I waited in line.

"Should I have my family here to register?" I asked the woman ahead of us.

She moved a baby from her back and placed it on her chest to nurse. "They don't have to stand here. They can come later for their pictures to be taken. It'll be hours before we get to the door." She rocked the baby. "When did you get here?" she asked.

"Just this morning."

"You are lucky to have come today. They only see new refugees on Wednesdays. I've been waiting since I arrived on Monday."

"How long did you travel to get here?" I asked.

"Nine days. We walked on some days and took a cattle truck on others."

The way she spoke suggested she was from my parents' tribe. The distance she'd come confirmed my suspicion. "Did you travel alone?" I asked.

"No. I was with my husband and his mother, but she got sick on the way, and he decided to take her back to die among her own people. I wanted to go with them, but my husband said, 'Go with our little one. Get away from here, now!' He yelled so loud that I had to leave, may Allah forgive me." She stopped as if she'd noticed something. "Where is your husband?"

"I am a widow," I said. "I came with my husband's mother, brother, and my two children."

"Your husband is dead?" She hesitated. "Was he shot? Did a gun take your husband?"

"No, he wasn't shot. He just died."

"At least there's some comfort in that. The sick and dying give us time to accept that they are leaving. A gun takes them without warning. They're here one second and gone in an instant."

We both fell into complete silence as we waited. The woman was right. We stood in line until the sun reached the middle of the sky, pouring down stifling heat. When we were close to the door, I asked Hasan to go and call his mother and the children.

The woman stared at Adam and Amina as they came our way. "These are your children?" She pointed an accusing finger and pulled away as if she were ready to leave the line she'd stood in for hours.

"Yes," I replied, drawing them to me and raising my chin defiantly.

"They don't look like you." She glared at the rest of the family.

In the refugee camp, we might have been far from the reach of our immediate enemies—Father, Omar, Rhoda, Jamac, and Ahmed—but we were not safe. The tribal hatred that had devastated us at home was here in the snickers of the others in line.

"Your children are..." She didn't finish the sentence. She didn't need to. She turned to the woman in front of her. "Those are her children," she whispered loud enough for me to hear. "Why in the name of Allah would she marry a Boon man and still walk around with such children after he died? I would have abandoned them in a heartbeat." The woman spoke as if I were not there.

"She is brave. To drag the Boon's children and his mother after the Boon died is the mark of courage."

"Courage or stupidity?" the first one questioned.

I kept my eyes on the front of the queue.

❧

The process, once inside the office, was much easier than the wait. They wrote all the names of the family members, took pictures, gave us identification cards, assigned us a piece of land to build our tin hut and handed us an ID card. After that, we were asked to register with CARE for our rations and the Red Cross for contacting any relatives we might have outside Somalia. I wrote Elmi's name and gave the address on his last letter, sent two years earlier.

"Why was that woman so mean?" Amina asked as soon as we were well away from her.

I took her by the hand with a weak and weary smile. "I am sorry."

"Why do people hate us so much?"

I could offer no protection from the ever-present bigotry that would follow Amina wherever she went. "Because we are different."

"So?"

Mother's threat to send me to Timbuktu when I had asked why she hated Sidow rang in my ears. "Never mind. We won't allow them to hurt us because they don't matter," I said. But I knew they did matter. Oh, how I knew they mattered.

❦

A messenger from the Red Cross office handed me an envelope a month after our arrival at the camp. *Your brother Elmi has been located. Come to the office tomorrow morning at 8:30.*

I read and reread the note that night and the following morning, until I started out for the office much earlier than necessary.

I spent most of the ten minutes they gave me on the phone with Elmi trying to speak, but I ended up crying each time I opened my mouth. The words of joy and gratitude that formed in my mind, weren't reaching my tongue.

"I have been looking for you ever since Father told me you left Mogadishu. I am so happy you have contacted me."

"Father?" I repeated.

"Yes. Father said you were at his home, but you…" Elmi's sentence, naked and incomplete, hung in the air.

"I did what?" I asked.

"Father said he wanted to make sure you were safe, but you refused to stay."

I laughed bitterly. "He has a strange idea of what *home* and *safe* means."

"Why? What happened?" he asked with concern.

Maybe it was good that Elmi didn't know. Part of me wanted to tell, to make sure he knew how evil Father, Omar, Jamac, and Rhoda were, but I couldn't—not on the phone, not like this. "You should ask Father, or better yet, Rhoda."

"I'll ask Father, then. I don't talk to Rhoda, or Omar for that matter." Our time was running out and Elmi changed the subject abruptly to deal with more urgent matters. "I'm coming to visit you as soon as I can. Send me the names and ages of everyone in the family. I'll try to apply for immigration visas to Canada before I leave."

Elmi called me six weeks later to say that with the help of a local church and a financial guarantee of twenty thousand dollars from him, our visa process would start soon.

"All that money for us." I was in awe for the depth of the commitment needed to get us out of the camp.

"It is to ensure that the people who come are not a burden on the existing society," Elmi explained.

"We'll not be a burden to anyone, not to the country, not to the church, not to you."

"I know, you won't."

I shared the good news with Hasan and my mother-in-law. The whole family rejoiced at the hope brought on by Elmi's call.

❄

Three months after his first call and four months after we came to the camp. Elmi visited. I cried more than I spoke for the entire two weeks he was with us. Elmi's coming coincided with the notice of an intake interview scheduled by the High Commission of Canada.

"My immigration lawyer in Canada told me there would be an interview in the next few days, so I decided to be here with you for that," Elmi said us as soon as he arrived.

On the morning of the interview, our neighbors visited in droves, congratulating us on the quick opportunity to leave the camp. Amina, and Adam waved us good-bye for children weren't required to attend, but the walk to the office where the interview by the High Commissioner of Canada was to be held felt long.

"Do you want to sit?" Elmi asked as soon as we entered the waiting room.

"I am not tired, just afraid."

"I know, but it will be over soon. The wait is the hardest part." Elmi sat down and patted the chair beside him.

Sitting next to Elmi, I tried to calm down, but the old wooden chair wasn't large enough to contain me. A wave of uncertainty rumbled within me, so I got up and paced around the waiting area to soothe my frayed nerves. "What happens if they reject us?"

"There is no reason to think like that. This is a family class application. It's already been approved in Canada. This is just to make sure everything matches what I put on the application."

"What's taking them so long?" I wondered aloud.

An hour later, an attendant opened the door. "Moallim family." His raspy voice startled me. "Come." He motioned for us to follow him inside.

Elmi smiled at me. "I'll be right here when you return."

Hasan, my mother-in-law, and I followed the attendant.

The man sitting behind a large oak desk looked up from a folder when we entered. He pointed at the wooden chairs lined up against the wall. "I'm Mr. Hanson. Are you the Moallim family?" he asked through an interpreter—a young Somali man sitting to our left.

"Yes," I responded.

"Do you have a husband?"

When I told him I was a widow, he asked the details of Sidow's death, the way I found him, who told me where his body was, and what condition he was in. The painful memory prickled my senses.

The officer allowed me to stop several times to compose myself and continue. "Do you have a death certificate for your husband?" he asked.

I looked at him, surprised. I explained that due to the war there was no way to get any certificate: birth, marriage, or death.

Mr. Hanson spent the next few seconds searching though some folders. He finally found what he was after and handed me an official-looking sheet of paper. "Here. Please fill out this form."

The paper required the date of Sidow's death, the cause of death, and his age at the time of death. Upon completion, I handed it back to him.

He gave me a blank piece of paper. "Describe the position of the body as you remember it."

It was not too hard to locate the image of Sidow in my mind, but it was very difficult to look at it. I had spent so much energy suppressing the horror that the road back to it was treacherous. I stared at the page, unable to start.

"Just do as much as you can," the officer urged. He wanted me to include the location of Sidow's wounds. Finally, he took the paper from me and examined it carefully. "Thank you. This will do." He turned the paper face-down and wrote notes on the back of the page.

The officer moved on to inquire about my relationship with Elmi, our sponsor. He listened to the rest of my narrative and the reasons behind my application.

"How many children do you have?"

It was a simple question, but I gasped. The man raised his eyebrows, peered at me, stared for a few seconds, and turned to the interpreter. "Madam, how many children do you have?" he asked again.

"Two," I answered. The hesitation that came with the word planted itself between us like a pack of hyenas. I waited for his suspicion to transform into a question, but nothing came except that distinct kick in my belly. It jolted me back to reality just as it had absorbed my attention for the past few weeks.

"And their ages?" He was now looking at papers, taking notes, his demeanor less suspicious, almost indifferent.

I corrected my error through the second answer. "My daughter is eleven, my son is nine, and I am almost five months pregnant." The truth had to come out.

The man impatiently sifted through the heap of paperwork. He pulled out a few sheets that were stapled together, flipped through them until he located what he was looking for. He took his reading glasses off and trained his pale blue eyes on me.

"Your application says your husband died quite a while ago." He kept his eyes on the form as if the information would disappear if he looked away.

"I was raped," I whispered, the shame and despair burning my face.

The man didn't flinch. The stories he heard in these interviews must have made it impossible for anything to surprise him. For a fleeting second I felt sorry for him. It was painful to tell my dreadful tale, but what must it be like to receive such tales daily and document the horror?

"Were you raped here, in the refugee camp?"

"No, in Somalia," I forced a response.

"Did you know your attacker?"

The memory of that horrible night came back. Jamac's eyes, wild with lust, stared out from the recesses of my mind. I tried to wipe the hideous image away by blinking several times, but it was impossible. My stomach lurched, and I had only enough time to turn before emptying my meagre breakfast onto the cement floor. Tears produced by my effort to quell the memory filled my eyes, and I couldn't see. No one said a word.

My mother-in-law used her shawl to wipe my face and mouth. "I am sorry, my dear."

"So am I." I wept more.

Mr. Hanson ended the interview and closed the folder

with an audible clap. He got up, stood next to the desk, and handed me a paper. "Take this and get a pregnancy test at the clinic. Have the nurse fill out these forms and send them back to us as soon as possible." He called for someone to clean up the mess on the floor, announced a lunch break, and, with a twist of his heel, left with his interpreter in tow.

"Sorry," I apologized to Elmi when we got outside.

"Sorry for what?" he asked.

"For telling the man about the rape—messing up the interview."

Elmi gasped. "You were raped? By whom?"

"Your father's people," my mother-in-law responded, her voice stern.

My stomach heaved again, but I had nothing more to purge.

"Jamac? Jamac *raped* you? Why didn't you tell me that when I first called? He did it in the house? It all makes sense now; the way you left, and how Father said you refused protection. I knew how devastated Jamac was when you married Sidow. After you left, Father and Mother tried to soothe his damaged manhood with false praise about how he deserved a better wife than you. Still, he studied your photos as if he could summon you from the images. I was afraid he'd come after you that same night to show he wasn't as cowardly as others labelled him. I stayed close to him, but all he did was mutter, 'Idil must experience what she's missed,' but then he went home with his parents the following day." Elmi was angrier then I had ever seen him.

"You didn't tell me this when you visited me before the wedding," I said.

"There was no point. Jamac went home, and I thought he would eventually forget about you and marry another girl. Did Father help him? Did Omar or Rhoda? Who else was involved? I will go to Somalia and kill all of them." Elmi wasn't speaking to me anymore. With one look, I could see the plan forming in his mind.

"No, don't do that. You can't go after them; you can't talk about this at all. Forget I said anything. My children and I— this whole family—all we have is you. Please leave this alone."

"After what they have done to you, how can I?" Elmi was near tears. In the safety of the UNHCR compound, he gathered me in his arms and gave me a warm and soothing hug. "I am sorry you had to suffer so." He kissed me on the cheek.

"Please, you must forget about this because without you, we will all be lost," I pleaded.

"Elmi, Idil is right," Hasan said. "The best thing to do right now is to help us leave this place."

My brother relented and gave me his word.

Two days after the interview, we said good-bye and Elmi returned to Canada. "Don't worry. You'll get through this," he promised.

The five of us stood by the road that led away from the camp and waved as Elmi entered the rented car that would take him to the airport.

# CHAPTER TWENTY-EIGHT

THE PREGNANCY TEST showed nothing more than what I'd known all along; the result was positive. Even so, I had hoped the nurse would tell me otherwise. I so wanted her to say the baby was growing in my mind, not in my womb. She didn't.

My mother-in-law, sitting next to me in the small office, put her hand on my shoulder. "Place your trust in Allah, my dear," she said.

I held on to her so I didn't float away into the nothingness that surrounded me. The nurse looked at me with kind and caring eyes. "You're too late to have an abortion," she said.

I wouldn't have had an abortion in any case, but the fact that I'd had no choice about getting pregnant and no choice to terminate it tugged at my heart.

The nurse pulled out the papers she had received from my file and filled out the forms. "How many other times have you been pregnant?"

"Two full terms, one miscarriage, and this." I pointed at my belly.

She signed the papers, and put them in an envelope. "I'll send these to the office," she said, and walked us to the door.

"I am pregnant," I told Elmi when he called me three weeks later.

"I know," he replied. "I received a call from my lawyer here, and he says you are approved for travel, but they have to wait until after the baby is born. Once you provide a birth certificate, you'll all get your visas."

Elmi took a deep breath before he spoke again. "Every time I think of what has happened to you—the way they treated you—I want to kill them all."

"Don't think like that," I said. If it was possible for anyone to comprehend the depth of the violation, Elmi did.

"Remember to notify the office as soon as the baby is born," Elmi reminded me each time he called.

❧

A healthy seven-pound baby boy arrived two weeks past his due date. If the baby had known the trouble that waited outside the womb, he would have stayed inside even longer. It was a short labor, but there was no Sidow to rush in and cover me with kisses. Oh, what I would have given to be in his embrace right then.

My mother-in-law stood next to the midwife, smiling and took the baby to clean him.

Caught somewhere between the joy of the new life and grief from the misery around us, I would've cried, but for the gift of her strength.

"Look at him!" She brought him to me. "Such a blessing." Her face wore the bright smile I hadn't seen for a long time. "Can we name him Sidow?"

I wasn't sure I could handle the constant reminder. "That's his father's name," I said instead.

She turned with raised brows. "He'll be his father's son." Her smile lit up the whole room.

"If that's what you want." I forced a smile. "He'll be Sidow's Sidow." I laughed at the thought.

"Let us call him Sidow Moallim Sidow." The sound of the name on her mouth was soothing. "Could we do that?" she asked.

"Why not? He's ours and we'll call him whatever we want." If I looked close enough with my eyes half closed, the baby shared similarities to Amina and Adam; the extended jawlines and the large, dark eyes.

❧

A month later, my mother-in-law entered the hut in a hurry while I was nursing the baby. "Rhoda is here." She took a blanket from the basket next to me and draped it over little Sidow to hide him from Rhoda.

I massaged my throat to loosen the lump that was lodged inside. "What does she want?" I asked, alarmed that she had tracked us down to the camp.

"I don't know, but she is asking for you. Should I let her in?"

I nodded.

"There you are." Rhoda entered, cradling her purse.

"How did you find me?" I asked unceremoniously.

"What, no greeting?" Rhoda asked innocently.

"Why are you here?" I had no intention of being civil to her.

As if she had read my thoughts, Rhoda's tone changed. "It turns out Omar needs your help."

"And what makes you think I would help Omar, or any of you?"

"You will if it means we leave you and your children alone. I promise not to say anything to my brother about the baby if you cooperate."

"What does the baby have to do with anything?"

"You got away with wrongdoings twice, once for marrying the Boon instead of Jamac, and the other time for escaping after he'd planted his seed inside you. You won't be as lucky the third time. This is Jamac's son, and you are raising him among Boons. That would not be tolerated, but I'll keep my mouth shut if you agree to help." Rhoda winked slyly as she finished speaking. "You might be out of Somalia, but you are not out of our reach."

She was right. The tribal troubles I faced in Somalia didn't end at the border. However, the mention of my child and Jamac in the same sentence sent tiny filaments of worry spreading through my lungs. I struggled to breathe. "What do you want with me?" I forced the words out.

Rhoda grinned, having gained my full attention. "Jamac is holding both Omar and your father hostage for your wrongdoings. At first, Jamac agreed to a payment for the broken deal your parents made, and the gaalo whore was supposed pay him. But she bought an airline ticket and left as soon as she was in Kenya. And guess who is here after Omar's precious wife disappeared with the money! Me, his *real* wife! Now that she and the money are gone, it is you and I who must fix this."

Rhoda continued listing Sheila's transgressions. "That whore fooled everyone—the elders, your parents, and Omar—but I knew she was nothing more than a lying swindler, in it for the money and nothing else."

"I am not interested in your complaints about Sheila or about the so-called deal." I hated Rhoda's presence just as much as I hated dealing with her. "You forget, Rhoda, that *I* made no agreement."

"Nevertheless, you will visit Omar when he is brought to Garissa in the custody of our tribal relatives there. You will hear his request and fulfill it, or I will call on the tribe to come and take your baby. You will help Omar gain his freedom and in turn secure your own."

"I *am* free, you—"

"You will *never* be free, not while you are raising my nephew as a Boon child." Rhoda cut me off. "Can you imagine what Jamac would do if he found out you have his son among Boons? It must be apparent by now that we can reach you wherever you are. This way you don't have to look over your shoulder, and Omar will be happy to answer all the questions you have."

"What questions?"

"You must want to know about Sidow, and what Jamac did after you eloped."

I sat forward. "What about Sidow?"

"Ask Omar. I wasn't there."

Rhoda had me and she knew it. "I'll return and tell you when you can visit Omar. May I hold the baby?" Rhoda extended her hands for the child she had just threatened to take from me.

I held him even closer.

Rhoda dropped her arms at her sides. "Idil, you are a lucky woman, and I am happy for you. You have three children, but you must do this to keep the third one!"

This threat was not even thinly veiled. Rhoda was more than willing to play her final card and tell Jamac he was a father. Our eyes met, and Rhoda smiled knowingly before she turned to leave.

⁂

"Rhoda wants me to visit Omar and help free him," I started our phone conversation when Elmi called a day later.

Elmi didn't ask why, how, when, or where Omar was, but his response was clear. "You can't visit him. Please tell me you won't. After everything they have done to you, surely you recognize this as a trap."

"I have to go."

"You don't have to! Why do you have to do anything? You don't need him; he was never a brother and he never will be."

"Elmi, Rhoda knows the baby is Jamac's. They'll take him from me. She said they would leave me and my family alone if I visited Omar. If I refuse, she could send someone to snatch my child."

"And you believe her? The woman who said she would

give you a ride and set you up to be raped? What makes you think she'll leave you alone after you do what they want?"

"They know where I am. I can't get away!" The fear I'd been pushing down, rose to the surface. "This way, I can buy time until I leave."

"You can leave the camp. I'll send you some money to rent a place near the airport. You have less than a month to wait for your visa."

"Elmi, I don't want her to find out I am leaving for Canada. It's safer to pretend to work with her until it is time to go."

"If you are determined to see him, don't do it without me. I'll come as soon as I can, so don't go before I get there. Promise." Elmi wouldn't hang up until we reached a firm agreement.

Two days after Elmi's return and two weeks after she'd first visited me, Rhoda met me on my way back from the ration queue. With the passing of time, I had begun to hope that whatever help Omar had needed from me, he didn't anymore. My heart sank when I saw her coming.

Breathless, Rhoda started talking in short, choppy sentences before she even reached me. "Omar is in Garissa. He is being held by members of our tribe who live there. They are supporting Jamac because they think he was wronged. Omar is waiting for your visit!"

"Why did they bring him all the way to Garissa?"

"Jamac was afraid the two factions of the tribe—the group that supported Jamac and the others who are on Omar's side—might start fighting if he kept Omar closer to home. He told everyone that Omar left the country on a business trip. Since Jamac was living with your father before the fight, no one suspects anything."

"Where is Father?"

"Omar will tell you. It is two hours away. Do you need a ride?" Rhoda's eyes landed on the baby strapped to my chest, but she didn't threaten me this time.

"No, I have a ride." I didn't want to mention Elmi was here. The less they knew, the better.

Rhoda walked away, but after a few steps she stopped and turned around to face me. "Idil, remember. In the end, Omar and you will be free. You'll get to raise *all* your children, and Omar will be able to take his money back from the whore. And I will have my husband back. We will all win."

"I will visit Omar tomorrow," I said.

Rhoda pushed a paper with hastily scrawled directions and an address into my hand then gave me a cheery wave before she left.

# CHAPTER TWENTY-NINE

"IDIL, WE HAVE to go. It's a long drive." Elmi walked to the door and back.

I was anxious to have my questions answered by Omar, but apprehensive at the same time. I'd heard parts of the story about Sidow, Mother, and Father. There was the one bracelet and the money, and Jamac's comment about Mother's accident. Two deaths with no satisfying explanation. "I don't want to see Omar, but I have to protect little Sidow and hear the facts about what happened for myself," I said aloud, trying to justify the madness of my actions. "I must convince everyone that I'm cooperating until we are able to leave."

Elmi walked me out to the rented car. He got in, adjusted the rearview mirror, and we were on our way. "You know how I feel about this," he said. "I am only going because you won't be talked out of it. But I want you to know you can change your mind right up until you are sitting in front of Omar."

He swerved the car to avoid hitting a dog that ran across the camp road.

My head was spinning with thoughts, and they kept me quiet. *Is this another trap? Will we be in danger? Will Omar answer my questions? Can I stand to hear the truth, or is it better not to know? Will Rhoda keep her word to leave my child alone?*

"I don't like this," Elmi continued, "but I'll play this game if I must, until your visas come through." Elmi rested a hand on the gearshift as we left the dust-filled refugee camp behind and reached the main road.

The tires hummed against the pavement. After two hours of driving, Elmi parked the car in front of a wire mesh fence. "I'll be right here," he said.

I walked away from Elmi and toward the gate.

"Who are you here for?" an armed guard asked.

"My brother, Omar Hussein Nuur."

The guard led me to a small room. "Wait here, I'll bring him in."

The furniture in the room consisted of a metal table and four folding chairs.

The door creaked. I turned instinctively, and my eyes landed on Omar. Big, rusty shackles looped around his hands and legs. Metal chains clanked with every step he took.

The guard ushered him in. "You have thirty minutes," he said.

I saw the bracelet on Omar's wrist under the cuff before he reached the table. "Where did you get that?" I asked, pointing to his wrist.

Omar didn't answer. He walked slowly to the chair across from me and sat down. Unlike the pressed suits and stylish clothes he was used to, he wore an old pair of filthy cream-colored pants, an oversized T-shirt that hung loosely around him, and sandals made of tire inner tubes. His exposed skin was dry and ashen, making him appear as though he was suffering from an acute case of malaria.

After a long and agonizing minute, our eyes met. Before he even began, the debate to stay and listen, or walk away raged inside my head. I knew I wouldn't like what I was going to hear, but I needed to stay for my child and to get to the truth. "Where did you get that bracelet?" I asked again.

Omar glanced at his wrist and looked up. "You married a Boon man, and I did nothing." Omar was angry.

"What does that have to do with anything?"

Omar didn't hear or didn't want to hear. "I avoided gatherings because others mocked me. Even my closest friends, people I would have expected to support me, whispered as I approached and stopped talking when I joined them. But I didn't blame them. I deserved such treatment because I was the coward who didn't rescue his sister from a shameful existence." He continued to stare at the shackles on his hands.

"Where did you get that bracelet!" I tried to force Omar to focus on the question, but he was moving farther and farther away from it. My plan to gather information and keep the meeting under my control was going up in flames.

"I should have done it sooner. Before the children. You weren't supposed to have any. Mother said she was sure you wouldn't have children, but you had two. None of that would have happened, if I'd done right from the start." His hand caressed the rough surface of the table, and his lips quivered.

"All I am asking is where you found that bracelet."

Omar slammed the table with his shackled hands. "Please forgive me! I failed you. Jamac couldn't understand why we allowed such a travesty to take place. He wanted you so badly."

Jamac's image, violent and vicious, filled my mind. I felt nauseated and swallowed hard. "So, he raped me instead."

Omar sat up, strong and unwavering. "I know Jamac is selfish, but he didn't rape you. He made love to you, showed you what you'd given up when you married a Boon."

I rose so quickly that the chair clattered to the floor behind me. The guard looked in, his ample body filling the doorway and blocking the light. I moved backwards, away from Omar. He had limited mobility, but I was still afraid he might come after me.

"Wait! You didn't hear Sidow's story." For the first time, Omar called Sidow by name.

I hesitated for a second, wanting to go back, but my insides twisted. I had to leave before my stomach heaved again. The guard stepped aside to let me pass.

I staggered toward Elmi. He opened the car door and let me in. "What happened?" he asked as he climbed in the driver's side.

"He apologized for not protecting me from marrying a Boon."

"You should never have come here. Nothing good is ever gained from dealing with him." Elmi took a deep breath. "What did he say about Sidow?"

"Omar spoke about his cowardice for not 'taking care' of Sidow sooner."

"Even when we were children, he viewed torturing living creatures as a sport," Elmi said.

"He says Jamac didn't rape me." I covered my face with my hands, trying to piece together what had happened.

"We share blood with such evil." Elmi inserted the key in the ignition, but didn't start the engine.

For a few minutes, I sat in the car, trying to calm my racing heart and sick stomach. "I think I have go back," I told Elmi.

"Are you sure?"

"If I leave like this, they'll think I don't want to work with them."

Elmi removed the key from the ignition, walked around the car, and opened my door without another word.

❦

Omar was still where I had left him, his head between his hands, that same guard sitting across from him. The man stopped talking and got up as soon as I entered. "I will wait by the door," he said and stepped out of my way.

Omar looked up. "Thank you for coming back."

"What did you say about Sidow?" I asked, trying to take advantage of Omar's relief at seeing me.

"I did what I should have done in the beginning."

"What did you do?"

Omar stared into the distance as if watching the events unfold before him. "Sidow wanted to leave as soon as he realized it was all a trick, and there was no job for him. He wanted to run home to you like a whipped dog."

"You…" I couldn't finish the sentence.

"He had no right to be with you."

"*What did you do?*" I forced the words. I had suspected my family played a role in Sidow's death because of the way Mother had found him in that alley, far from where she had any business being. Still, it was hard to take in.

Omar shook his head. "It was my duty as your brother to protect you, to make sure you did what was right by marrying Jamac, whether you agreed or not. But I didn't."

"So, you killed my husband, the father of my children?"

Omar spoke again. "Sidow laughed at me when I proposed that he divorce you. I promised him no harm would come to him or his children if he gave you your freedom. I even offered him money, but he looked at me as if I was crazy for suggesting such a thing. He said no, so I struck him. I knew you wanted to be rid of him, to be free from your mistake." Omar tried to reach for me, but the chains on his hands prevented him.

"Sidow fought back. During the struggle, he reached into his pocket for this." Omar extended the wrist with the bracelet and held it out. "There were two. What happened to the other one, I can't say."

I proceeded to remove the bracelet from Omar's wrist, and he didn't stop me. As I unfastened it, I could imagine Sidow reaching for the bracelets and taking comfort from them. I closed my eyes to shut the image out, but only succeeded to blur it for a couple seconds. Soon it was in focus again.

Omar continued with the story. "I kicked and punched him until all the rage and anger left my body. Finally, I had done the right thing. I took care of you as a brother should." Omar leaned over the table as far as the chains would allow and smiled.

"You killed my husband!"

"But you understand why it had to be done. It was long overdue, I admit, but I was no longer the man who let his sister marry a Boon and did nothing about it." He dropped both hands in his lap and looked at me with those evil eyes.

"You didn't free me, you selfish moron. *You killed my husband!*" I yelled so loud that the guard poked his head in and cautioned me to keep it down.

Sweat dripped from Omar's face as he relived the memory of killing Sidow. "Instead of acknowledging my selfless deed, Father yelled at me for killing Sidow, instead of convincing him to divorce you. Father and I had tried once before to scare Sidow into giving you your freedom. First I had my men beat him and tell him that if he didn't bring you back to your family, he would pay the price. They brought him back to you and he was given a week to do right. He didn't seem to understand the message."

"Sidow said he didn't know his attackers."

"Why would he tell you when he knew you would leave him and return to your family?"

"Sidow knew I loved him and would never have left him."

Omar rested his head on the table. "Clearly he didn't. I tried to make him divorce you, but he refused. You see Idil, I had to kill him to secure your freedom."

My heart raced. "I *loved* Sidow with every ounce of my being!"

"Well, the man is dead now. No harm in saying you loved him." Omar's words were hard and cold. "Now that you are free, I need your help." Omar smiled. "It is time for *you* to protect *us*."

The switch from telling me he'd killed Sidow, to asking for my help came at a dizzying speed. I wiped my tears on the sleeve of my dress and sat up straight. "I have nothing left to protect."

Omar smiled, mocking. "Ah, but you have so much to lose starting with that baby of yours." His voice was even. The statement was not only a threat, but a promise with precise consequences.

Omar was just sitting across the table, but his words came from far away. "I want you to tell the tribal elders that you will marry Jamac. You don't have to marry him; you just have to say you will."

"Are you crazy?"

Omar lifted his hands in full view and the clanking from the metal rings filled the room. "I've done my part and made you free. Now it's your turn to return the favor. Free me from these shackles by promising to live up to your end of the bargain." Omar let his hands drop on the table to punctuate the sentence.

"Speak to the elders Rhoda takes you to next week and tell them you are ready to honor your the commitment to marry Jamac. Tell them you'll marry him in two weeks, but that you want to go back to Somalia to do it. I will take care of the rest."

"Why go back to Somalia?"

"Jamac was angry when you married the Boon, but he was enraged when you escaped the second time. He blamed Rhoda for not letting him guard you until the marriage was complete. He blamed Mother for not delivering her part of the bargain, and me for not convincing the Boon to divorce you. Above all, he hated Father for suggesting that he forget about you and find another wife."

"So Jamac is holding Father until I agree to marry him?"

"You see Idil, it is not the marriage so much as it is the man's pride that was damaged by your actions. Father allowed Jamac to move into the house with him so he could help Jamac get over your betrayal. I told Father it wasn't safe to keep him around. Anyone could see he was a dangerous man. But Father thought that keeping him close would prove to Jamac that we were on his side. Father even searched for another wife for Jamac, but that only made the situation worse."

Omar shook his head. "Jamac is such a treacherous man. He asked Father to bring you back, or to give him one hundred thousand dollars to compensate for your escape. We agreed to pay him, but then Sheila left with the money.

"In the end Father told Jamac to be a man and find a woman who wanted him. Father tried to walk away, but Jamac shouted after him to come back or he'd regret it. Father continued walking to the door, and I followed. That's when Jamac pulled his gun and fired into the ceiling. When Father and I turned around, we saw that our guards were suddenly working for Jamac. We had four guns pointing at us."

"Father's guards sided with Jamac?"

"They believed Jamac had been humiliated and that he should earn his dignity back. A little extra money in their pockets probably helped too," Omar said.

"Where is Father now?"

"He is here in this compound with me. As you know, he is a very proud man and he didn't want to come to you, asking favors." Omar rubbed his neck. "Jamac claims that if you marry him, he will free both Father and me. Otherwise, we will have to pay him off, or die."

*Now I am expected to sacrifice myself and my children to save Father and Omar.*

The room was profoundly quiet, until Omar asked, "Did Rhoda bring you here?"

"I didn't come with her. Elmi gave me a ride."

Omar became visibly angry. "I cannot believe this! Elmi is here and he didn't come in? Why not?"

"Did you want him to?"

"Why wouldn't I? I need help. If he were in my place, I would have done anything to free him. He doesn't want to face me because he is a coward. He is afraid I might ask him to stay here and take care of his family, instead of running back to Canada." Omar sat back filling the room with rage.

My thoughts reeled. I knew, without a doubt, I was dealing with a madman. I regretted mentioning Elmi's name. "Rhoda didn't—"

"Rhoda! I don't want anything to do with her! I am only pretending to love her until her brother releases me. Then I'll get my money back from Sheila and kill Jamac for what he's done. Our family needs to band together. And like you and me, Elmi must do his part. Mother is gone and Father is no longer in charge, so we must take care of each other. As for Rhoda, if she thought I would keep her, and she'd become the woman of the house now that Mother is gone, she would kill Jamac herself. I don't want either one of them anywhere near me."

Truly, Rhoda, Omar, and Jamac deserved each other.

"I need you to free me from Jamac and Elmi to help me get my money back from Sheila," Omar continued.

"And where is *she* now?" I asked.

"Sheila's disappeared. She withdrew all the money from the business because her name was on the account. Everything is gone. That's why you must pretend to consent to marrying Jamac. It's the only way to free Father and me. If you do as I say, you can have anything you want: money, Mother's house, anything."

"I don't want your money or the house. I need nothing from you."

"The Boon is dead now, so just apologize for marrying him and never mention the children again. We can even send them overseas so they get a good education. No one ever needs to know about them."

"Deny my children?" I got up to go at the same time as the guard entered the room.

"Time's up," he announced.

The sight of the large man was a relief, but Omar continued to rant. "You will help me, won't you?" He spoke urgently to fit in as many words as he could in the seconds he had left.

The guard's impatient command came again, this time with a yank on Omar's shoulder. "Time to go."

Omar rambled. "You will come back. We will plan this together next time you visit."

"All right," I promised. "I will go with Rhoda to the elders and promise them to marry Jamac." I prayed with all my being there would never be another visit.

Rhoda was sitting in my shack when we got back to the camp. "What did Omar say?" she asked. She had waited for our return and was obviously intent on hearing the result of my visit with her husband. I hated that she saw Elmi with me, but it couldn't be helped.

"You know very well. He wants me to marry Jamac," I said.

Elmi was livid about what I'd told him on the way back in the car. He stared angrily at Rhoda.

"Idil," she said, "you only have to tell the elders you will marry Jamac. You don't actually have to. That is the only way Jamac will allow your father's or Omar's release."

"You want me to help the man who admits—who is proud—that he killed Sidow because it was his duty?"

"Sorry." Her apology was brief and insincere.

"Did you know of the plan to kill my husband?"

"No…I didn't," Rhoda said. The hesitation said more than her denial.

"What *did* you know?" I demanded.

"I asked your mother if Omar told her where to find Sidow's body, because he came and spoke to her right before Sidow was found. Your mother said Omar wasn't involved— that one of the workers told her where to find the remains."

The hair on the back of my neck stood up. "Omar admits he did it. He gave me all the gruesome details. He was wearing this bracelet. Sidow had two when he left. The other one was in that can Father gave me at the funeral."

Rhoda's eyes opened wide as she confronted the undeniable evidence. "So that's what was in that can! Your mother kept it so close to her. This is the first time I've heard anything

about Omar's role. I didn't know he was in any way responsible. Believe me." Rhoda was doing her best to stay calm.
"Let's just concentrate on getting Omar out of Jamac's control so he can get the money back from the whore."

"We don't care about the money," Elmi said.

"Well, maybe you don't, but Idil has another reason,
more important than money or pride, to do this." Rhoda's
tone was calm as she played her last card. The renewed threat
of losing my baby was not lost on me.

Elmi opened his mouth to say more, but I placed my
hand on his upper arm. "Elmi, let it go." His muscles relaxed
under my touch.

I turned to Rhoda. "I will do it. Let me know when the
elders are here, and I will say what you want me to say."

Rhoda smiled, believing she had maneuvered us
brilliantly.

Elmi didn't say a word until she was gone. "Let us pray
your visas come before the elders do," he said.

※

For the first time in a very long time, our prayers were
answered. Only one week after my visit with Omar, I sat
across from the officer conducting the final interview. I was
uncomfortable under his scrutiny and shifted my weight
from one side to the other, trying to relax.

The officer acknowledged us quickly and got down to
business. "Thank you for sending the baby's documents. Is
there anything more I should know? Has anything come to
light since our last meeting?"

"No, nothing has changed," I lied. I was tempted to tell of Omar's involvement with my husband's demise, but I couldn't take a chance on delaying our departure. Legal complications at this point would cost me time I didn't have. If we were to leave with all three of my children, nothing could come to light. Also, Hasan and my mother-in-law were present, and I didn't want them to hear about Sidow's death like that. Later, once we were safe, I would have time to share the awful details of Sidow's last day.

"Mrs. Moallim, do you have anything more to add?" the officer asked again.

"No, I can't think of anything."

"I am satisfied with your application and I'm ready to issue visas for you and your family. You are leaving next Wednesday, five days from now." After wishing us good luck in our new home, he dismissed us, and the attendant led us out.

&

Five days later, we were looking up at the airplane that would take us out of hell, and into what we hoped—with no certainty at all—was heaven. I was grateful that Elmi was on the same flight back to Canada.

"Idil, come." Elmi hoisted the baby up and stood at the gangway. "It's time to board."

"Mom, we have to go," Amina yanked at my hand and ran ahead to catch up with Elmi, Hasan, and her grandmother. "Mom!" she yelled again. "Come on. Hurry!"

Adam followed her.

I suddenly felt caught between two worlds; the one I

knew didn't want me any more than I wished to stay in it, and the one I was not sure would be welcoming. Stoic and somber, I cried inside. I cried for the pain my husband had endured all his life, especially the years he was married to me, and particularly the three days he was held captive before he died. I cried because it was my own brother who committed murder under the guise of helping to rid me of my shame. I cried for Amina's and Adam's futures as they encounter those, including their own uncle, who believe people like them and their father are disposable. I cried for my baby because of his beginnings and his uncertain future. I cried for what might have been, what won't be, the void that will never be filled. I cried for my lost love, my husband, my friend, and the father of my children. I cried for my Sidow.

"Here I come," I said aloud and followed my family.

# ACKNOWLEDGMENTS

Although the book bears my name, there are so many people to thank for the fact that I am here writing this acknowledgment.

To my sister, Ruqia Kusow, who, when I was thirteen, gave me my first notebook where the outline for my first creative writing was formed. Your courage, support, and kindness are the light that illuminates my way to every success. To my children, your ultimate trust in me is an honor for which I give prayers of thanks every day. Your unconditional love and gratitude for all I do gets me through everything, no matter how difficult. For my nieces and nephews—you are the hope for the future. Thank you for being so much more than nieces and nephews. My brothers Abdi Kusow, Mohamud Bono, Abdulaahi Kusow, Ali Kusow, Ahmed Kusow, and Isaaq Kusow, who told me you believed in me when I needed to hear it the most. Without your constant support and unwavering belief this project wouldn't have been possible. My sisters Yasmina Bouraoui, Naciimo Huseen, Shukri Nur, Fadumo Abukar, Lul Omar, and Fadumo Omar, having you in my life makes a world of difference. Thank you. You have been there for me in more ways than my words can capture.

Special thanks and gratitude goes to my publisher, Margie Wolfe, for giving voice to my words. To my editor, Kathryn Cole, for believing in my worth as an author, while holding me to the deadlines for those rounds of revisions and rewrites. Thank you for all your questions about the words and ideas I assumed were clear to the reader. You are the champion for this story.

Thank you to Lorie Schofield, Donna Priestyeski, and Leslie Harper-Reid for reading the roughest of drafts and pulling the story out of the mess. Your commitment and time is greatly appreciated.

To my Ann Arbor Area writing group, Karen Simpson, Patricia Tompkins, Shelley Schanfield, Ellen Halter, Kim Peters Fairley, Karen Wolff, Skipper Hammond, Dave Wanty, Yma Johnson, Ellie Andrews, Rachel Lash Maitra, Naomi Petainen, Leslie McGraw, Kay Posselt, Ray Juracek, Danniel Kurt Gilbert, Donnelly Wright Hadden, and Beth Neal, you have taken me in at my loneliest of times when I had nothing more than hope and helped me find the story hidden beneath the confused sentences and complicated plotlines.

To the Write on Windsor writing group, Mick Ridgewell, Ben Van Dongen, Christian Laforett, Alberto Bernal, Jessica Gouin, Rand Hoppe, Roy James, Kathleen Rockey, and Christine Haydon, thank you for keeping me vigilant against pitfalls of repeated words and information dumping.

I am especially grateful to Michael Drakich, Rachel Pieters Mumford, and Lori Lorimer for giving so much of your time to read the complete manuscript. Your keen eye to the details and spotting both the big and smallest of mistakes moved the writing from readable to publishable.

To my friends, Venus Olla and Allison Forbes, for all the late-night tea and chats. Your support means so much more than I can say. My deepest gratitude goes to Arline Calvert and Stefan Adjetey for keeping it real. Your unfailing support makes every workday a joy.

# ABOUT THE AUTHOR

FARTUMO KUSOW was born in Somalia and immigrated to Canada at the start of the civil war. Her first novel, *Amran*, was serialized in *October Star*, Mogadishu. Since her arrival to Canada in 1991 she has earned a B. Arts Honours in English Language and Literature and B. Education from the U. of Windsor. She teaches English literature for the Greater Essex County District School Board. A mother of five adult children, Fartumo lives in Windsor, Ontario.